PRA
HEROES OF '
MURDOC

"A thrilling seafaring fantasy packed with swords, magic, inhuman foes, and endearing heroes."

—BOOKLIFE by Publishers Weekly

"An adventurous fantasy series starter that follows a captain and his crew as they search for the fabled Grimstone. An enjoyable questing tale."

—KIRKUS REVIEWS

"This is an enjoyable adventure with some hilarious, tongue-in-cheek, and exciting moments. A rich adventure!"

—AUDIOBOOKREVIEWER.COM

"An enthralling treasure hunt on the high seas with a colorful cast of characters, Murdoch's Choice sucks you in and refuses to let go."

—E. R. PASKEY, Author of *The Guardians* and *Finder* Series

"*Murdoch's Choice* will take you on the fantasy high seas! Prepare for mystery, engrossing characters, and heart in this adventure! The plot's great, but it's Captain Murdoch and his lively crew that keeps me hungry for more!"

—JMD REID, Author of *The Storm Below* and *Jewels of Illumination* Series

"From the first page, this book transported me to another time and place that was beyond magical. This is what great writing is all about and I can't wait for more!"

—SHANNON EVERHART, Author of *Moments at McBride*

"Unique magic system . . . pirate and heist theme. . . . It's *Mistborn* on a boat."

—ALEX MCHADDAD, News Director at EOAlive.TV

HEROES OF TIME LEGENDS

A NOVEL OF THE HEROES OF TIME SERIES

MURDOCH'S CHOICE

BY WAYNE D. KRAMER

Publisher's Cataloging-in-Publication Data:

Names:	Kramer, Wayne D., author.
Title:	Heroes of time legends : Murdoch's choice / by Wayne Kramer.
Other titles:	Murdoch's choice.
Description:	[Revised first edition].	[Louisville, Kentucky] Heroes of Time Productions LLC, [2021]	Series: Heroes of time series.	Audience: young adult.
Identifiers:	ISBN: 978-1-955997-30-0 (hardback)	978-1-955997-14-0 (paperback)	978-1-955997-01-0 (e-book)	978-1-955997-43-0 (audiobook CD)
Subjects:	LCSH: Ship captains--Fiction.	Voyages and travels--Fiction.	Daughters--Fiction.	Merchant ships--Fiction.	Magic--Fiction.	Seafaring life--Fiction.	Adventure stories.	LCGFT: Fantasy fiction.	Action and adventure fiction.	Sea fiction.

Classification: LCC: PS3611.R3636 M871 2021 | DDC: 813/.6--dc23

*For all the family, friends, and
colleagues of the late Daniel "Skip" Person,
our real-life Captain Murdoch.*

PREFACE & ACKNOWLEDGEMENTS

This book is an answered prayer.

So many authors probably feel that way when their books get published, especially when it's their first one. You also sometimes hear of those authors who have dreamed of getting published for more than twenty years before they finally did. I'm thrilled and honored to join their ranks.

I actually wrote another "first" book for the "Heroes of Time" series, called *Heroes of Time: The First Ethereal*. Strategies shifted, plans changed, elements aligned ... and so *Heroes of Time Legends: Murdoch's Choice* came first.

And I think that works wonderfully. *Murdoch's Choice* provides an apt, fast-paced entry for the series. In fact, either book is a great place to start.

The extensive worldbuilding I had done in creating *The First Ethereal* fed nicely into the writing of *Murdoch's Choice* and, I believe, allows it to be a richer experience packaged into a relatively snappy, smallish debut novel. These two novels are indeed both part of the "Heroes of Time" series, but rather than running purely in sequence they run more in parallel, supporting the broader narrative at different angles that will, eventually, intersect. This makes *Murdoch's Choice* something of a tie-in novel to the larger story and thus why the word *Legends* is also added to the full title. It is, even more specifically, Captain Murdoch's part of the series.

Murdoch's Choice carries extra special meaning for me as a dedication to my late friend, colleague, and part of the family, Daniel "Skip" Person. Captain Zale "the Gale" Murdoch was born in my notes and outlines over the year or so prior to Skip's passing in December 2018, a character based directly on his larger-than-life personality, token sayings, and intelligence. It was Skip himself who came up with the character's name (offering "Augustus Macpherson" as an alternative) and suggested that he should captain his own vessel. Somewhere in all of that we brainstormed a feisty red panda to accompany him.

And so my acknowledgements start with him. Thank you, Skip.

Also, thanks to your long-departed cat, Queenie.

My long journey to finally becoming a published author carries far too many people to list. I want to thank those on the professional end who rallied to make all the pieces fit so that publishing in our desired timeframe could become a reality: Allyson Machate of The Writer's Ally for her coordination of the copyediting, proofreading, and publishing details; Emily Hitchcock and Michelle Argyle for a job well done on typesetting, interior design, and putting all the technical pieces together; Ron

Kadden for helping me with strategies that really set things in motion; and Nathan Bransford, my editor, who lent me some of his valuable experience and challenged me in all the right ways. Also, thank you to Eric Poggel for his skillful development of my website and online beta reader system.

Jade Zivanovic of Steam Power Studios did a marvelous job on the cover art, character art, *Queenie* ship drawings, and the ship's log. Especially cool about the ship's log is that it was created using Skip's real-life handwriting, in particular notes from within his old Bible.

Chris Jackson, author of the "Blood Sea Tales" series, was an awesome source of nautical knowledge and experience, which added a great flavor of authenticity in the final revision of this novel.

Many special thanks to Jacob Kuntzman, who has supported my writing endeavors over the years with such humbling and appreciated enthusiasm. He is the absolute best kind of alpha reader I could hope to have, always ready with candid feedback and ideas, and always willing to go over all the changes made along the way.

I also want to thank all of the beta readers who provided feedback on this novel, even when the timeframe got tight: Jackson Utz, Jason Holmes, Ryan Harger, Joe Sammons, Alex McHaddad, Jade Zivanovic, Luke Dupps, and William Colaw. You guys are awesome!

A special shout-out to my long-time buds Luke Dupps and William Colaw. Luke is the real-life "Fump" Willigan—a nickname given to him by Skip. His giving me the video game *Chrono Trigger* back in 1996, which I later endeavored to novelize, is quite possibly what kindled the fire within me to become a published author. William has always been there to listen to the ups and downs of my journey to finally becoming an author, offering much-appreciated encouragement and support.

Thank you to Lona Person, Skip's wife, for being an awesome mother-in-law and Mamaw Gangy to our kids.

A most heartfelt thanks to my parents, Greg and Joy, who worked hard to position me for success in life, and also to my brother, Brandon. We are all blessed to share so much life together, which has built and enriched the person I am today.

Finally, thank you to my wife, Kaly, and our daughters, Dawn, Brooke, Holly, Ivy, and Jade. They get to see and put up with all those moments of my stressing over work while stubbornly pressing ahead to pursue my dreams as a writer. Even so, when Kaly surprises me with a "Best Author in the Galaxy" T-shirt or a "Future Best-Selling Author" mug or a "Writer's Block" candle (scented of regurgitated ideas) ... *that*, folks, is true love.

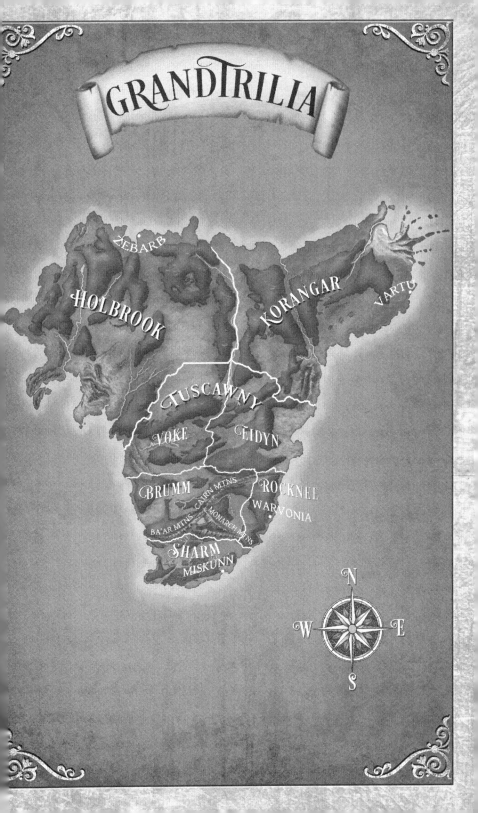

Ekron
Whiteland
Kelan
Grandtrilia
Coral
Ash
Islands
Holbrook
Koranga
Tuscamon

THE GREAT CRESCENT

Eukhan

Ska'ard

Zoar

Akkadia

Aviania

The Border Crescent

N

W E

S

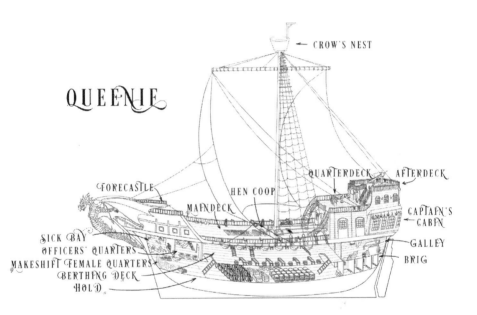

QUEENIE

CROW'S NEST

FORECASTLE

HEN COOP

MAINDECK

QUARTERDECK

AFTERDECK

CAPTAIN'S
CABIN

SICK BAY
OFFICERS' QUARTERS
MAKESHIFT FEMALE QUARTERS
BERTHING DECK
HOLD

GALLEY

BRIG

CENTERPIECE

6/33/3201 P.A.

Fiddles and flutes trilled like the skipping of children, punctuated by lively drumbeat. Men guffawed in raucous laughter and clapped the shoulders of comrades, and enough mulled drinks had been consumed to poison the ocean. Here, upon the rooftop terrace of The Wayward Sailor's Inn, it was just another celebration of old salts and jolly tars from the seafaring mercantile guild.

Starlina Murdoch was neither a salt nor a tar. She wasn't old or particularly jolly. She was simply here, hoping to prevent disaster.

She flipped long, brown hair with streaks of light blue away from her lean, well-tanned face, a wineglass steadied in her other hand. With a piercing glare, she looked throughout the gala, scanning the cluster of motley riffraff and quietly snorting her distaste.

This was an inn of Warvonia within the province of Rocknee,

an old town situated along the kingdom of Tuscawny's eastern coast. Not much had changed here for centuries, and many of its inner workings happened out of the light of day, but at least one of its constants was the simple, subtle charm of a seaside town, with its rich, salty air and its maze of curvy, sloping streets that seemed impossible to navigate save to those who knew them.

Tonight's celebration revolved around the return of one of the guild's most renowned captains: her father, Captain Zale "the Gale" Murdoch of the *Queenie*. The ship had become one of the most famous merchant vessels in the kingdom, if not the entire continent, under her father's command.

It didn't take long for her to spot her father. He stood across the terrace, a stout, boisterous man surrounded by fawning sailors rapt by his every word. Even from this distance she heard his gruff yet gentlemanly voice overpower everything else.

"It was a fish monster alright, with arms like a giant squid and legs like a frog. As soon as one appeared on deck, I speared it with a pike like a pickled herring and launched it from the ballista!" Those around him stared agog, as though in the presence of greatness incarnate. He lifted his hands to calm their apparent adulation. "Not saying I'm a hero. Just saved my entire crew *and* our bounty, like any captain worth his salt should do. We slayed the rest of those gilled demons right there on stern in glorious victory." He raised his arms high. "And I said, 'Men, tonight we dine on *fish*! *Ah ha ha ha!*"

Shaking her head, Starlina downed the rest of her honey-mulled wine, relishing its smooth yet spicy bite.

She wasn't really here for her father, nor was she here for the hearty libation.

She was here to see the best friend that her father was already stealing from her.

Jensen Karrack, a young man of sixteen, and Starlina had known each other since childhood. Their relationship was a coy evolution beyond friendship—an innocent hand-hold here, a little shoulder-rub there, arms touching in the tavern when seated among other friends. They finished too many of each other's sentences, laughed just a little too much at each other's jokes. Starlina loved every bit of it.

Attending this soirée had been a last-minute decision. She hadn't told Jensen she was coming, and already she wondered if it was a mistake. So far she hadn't even spotted him among the scallywags ambling about the terrace, some steadier than others.

Jensen had talked often about sailing. It wasn't until recently, as he approached university age, that Starlina realized how serious he was about pursuing it for his actual career. That didn't make it inevitable, nor was it easily accomplished. Long-haul sailing positions in Warvonia's guild were in high demand, especially with the most successful crews. Most likely he would have to accept something less elite, perhaps at the harbor, or something administrative.

Then came the opportunity of Jensen's lifetime. It jostled Starlina to the soul.

He'd won a contest, besting dozens of other seafaring student hopefuls. This granted him an opportunity that didn't usually come until well along in the university program—the opportunity for firsthand experience aboard an actual ship of the guild.

By some horrid knife-twist of fate, Jensen was able to choose her father's ship.

Supposedly they'd sailed just beyond the edge of the Great Crescent. Supposedly they'd battled gyllians—giant mythical fish monsters, slaying every one. Supposedly they'd plucked ambrosial grapes straight from the Ethereal Realm, parted the waves with their valor, and snuffed the fires of Gheol with naught but their unfathomable bravery. With sailors, who really ever knew what to believe?

Starlina took another glass of wine from a passing servant's tray and leaned against the stone plinth of a statue as she sipped. At this vantage point, she was a few steps higher than the main terrace, giving her a broad view of the attendees. She sighed and glared at the statue's face. It was of a sea captain, pointing his cutlass in the direction of the ocean.

She frowned at the scene before her. She had been certain Jensen would be here.

Swirling her glass absently, it occurred to her that she was likely the youngest one here. With her fifteenth birthday less than six months away, she was nearly of the "young adult" age class. She already felt mature beyond her years. She lived alone, bused tables to support herself, rarely saw her parents, and knew her limits with wine better than most of the tipplers roaming this place.

She downed that glass and grabbed another.

Her mother had left months ago, supposedly for Sharm in the south. Good riddance, as far as Starlina was concerned. They'd had little more than fight after fight over her mother's destructive life choices with countless men. It was a relief when her mother finally left Warvonia. Starlina still wished the best for her, that she might find a better way for herself in a different place, although she doubted it.

The four hundred twenty-five days of each of Starlina's fourteen years already felt like a long slog toward adulthood. There were exceptions, of course. There was the time she spent with Jensen, when twenty-eight hours never seemed long enough for just one day.

Her reverie was broken by her father's roaring voice as it carried across the terrace.

"Blubberpots, sots, and jigglequeens, every one of 'em! *Ah ha ha! Pop-Pop!*" He did some goofy little jig that earned endless claps and chuckles from everyone around.

Starlina rolled her eyes and looked away, beyond the inn, where below stretched a calm and deserted plaza, one of many that was relatively unchanged since feudal times. Soon enough that plaza would be filled with the boisterous din of drunken sailors stumbling away from this place.

She'd been here long enough. Maybe it was time to give up on her hopes of talking some sense into Jensen. She took another sip of wine.

"*Another* glass, milady?" spoke a luscious voice from behind her. "Shall I arrange a carriage for your safe return home?"

She gave a lopsided smirk and spun to face the source. There stood Jensen, staring at her with those beautiful hazelnut eyes that had hypnotized her since their childhood. His brownish hair had hints of muted yellow throughout, and his lean, square face had a handsome, angular jawline.

He still smelled like the sea, like a sailor—salty, rugged, with hints of heedless adventure. Not a bad scent, necessarily, but it stoked a sense of urgency within Starlina. She was already losing him.

"A carriage for two, Mister Karrack, so that you may whisk me away from this place at once."

Maybe that was a little direct, but she wanted his attention. She wanted him alone with her, away from all of *this*.

He raised an eyebrow. "*Mister* Karrack?" He shook his head, looking dejected. "And I thought we had at least achieved a first-name basis, Miss Murdoch."

She fixed him with a glare, about to respond when a portly, glossy-skinned man pushed between them with a guttural belch. Her mouth fell open in disgust as she watched the man hobble away.

"Jensen," she said sharply, "let's find someplace less obnoxious. A stroll on the beach, perhaps, or the market square, or even the harbor."

He laughed. "So soon? The fun is just beginning!"

She sat her half-emptied glass upon the statue's stone plinth. "I've had quite enough of sailors for one night, thank you. All I can smell in the air here are sweat and alcohol."

"It's not so bad once you get used to it."

Starlina and Jensen turned at the sound of her father's coarse laughter bellowing into the air.

"The guy just looked at me and said, 'I never met a bridge I didn't burn!' *Ah ha ha ha!*" Cackles erupted all around him like a pack of hyenas.

"Well," she said, turning back to an amused Jensen, "I suppose I don't *want* to get used to it."

There was a flicker of conflict in his face, but it vanished with a stroke of his goatee. "You should've seen us out there, Starlina." Now he was outright giddy. "Fog everywhere, utter stillness, just us out there in a quiet cove right at the mouth of the Border Crescent, where the prize rested in an underwater cave. The *Border Crescent*, Starlina, on my very first voyage!

"And then they came—the gyllians. They're *real*, as real as badger anthropods. They actually *climbed* up the ship, some of them even to the deck. Your father's crew…" He paused, over-taken with awe, drawing a breath. "…they're true fighters. Those monsters were vicious, like nothing I've ever seen. I actually took down one with a hatchet."

She gaped at him. "That sounds absolutely horrific!"

"If only you could've seen your father! He spiked one like a kabob and bolted it from the aft ballista!"

Starlina hardened her stare. "So I've heard."

This was worse than she'd thought. Now he'd triumphed in the face of true danger. What ambitious sea-bitten young man could resist *that*?

Of course, the excitement was fresh. Her father and Jensen had been away for nearly a month, returning just two days ago. She'd already grown up wishing her father could simply disavow the seafaring trade. Was she now destined to wish the same of Jensen?

It's this town, she seethed inwardly. *Boys enamored with the ocean since childhood, like some vast rite of passage, as if everything else were meant for lesser folk.*

Jensen looked out toward the lower terrace, where they could still hear her father's laughter. "Even here, your father is quite the centerpiece."

"So that's it, then?" asked Starlina. "You'll be joining my father's crew, sailing off into the great beyond?"

"That's far from official, and anything could happen over my time at university. I can't deny being excited, though, for I think my chances are much greater having joined in that voyage."

Starlina flashed him a glare. "Why must every man in this town take to the sea? Is there not enough to be done here upon the land?"

Jensen chuckled dismissively. "Let the land be for those who like their vision hampered. Give *me* a clear horizon—the promise of adventure and discovery!"

"Overrated tosh, if you ask me." If not for the dark, he might've seen the heat rising in her face. "I don't think I could ever be with a man in the seafaring guild." She ignored the sudden concern in Jensen's eyes. "They're far too absent."

"Some voyages are long," he said, "and some are short. But

they come with great reward, and is it not true that time apart makes the heart grow fonder?"

"Time apart leaves the heart to ponder, more like."

"Well," said Jensen, "*I* think you should keep an open mind. If I one day get to join with your father's crew.... Well, there's none closer to reaching the guild's mastery bar. Imagine he *does* reach it. I could be one of the few sailors in history to be part of a crew under grandmaster status. We can take fewer jobs...and the best jobs."

It was Starlina's turn to laugh. The mastery bar was basically a guild-wide goal, more like a challenge, set by the officials. Reaching it was like trying to reach a rock from out of Eliorin's planetary rings. "They raise that bar every year! You might just grow old chasing after it. All they do is make it so no one could ever hope to achieve it."

"Your father will," Jensen replied with an air of finality.

There would be no arguing with Jensen. Ever since he was old enough to know what sailing was, it seemed, he had idolized her father. Maybe Jensen was a lost cause after all.

"There are plenty of sea-related occupations that don't require sailing, you know."

He tittered uncomfortably. "A little late for me to change course now."

She arched an eyebrow. "It's only the thirty-third of Jervens. Plenty of time to make a change." His seventeenth birthday was fast approaching, on the fifth of Jovidor, only a few short weeks until those hoping to be students would declare their desired disciplines before a panel of university professors.

Jensen looked dreamily toward the planet's rings in the sky. In the hazy air, they illuminated the terrace in an almost ghostly nightglow. "After that last voyage, I'm all but certain to earn admission."

"That's what I'm afraid of."

He ran a hand gently through her hair. She inhaled at the touch. "Ah, Starlina, I so long for the day when you can join me upon a ship. Then you might see how truly majestic it is."

She shoved his hand aside. "I've been on a boat before, Jensen."

"Not with *me* on it," he said with a wink.

She stabbed him with a sharp glare. "I'll stay on solid ground, thank you, where humans are meant to be."

"Then you've decided upon your own university declaration?"

She hadn't, but she still had time for that. "I suspect it shall be whatever keeps my feet firmly upon the land, sir. Something here in Warvonia. I'll make this town so striking that the eyes of every citizen can't help but aim within, instead of toward the ocean." Starlina loved all forms of design—fashion, architectural, interior—and so she imagined her career aspirations leaning in that direction.

"Anything might develop for me while you're away for weeks and months on end," she added before he could comment. "It might be time for me to leave this old place. Miskunn might suit me better...or Ruca, with a view of the palace."

"You could go anywhere, Starlina, and it will always be my mission to find you there, if even to view your beauty from afar."

Curse him to the fires of Gheol, she thought. *He's completely unflappable.*

Her icy countenance melted into a thin smile. "You would, too ... and I'd be all for it, waiting for you like a fool."

Lute and cello chords sang out, whilst kettledrums pounded a beat. Brightly dressed minstrels in an upraised gallery took over to liven up the occasion.

Jensen held out a hand. "I hope your feet aren't planted *too* firmly. Care to dance?"

She took his hand, he took her waist, and together they floated about the terrace like youthful swans on a lake. As children they had danced together countless times to music much like this. Yet, as Jensen's strong hands clasped her sides and twirled her with such control, suddenly the dance felt anything but childish.

For countless songs they spun and glided about, until nearly an hour had passed like a few minutes. Everything around her disappeared, all of it a trifling blur. She saw only Jensen.

Finally, the music stopped, leaving Starlina breathless in Jensen's arms. Shouts and laughs and conversation of the gala again reigned around them. Her attention was only on him. He held more than her sides. He held her heart. In truth, he always had. If only she could make him see the joys of life—life with *her*—without so itinerant a job as sailing ... then all could be perfect.

Jensen released her. "You've only gotten better at that," he said.

She drew in a breath. "As have you, good sir."

"I have something for you." He reached into his pocket and pulled out a polished gemstone like pinkish-purple glass. "This is lilac kuntupite. It's said to align the hearts and souls of people who care for each other over great distances. Might be a load of rubbish, but who knows? I got a pair of them from a friend in the guild. So, now I have one . . . and so do you."

She took the stone and looked it over, not quite knowing how to react. It was a genuine gesture, but with it came again that promise of "great distances," a constant she'd already had to endure growing up with Zale Murdoch as her father.

"It's beautiful," she said. "Thank you."

Their moment was interrupted by her father's voice, which had a remarkable ability to carry a broad distance.

"Let's hang 'em first and *then* have the trial!" The men around him were in stitches, their faces red, likely as much from the drinking as the laughing.

"*That* silly man will be the one to break the mastery bar?" she asked. "And I thought *I* was the one who's had too much wine."

"He will, alright. You just wait and see. Your father's unstoppable. Captain Zale 'the Gale' Murdoch—the man, the scourge, the legend." The nut-brown eyes of his dashing face looked into hers. He moved closer, very close, his face inching toward hers.

She jolted back, despite the playful smirk tugging at her

mouth. "You haven't asked my blessing to approach like that."

He stopped, only a breath between them. "Sailors don't ask questions. They take action."

He kissed her cheek and walked away, Starlina's heart racing and her mouth grinning from ear to ear.

Chapter 1

THE GALE

7/19/3203 P.A.

There comes a time for any ruthless seafarer at the top of his game, once well along in years, to set aside the rough-and-tumble manner of his occupation and gird himself with the kinder, gentler mien of the Pop-Pop.

Captain Zale "the Gale" Murdoch was no small amount of man. Just shy of fifty-five years old, he had grown and shaped himself a magnificent ale-gut, a solid round and impenetrable protrusion. A thin carpet of cropped, silvery brown and auburn hair covered his head and flowed into the whitening hairs all about his face. His legs were thin and his wrists were small, but he had all the muscle he needed. His greatest muscle, after all, was his brain.

Lola, his darling wife, stood just behind him. She was well-built and broad-shouldered, the sort who could stack two mounds of firewood in the dead of winter while tending a pot of stew and scouring the tub all at the same time. She had dark, discreetly graying hair and an endearing round face.

They approached the home in which Lola's daughter lived with her husband and children. It was a modest abode of sand-colored bricks, situated in Warvonia's southwestern residential district.

Zale was just in from yet another profit-rich voyage sure to be the envy of every other merchant in the guild. A self-satisfied smirk stretched his broad, whiskery face. He would have his reward.

But that was no matter now. What mattered now was beyond the humble, wooden door before him. He pushed it open with a flourish, ready to demand the tribute he'd so rightfully earned.

"Give ol' Pop-Pop a smooch!" He belted out a belly laugh, shaking his girth. Squeals of delighted children welcomed him.

Four children to be exact, and not just any children. His granddaughters. Fawn was age nine, Sage was age six, and little Nova was turning four on this very day. Hazel, reaching out and babbling from within her mother's arms, was not yet two.

"Oooh, I hear someone's having a birthday!" Zale teased.

"Me! Me!" piped Nova. She had bouncing pigtails of white and golden hair.

Zale stooped low to accept the incoming barrage of hugs and kisses. Ecstatic little arms yanked him beyond the threshold.

Lola followed him in and eagerly accepted her own bounty of cuddles.

"Grammie Gangy!" greeted Fawn.

"Well hello . . . and happy birthday, Nova!" Lola replied.

Zale took care not to stumble as the kids pulled him farther in.

The lower half of his left leg was composed entirely of graphenite, a dark-gray metal-gemstone alloy considered to be one of the strongest and lightest available. Rarely was it spared for the needs of an ordinary civilian, but Zale was anything but ordinary. He'd proven his service to the crown time and time again, starting with over two decades in Tuscawny's naval Sea Force, years spent with obsequious buffoons who specialized more in bootlicking than navigating vessels. He bested his nitwit shipmates at every turn, whether rigging a ship for prompt departure or locking blades with marauders.

Things got interesting when the seafaring mercantile guild sought him out.

The pay would be better, the work more exciting, and he'd be among true professionals. Unlike the mercantile guilds of other provinces, crews from Rocknee, and more specifically its prominent port city of Warvonia, were often entrusted with the most specialized and rare of cargo runs.

It became almost an afterthought to Zale that this was one of the kingdom's iffier mercantile guilds. Most assumed it was a guild of criminals—bootleggers, privateers, and smugglers sanctioned by the crown to sail their private vessels, without the colors of their land, and retrieve the kingdom's less-than-virtuous bounties. Zale saw it as a guild of the competent.

He received a quick lesson in the magnitude of his new charge during one of his earliest assignments, a secretive mission of military import. As his ship approached the jagged sea stacks of Aviania, just outside the Great Crescent, their ship was attacked by terons, bipedal winged creatures that could best be described as humanoid dragons. Few in the kingdom had ever actually seen these creatures. With talons like giant fishhooks and teeth like spearheads, they were like things of legend.

Zale fared the worst in the encounter, his leg ripped beyond saving. He never even knew what they had come for.

The guild showed remarkable diligence in arranging to have his limb rebuilt. Medical breakthroughs, it turned out, were quite possible for those whom the officials deemed worthy of the resources. With his new leg, Zale felt stronger than ever before, like something more than a mere man.

He returned to action in full pomp and circumstance, sailing from port in his new ship, the *Queenie*, one of the sleekest, fastest, and well-outfitted square-riggers to scale the seas, named after what Zale proclaimed to be the greatest cat that ever lived. He chose a gilded, roaring teron as its figurehead, touting his survival of that voyage past.

The great tale of Pop-Pop's metallic leg was a favorite of the grandchildren's.

Technically these were grandchildren only by marriage, the daughters of Lola's only child, Haly, and her husband, Dane. That made them no less family to Zale. They were every bit as much so as even his own daughter, Starlina, borne by a woman of his wilder past. For a while he wasn't sure which one. He had no children with Lola, but she had every assurance of being the only woman for him till death. With this gal, he was convinced that he actually meant it.

He relished the bliss of Nova's birthday party, enjoying great food and conversation. He lowered himself into an armchair, the kids clambering all around.

"So, a birthday!" Zale spoke grandly, taking Nova into his lap. "How old are you—two? Three?"

"Four!" Nova insisted, holding up three fingers. Fawn corrected her hand by lifting one more of her fingers. "Four! Four! Four!"

"Oh, it can't be! *Four* years?" He turned to Lola. "Can it be, sweet Dwoey?"

"It can," sweet Dwoey confirmed.

"Let's see. Born in 3199, on this nineteenth of Jovidor ... with this year being 3203 .... By the stars! You *are* four!"

Sage, a round-faced jewel with wavy locks and sheer joy in her gait, thrust a wooden sauropod toy in his face. "Sing the song, Pop-Pop! Sing the song!"

Zale chuckled as another of his many gifts garnered the appreciation of present company. He took the toy in one hand and conducted the tune with his other, as his pleasantly coarse voice sang out:

> Diplodor the Dinosaur,
> he went down to the knickknack store.
> Got some snacks and a whole lot mooooore!
> Diplodor the Dinosaur.

Once, of course, was never enough, so he repeated the song three times more before finally giving ol' Diplodor the sendoff. He joined his family in mirthful laughter, thanking the divinity of Eloh for the gift of this joyful respite before seeking his next adventure.

Warvonia was oft considered the gem of Tuscawny's eastern coast. Largely unchanged for hundreds of years, many of the town's outermost structures and walls were composed of old stone blocks quarried from the Monarch Mountains in the south. Red-roofed turrets prodded at the sky from its ancient wall towers and gatehouses. Farther inside the town, colorful, half-timbered houses lined narrow, cobblestone streets. At the locale's nucleus was an expansive town square famous for its aisles of market booths, which throughout the year were themed to seasons and holidays.

It was here that nineteen-year-old Jensen Karrack chanced a chance meeting with Zale Murdoch that was, in fact, not really chance at all.

Jensen sought Captain Murdoch's blessing to ask for his daughter's hand in marriage.

He had played this moment in his mind countless times. Even so, his palms were sweaty and his heart raced. He couldn't quite pinpoint why he was so nervous. Starlina and he plainly loved each other. They had for years. It had never been abundantly clear how the captain felt about this relationship. He had, at least, never spoken out against it.

Of course, he had never spoken out in favor of it, either.

Perhaps Jensen's nerves came simply from the fear of rejection. Perhaps he feared rejection in the form of being hung from the *Queenie*'s rigging or drowned in a barrel of brine.

Then there was his career to consider. Securing his position in Captain Murdoch's crew between his final two terms at the university had taken no small amount of persistence. The captain and other shipmates had seen his proficiency with weapons. High marks in helmsmanship from his instructors had empowered him to seek the role of boatswain's mate, while his skills in carpentry had helped to seal the deal.

Now he just hoped he wasn't about to put all of that in jeopardy.

But it had to be done—it was simply the proper way—and so here he was.

He already knew, thanks to a tip from one of his shipmates, that the legendary captain would be here today. Nervously he stood at the end of one of many streets spilling into the town square, running a hand through his brown-and-buttercream hair and stroking the goatee on his chin.

Finally, he saw his target. Captain Murdoch, dressed in a dark-red tunic and off-white trousers, strolled alone toward the market booths. Inhaling a deep breath, Jensen stepped lively into the bustling town center.

"Captain!" he called out, his voice cracking a little. "What a coincidence seeing you here!"

Murdoch turned with a scowl. His eyes softened with recognition, although the look wasn't exactly a cordial greeting. "Afternoon, Jensen."

"Gathering some essentials, sir?" Jensen cursed inwardly at this weak attempt at small talk.

"That's what the market is good for, so I hear," Murdoch replied.

"Uh . . . yes, sir. That it is."

Jensen followed Murdoch toward an aisle of produce stands, all freshly spread with the season's latest bounties. Summer, sub-season of harvest, had ended with the start of Jovidor, and the fall sub-season had begun. Indeed, crops had produced aplenty, with baskets of colorful berries, piles of melons, and carts overflowing with peppers, cultivar beans, and all manner of vegetables.

The captain paused to pick through a cart of apples. "What're *you* after?" he finally asked, not taking his eyes off the fruit.

"Hmm, yes, an apple will do nicely," Jensen stammered.

He grabbed the first apple within reach and absently handed the merchant a five-lat coin.

Murdoch turned and walked off.

"Actually, sir . . . I'd like a word, if you please."

The captain's stony expression remained unchanged. "Well, we *are* both here, after all."

Jensen's mouth felt very dry. "Sir . . . it's about your daughter,

Starlina. As you know, we've known each other since childhood, and we have grown into fine young women—uh, woman—rather, *she* has grown into a fine young woman . . . sir." Murdoch's agog expression bore into him. "I find that I'm . . . well, I'm in love with her, sir. I've a mind to propose marriage. I'd hoped I might have your blessing."

Murdoch looked him up and down. Jensen wondered if this might be a good time to turn around and run. He watched for the captain's reaction, hoping he hadn't signed his own death warrant.

Murdoch's mouth fell open. "*Bah hahahahaha!*"

A few passersby flinched at the sound, widening the space between them.

"You're a fanciful one, Jensen. Never forget—the sea is an unyielding place. See that your earnest whims and callow impulses don't get the better of you."

His mouth frozen agape, Jensen watched Zale Murdoch disappear into the market crowd.

Nova's birthday two days prior still replayed merrily in Zale's mind as he made his way toward The Wench's Tavern. He took in a sliver of nighttime sky as he walked the streets, Eliorin's planetary rings painting a bright band across the starry tapestry. Despite being nestled along one of the town's lesser-traveled alleys, the tavern tended to host some of the land's most travel-seasoned patrons. It was the preferred hunting ground for new mercantile work, and it was one of very few places where those seeking Zale knew they might eventually find him.

Their next job would be especially important.

Zale's crew was but one solid catch away from breaking the guild's mastery bar, a goal set every year by the guilders. It was a number based on the value of a crew's lifetime catch. Every year, of course, it only increased, always pushing more hopefuls out of the running. Zale and his crew were already well beyond goals of the past. To reach this goal granted the crew's captain "grandmaster" status. Reaching the goal was practically unheard of, with the exception of certain legendary crew masters of the past. With it came the promise of greater authority within the guild, quota flexibility, and riches aplenty.

The rules of the bar were clear: only one crew would ever be awarded grandmaster status within a given year, and they had until the end of Agust to do it. After that, the bar would be moved again.

This year Zale's crew was especially close. One more run of reasonably high value would do it. With this being the twenty-first of Jovidor, they still had just shy of nine weeks before the current goal expired.

Zale threw open the tavern door like a gust of wind, blowing the room into a curious silence. His eyes surveyed the environs as he took measured, clomping steps toward the bar counter in the back.

"The Gale."

"Zale the Gale."

"Murdoch, Captain 'the Gale' himself."

His name traveled throughout the room in a chorus of whispers—music to his ears. He pulled a chair at the bar and sat with a groan, the room behind him returning to its usual din of chatter and thumping mugs.

When the barkeep arrived, Zale greeted him with a polite smile. "Dark stout ale for me, good sir. Thank you."

His drink arrived in tandem with a lanky man in a long, dark coat. He had a lean, almond-shaped face and short, dusty-blond hair.

Zale kept his eyes forward as he lifted the glass for a drink. "Evening, Dippy."

"Good evening, sir."

Dippy was first mate of the *Queenie*, essentially an extension of Zale when it came to finding new jobs and, if needed, additional crewmembers. Dippy wasn't his real name, of course. His real name was Daubernoun. He looked like a Dippy to Zale, and so Dippy he became.

"What's the report?" Zale asked.

"A few private jobs," Dippy replied. "Some collectors seeking rare minerals like gold-veined lapis and green moonstone."

Zale raised an unimpressed brow. "Lapis? Do they take us for land-rats? Tell him to go up the coast into Korangar, and turn left at Boring Town. Luxorite I'd have found interesting, for a zesty chance at bilking foreign royalty."

There was a loud *thump* across the room, accompanied by a frenzy of shuffled chairs. A man fell to the floor, completely still. In this place, it was just as likely to be from drunkenness as poison. A bald man wearing a frock coat leapt to his side.

Zale was about to turn back to his drink. In spite of himself, he kept watching.

The bald man seemed to be tending to the man on the floor. He leaned in close, placing his hands delicately on the man's head and chest.

"Bizarre," Zale muttered.

The bald man looked up and made eye contact with Zale. Seconds later, the fallen man gasped, scrambled to his feet, and stumbled out the exit.

Dippy pointed toward the spectacle. "Did that guy just heal that other guy?"

The bald man stood slowly and went back to his table as though nothing had happened.

Zale took a swig of ale. Strange sights were not uncommon here in the tavern.

"What other jobs, Dippy?" he asked.

"There's another seeking quandalite."

Zale scratched at the thick stubbles of his chin. "Don't hear that one every day. Does he have the lyra to show for it?"

Dippy faltered a bit. "Says he's willing to pay more than market ... but only with a ten percent deposit."

"Bah ha!" bellowed Zale with a slap of the counter. "Hire the Gale on such nominal dosh? And my papa's Grimy the Grimkin."

"Well, I thought you'd say that." Dippy ran a hand through his hair. "There is one more, Captain. Fella claims to represent nobility, here on business for the Palace."

Zale frowned. "Curious case. Are you sure about this? *The* Palace—*Metsada* Palace?"

Metsada Palace was the kingdom's prime seat of governance, home to King Berosus Sar-Utultar and the legendary Throne of Light. The palace itself rested upon a star-shaped plateau said to have been formed by the divine using bolts of lightning. Zale, along with many others, assumed this to be just part of a larger narrative which insisted upon the King's divine right to the Throne.

"Does he claim to come *from* the Palace?" Zale asked.

"Says he's from Brumm, actually."

"Brumm?" This was a different story. The Palace was located in the province of Sharm, just south of Brumm, and between them coursed the rugged Ba'ar Mountains. It wasn't extremely far from Metsada Palace as the starling flies, but getting there was no quick jaunt.

On top of that, citizens of Brumm, compared to Sharm and Rocknee, were generally stereotyped as less refined. Their nobility, on the other hand, was a class all to its own—ruthless, always on the lookout for the most proper and sincere ways to stab each other in the throat, all for the sake of position and power. Brumm nobles looked down on those from the other provinces, rarely deigning to meet in-person. Instead, hired goons were sent to do their bidding.

Zale went back to his mug with a throaty chuckle. "Ask him why he married his sister."

Dippy's eyeballs darted back and forth. "Captain ... I think this one might be serious."

"Go on, man! Ask him!"

Zale watched as Dippy took timid steps away from the counter and stopped at a table by the farthest wall. Zale had already dismissed this prospect as codswallop. Seated there was a very plain man in very plain civilian clothes. He looked frail amongst this tavern of burly louts. His face was pallid, his black and white hair slicked back, his garb a simple brown suit.

Dippy asked the question. Zale took another gulp from his mug. *Insolent hound*, he thought. *Serves you right for wasting the Gale's time.*

The man's dark scowl caused such a transformation in his face that even Zale flinched. His words to Dippy seemed sharp and pithy. Dippy looked as though the man had just pointed a knife at his chest.

A minute later Dippy scampered his way back toward Zale. This time he motioned to the barkeep for an ale of his own.

"Well, that looked eventful," said Zale.

"He doesn't have a sister." When the ale appeared, he took a long drink. "What he did say is that he knows you have a wife, a daughter, a stepdaughter, and four grandchildren in the vicinity of Warvonia."

Fury filled Zale so fast that his vision blurred. "*What?!*"

Men at the nearest tables shifted their chairs uncomfortably.

Dippy leaned in. "Captain, please listen. This guy seems well-connected. He might be for real. He seems dangerous."

Zale considered that. It often held that the dangerous men were the more serious ones. "What's the job?" Zale rumbled.

"Says he'll talk only with you. But he did tell me it's enough to pass the bar ... and he's already talked to ol' Seadread."

Hearing mention of his long-time rival only galled Zale all the more. Captain Garrick "Seadread" Rummy—or Captain Puffypants, as Murdoch often called him—was also within striking range of the mastery bar this year. *Cheating ratbag*, Zale seethed at the thought. He was certain Garrick had somehow bribed the guilders into boosting his tally.

Zale downed the remainder of his ale and pushed back from the bar counter with a guttural moan.

"Look alive, Dippy. Let's see what we're dealing with."

They went straight to the man's table, Zale leading with a glare fit to kill.

"Captain Murdoch," the man greeted with a tilt of his head, his voice like slick oil. "I'm pleased to see I finally garnered your attention."

Zale eyed a black amulet around the man's neck as he sat down, skipping the formality of a handshake. "To Gheol with your pleasure. Why are you speaking of my family?"

"Relax," the man replied coolly. "We all need our edge, Captain ... and mine is knowledge." He motioned for a server. "Let's have drinks. Wine, perhaps?"

"Ale for me," Zale replied. "Helps me think."

"Make that two," said Dippy.

A young male server arrived, and the man ordered. "Two of your ... standard-fare ales ... and a glass of Eidyn oak-leaf for me, chilled." The server left them. "It is good you came to speak with me. I am here to make the choice of your next job much easier."

Zale raised an eyebrow. "Life is full of choices. I always say, choose the one with the best payoff."

The man cocked his head to the side. "Indeed."

"My associate tells me you're affiliated with nobility," Zale said. "I can't help but feel a bit ... skeptical."

"Guild Chief Dugard Pratt can affirm my station, should you feel the need. By the time we're through here, I rather doubt you will."

Zale stared at the man. Not only was he supposedly from across the kingdom, but now it seemed he had some familiarity with Warvonia's leadership.

"Who are you?" Zale demanded.

"I am Vidimir Tefu."

Zale paused, waiting for more. Finally, he said, "Should that name mean something to us?"

Vidimir looked amused, his smarmy grin reminiscent of a triangle. "The name of Tefu is among the Great Lineage delineated in the accords of our province. But I'm sure a fully dedicated seaman such as yourself has little time for the inner workings of nobility."

Zale grunted. "Why would a man from Brumm in league

with nobility venture all the way out to our quaint seaside village?"

The server returned with their drinks. Vidimir waited for him to leave before continuing. "I come to your town, because in the entire Grandtrilia continent, there is no stronger band of seafaring ... *merchants* ... to be found."

"Flattered," Zale replied. "So, what are we after here, fine silks? High-value minerals? A nice trinket for your baron's sitting room?"

Vidimir swirled his wine and took a delicate sip. "This is of far greater importance than our baron, Captain. More than the capital baron ... more than the grand vizier ... more, even, than the king himself. This concerns the heart of our realm, the divine blessing bestowed upon the Patriarch when the days of the Shadow Age were chased away."

"Now you speak of fable," Dippy chimed in. "Shadow Age doomsayer, Cap'n. Mayhaps we *should* let Seadread take this one."

Zale nodded. "I'm inclined to agree. Believe what you will about the Shadow Age. If that's what this is about, we don't have the luxury of chasing mythical trifles."

"This concerns the Light of the Land itself," Vidimir said.

The Light of the Land was an energy source, said to be within a holy hall of the Palace. It was established long before even the kingdom's existence, as a sort of blessing upon the land from the Ethereal Realm during cataclysmic days of the past. It's what many believed gave the entire Grandtrilia continent, of which Tuscawny was a part, its right to exist.

Vidimir continued. "Divine benediction might have been vital in the days of Birqu Umis and our conquering kings of the past. But, it would seem, the divine is moving on, and the blessing that once ensured our stability now wavers. The once-stalwart brightness of Zophiel's Light, these days, is more like a flicker. It's a matter of time before it gutters out completely."

Zale fixed the man with a hard look. "This sounds more like a matter for the divine than a seafarer. Have you tried praying lately?"

Vidimir sipped his wine, his eyes amused. "Fate is a dogged mistress, Captain. My first whim was to find you here... and here we are."

"We tend to prefer bounties a little more on the *tangible* side," Zale said. "*Real*, as it were."

"If money is your concern..." Vidimir reached under the table and lifted a canvas bag. He set it down with an unmistakable jingle of coins. "...I assure you the reward will be more than enough to shatter your guild's mastery bar. A bar, by the way, which has already been raised."

"Complete blarney!" Dippy yelped, nearly jumping from his seat.

Zale chuckled. "I'm afraid you're mistaken, sir. The bar is never raised till after Agust. Anything else is against the long-standing code of our guild."

Vidimir shrugged. "You'll soon see for yourselves. But I fear you'll find it quite an insurmountable goal in such a short time.

That is, unless you accept the offer at hand."

Zale had to admit, Vidimir's account was intriguing. He might indeed serve the nobility class and thus possess more knowledge than most about lore surrounding the Light and the kingdom's foundation, but this claim about the mastery bar was especially hard to believe. For one, why would this man from Brumm know about it before even Zale? It was a matter Zale intended to verify the first chance he got.

"For the sake of humor, what is it you want?" Zale asked.

"The ancient shard of *Ni'shan-qa Til'la-ni'tha* ... perhaps better known as the Grimstone. It is a fragment of the Great Celestial Entry which ushered in the Shadow Age. In the right hands, the power within this fragment can be harnessed to keep our land stable, even as the Light fades. You are to deliver the Grimstone to me at the port of Miskunn, from which you will sail with undoubtedly the single greatest payout of your career."

"Dark to replace Light. There's a twist," Dippy spoke wistfully.

Indeed, there it was again: the Shadow Age. If someone wanted to cast doubt on the legitimacy of a job, there was almost no better way than to center it around the Shadow Age. Even kingdom historians couldn't agree that such a time had even existed.

Zale stared into Vidimir's expressionless face and tapped absently on the table. "Look, we pull in shipments of pyritite for making household fuses. If it's luminous flocalcite ore you're after, we're your crew. We can pillage foreign crops, clear out mines, make off with livestock, or find you a nice gulobeast for a pet. You speak in fairy tales, and we're not very good at catching fairies."

Vidimir slid his glass to the side. He lifted his fingers before him, as if he were about to start knitting. Something disturbed the air around his hands, like heat distortion on a sultry day. His index fingers came together with a dark spark, and right before them he drew a tiny, purple rectangle in midair.

With a thrust of his palm through the rectangle, a flare of violet flame ignited upon the table, spreading slowly. Dippy jumped back with his chair. Zale remained still, keeping his hands clear. He expected to feel the normal heat of a fire. This fire radiated an unsettling chill.

Vidimir slammed his hand down upon the flame, extinguishing it. A cold gale of wind rushed through the tavern, momentarily snuffing lights and blowing over his wineglass.

Silence fell in the tavern. Every head turned toward their table.

Zale looked around at the faces staring in their direction. Then he burst out into a great laugh. "*Ah hahahaha!* That's some parlor trick, men!"

The general riffraff returned to their business. Zale spun back around to Vidimir. "Okay, so, is that some odd variety of flamethyst, or . . .?"

Vidimir eyed him darkly. "*That* is but a faint glimmer of the energy reminiscent of the Grimstone. In the right hands, the potential of this object is the envy of all lands."

"And supposedly where is this object located?" Zale asked.

"This is where I must face embarrassment." Vidimir stared at the table. "We were hot on the trail, certain we had found the Grimstone's location." He looked back up at Zale. "Our crews became lost in a tangle of uncharted islets near their destination. One ship returned in retreat. The other was ambushed by one of the black ships of Gukhan. It was my mistake. The crews I sent were not the best."

Dippy shuddered. "Gukhan?"

Gukhan was the one nation within the Great Crescent that most sailors went out of their way to avoid. Many crews that sailed too close never returned, and the reclusive Gukhanians were known as being especially hostile to outsiders.

Zale grunted. "Are you trying to help the kingdom or plunge it into a war with hellhounds? We don't poke at the secretive soldiers of Gukhan. Unwritten rule of survival."

"A rule or not, the need is real. An opportunity is before you, Mister 'the Gale.' Someone will retrieve the Grimstone for me and become a chapter in this land's redemption." He pushed back from the table and stood. "Whether or not you are that person is the choice you have to make." Without so much as a backward glance, Vidimir left the tavern.

CHAPTER 2

RAISING THE BAR

7/22/3203 P.A.

Z ale seethed within as he ascended a narrow cobblestone alley of Warvonia. He'd gotten very little sleep after last night's encounter with Vidimir. As he tossed and turned into the morning hours, he could not stop thinking about the mastery bar.

Dippy trailed in his wake. "Do you really think they raised the bar, Captain?"

Zale had eyes only for the road ahead. "I hope not... but I have a sneaking suspicion that something's amiss."

He moved as fast as his legs would carry him, which was not terribly fast, more of a swift hobble. Low groans escaped with his breaths, as much from angst as breathlessness. If there was current mischief concerning the mastery bar, he intended to get to the bottom of it.

The alley opened up into a vast plaza surrounded by gallant, columned structures of local governance. The largest of these was the residence of Warvonia's lord mayor.

Zale flashed it a glare and turned toward a much smaller but no less extravagant building of dark-green marble and gilded trim. Most of the seafarers in this town tended to keep a low profile in society, but the guilders who controlled them flaunted their power with nauseating arrogance.

In particular, within this building was the office of Dugard Pratt, chief mercantile guilder of the Rocknee province. Zale brushed sweat from his brow as he approached, exasperated over Vidimir's claim that the bar had been raised. If true, it marked a move by the guild as extraordinary as it was underhanded.

Zale's hand slid across a thick railing of burnished gold as he ascended the stairs. Not bothering to knock, he pounded through the door, stomping into a reception room of antique-green wood paneling. Two clerical ladies jumped from their desks with yelps of surprise.

"Master Murdoch," one of them sputtered. "To what do we owe—?"

"Dugard," Zale rumbled. "Is he in his office?"

"Chief Pratt is currently with someone. We can request an appointment."

Zale trudged forward. He didn't have time for this nonsense.

"Oh! Master Murdoch, please wait!"

He left Dippy in the foyer and pushed through a set of tall doors into an opulent office furnished with large, cushy chairs, shelves of record books, and console tables littered with local maps. This was the spendthrift office of Dugard Pratt.

Two familiar men stared back at Zale with round eyes. One was Pratt himself, a square-faced man with spiked hair and a thick beard of bright red and white, almost like snow on fire. Garrick "Seadread" Rummy sat across from Pratt's desk, a pock-marked, dour sight of a man with a lazy eye. Somehow the man's beard had managed to turn white with age, whilst the hair of his head remained perfectly black.

"Murdoch!" Dugard exclaimed in a big voice. "What in hell's fury are you doing?"

Zale weighed his response. Seadread's presence had taken him aback. He wasn't sure he wanted to have this conversation in front of his long-time rival.

"Captain Rummy," Zale nodded. "Have the winds fared you well?"

Seadread got up from the chair, standing nearly a full head taller than Zale. His lazy eye twitched in focus and his mouth worked a long, wooden churchwarden pipe.

"I need a word, Dugard," said Zale. "It's urgent."

"We're in the middle of something here. It'll have to wait."

Zale opened his mouth to protest, but the crackly voice of Seadread spoke instead. "No need t' wait." He turned toward Dugard. "Most like our purposes align."

"The mastery bar," Zale said cautiously.

"Aye, that be it!" Seadread said.

"Is it true then, Dugard? Has it been raised?"

Pratt rubbed at the bridge of his nose with a long sigh. "It's true."

"This is an outrage!" Zale shouted.

"Aye," Seadread hissed. "How fancies ye a nice, friendly mutiny t' get the point across?"

"Can it, Rummy," Dugard snapped. "Your crew might be one of the most ruthless to sail the seas, but your campaign would be short-lived against the Royal Guard."

Seadread answered with a derisive snort.

Zale spread his arms. "How can you *do* this? And *now*, so close to the deadline?"

"*Me?*" Dugard gave a disparaging chuckle and took a seat behind his desk. "I'm on your side here, gentlemen. I can't remember a time when two crews were so close to the goal. This order came from Fort Morga—from the capital baron himself, on authority from Metsada Palace. It seems, for now, that the crown wants the two of you to remain in full service."

"And what business does Lycus Char have with the seafarin' guild?" Seadread asked.

"*Baron* Char takes a keen interest in *all* the guilds throughout Sharm and Rocknee, not to mention an ever-tightening rein," Dugard replied.

Zale knew he spoke truth here, dissatisfying as it was. The baron's seat in Fort Morga was known in the kingdom as the *capital* baron. He was the only baron to preside over two provinces, Sharm and Rocknee, which also happened to be the two most populous provinces in the kingdom. Sharm contained the kingdom's capital city of Miskunn on the southeastern coast.

"This does not sit well with me at all," Zale grumbled. "It's completely against the code!"

"An ancient code," Dugard fired back. "You're lucky they haven't abolished it completely. Allowing entire crews to forego quotas for reaching an arbitrary goal, all while taking greater pay? It's a concept steeped in antiquity."

"Abolishin' it might yet be their goal, methinks," said Seadread.

"No other guild has any such thing," Dugard continued. "The kingdom might not pander to your lot quite as in days of old, but it seems the crown still has a soft spot. Despite mounting pressure— not the least of which is the constant possibility of starting war with other nations—they still want you scallywags to remain in service. At least for now, you're still considered *relevant*. Come now, gentlemen. You should be *flattered*, not dismayed!"

"How can we be assured the goal won't change again?" asked Zale.

Dugard shrugged. "You can't. But this is an unprecedented move, and I suspect the officials know when they're overplaying their hand."

"What has the bar been raised to?" Zale asked.

"It is now over ten million lyra," Dugard said.

Zale felt faint. More than one million lyra higher than before. In one fell swoop, he felt his hopes of respite slipping away. He had but wanted time to settle, to take only the jobs that most interested him, to spend his later years quietly with his family and granddaughters.

"And *this* be not overplayin' their hand?" Seadread asked.

"You're still both within reach," Dugard said. "Squeeze in the right one or two jobs, and you'll make it. Well . . . *one* of you, anyway. Now, get the blazes out of my office—both of you!"

Back in the foyer, Dippy eagerly hopped to Zale's side. He nearly tripped over a desk at the sight of Seadread.

"Sir," Dippy said, keeping his voice discreet, "is it true? Did they raise the bar?"

Seadread pushed through the exit ahead of them.

"It's true," Zale grumbled. "Go on and gather the officers as quick as you can. We need to go over our next move."

"Aye, sir."

Back outside, they descended the steps of the office building. Seadread stood below, watching them with his twitchy-eyed glare. Dippy cast him a furtive glance and skittered away down the alley.

"So," said Seadread as Zale reached the bottom step, "do ye fathom what job ye might pursue, Murdoch?"

"Not as such," Zale replied.

Seadread took calm steps toward Zale, stopping right in front of him. "Best pick a mighty coffer, Zale. 'Tis a high bar t' surpass."

"I'm still awaiting the strike of serendipity, as it were. And you, sir—have you picked up an apt assignment as of yet?"

Seadread's lazy eye seemed to shiver. "Might be that I have." He added a low grunt, his breath like old cabbage.

"May the best crew win, Captain," Zale said.

Seadread gave a dreadful, yellow-toothed smile. "Aye, just so, Zale. Best hope yer serendipity strikes fast. The seas of hesitation are filled with the carcasses of those who, at the brink of decision, waited and died." He clapped Zale on the shoulder as he made to leave. "Fair winds t' ye, Murdoch. Ye never know which way they'll blow."

Zale threw open the door to the rickety, sheet-metal meeting room where his crew officers had been assembled. Dippy had arranged everything, from securing the wharf-side locale to rounding up the officers. Shards of loosely mounted flocalcite minerals provided dim lighting from two of the room's opposite-facing walls.

"Look alive, men!" bellowed Zale as he entered. Cheery shouts of "*Captain!*" greeted him in return.

He shuffled his way toward a chair at the end of a long table that looked like a tall, smooth door sanded down and rolled over with brown paint.

He took stock of the other old salts seated around the table. It was time to make some decisions about their next job. He also needed to rally his crew around the challenge of the mastery bar situation, assuming they didn't first incite a riot.

Dippy, second only to Zale in seniority, puffed out his chest and tipped his sea-worn, black tricorn hat. "All the ship's top brass assembled, Captain."

"And then some, I see," Zale replied. "What's Wigglebelly doing here?"

Rapid chuckling responded from the other end of the room, from a gut that shook the table because it simply had nowhere else to go. The flushed, round face of Jaxon "Wigglebelly" Harper jolted back and forth, beady eyes glancing over his shipmates. The ring of wispy, white-gold hair encircling his head made him appear electrocuted.

"C'mon, guys." Wigglebelly pulled on his yellow suspenders. His zappy voice had the remarkable quality of sounding both light and thick all at once. "I'm the senior-most deckhand."

"You just want to know what we're meeting about," said Kasper "Beep" Gibbers. Beep stroked the long black and yellow hairs of his chin, a beard so thick that he was rumored to keep daggers stowed within. He was the ship's boatswain and the appointed deck foreman over matters such as navigation, rigging, sails, ropes, and hull.

"I'm an able-bodied seaman, man," Wigglebelly said.

"A *deckhand* is not an officer!"

Wigglebelly's smile disappeared. "I help all you guys out there. I can cook. I *fix* stuff, man!"

"You're *fat*, Wigglebelly!" Zale shot back. "And you can stay. Your jollity pleases me." Wigglebelly chuckled with glee, shifting the table a good three inches. Brash as it may have sounded, Zale's comment was chummy, making light of his own largeness.

Zale decided to start with matters of simple procedure. "Is the *Queenie* readied and provisioned for voyage?"

"So, we're *not* renaming the ship, then?" Beep asked. The subject, which Zale had dismissed at the time, had come up after returning from their last voyage.

Dippy rolled his eyes. "Again, Beep, it's named for the captain's cat."

"And—forgive me, sir—but that cat's *dead*, right? Mightn't that be bad luck?"

Zale felt a pang of sadness. Queenie had died during their last voyage, not two weeks ago, leaving Lola to the burial. Queenie had lived as posh and happy a life as any cat could hope for.

"That cat's better luck dead than half you slack-arsed lickspittles are alive!" Zale shouted. "Now, back on topic. Is the *Queenie* stocked and ready?"

"Aye-aye, Captain!" Yancy "Fump" Willigan saluted. Fump was the quartermaster, charged with the ship's stores of rations and supplies. A blue knit cap concealed his ginger hair, although his well-trimmed beard displayed it handsomely, and sunlight was the bane of his pale skin.

"Plenty of timber, nails, and sailcloth are all onboard," Fump said, "and victuals aplenty for a standard voyage. Barrels of drink get loaded in the morning, along with fresh wheels of cheese after Wigglebelly used up our whole supply."

Jaxon shifted his girth toward Fump. "You know what cheese soup calls for, man? *Cheese!*"

"Yeah, and usually *something* else! Elsewise it's just melted cheese. Gummed up my plumbing for days." Murmurs of agreement filled the room.

Zale slapped the table. "Stay on target, men! Chim, how's our armory stash? Are the crossbows and ballista all trimmed out?"

"Well, I haven't *shot* anyone for a real test since back in port," Rosh "Chim-Chum" Pureblood said, sounding mildly dissatisfied. Chim-Chum was nicknamed after an especially aggressive monkey they had encountered several voyages back. Rosh was Zale's one-armed master of arms, responsible for all weaponry aboard the *Queenie*. He had an oddly shaped, generally square head that flummoxed hat makers, glasses upon his nose, and receding sandy-brown hair.

"But the siege skein is well-torqued," added Chim, "and the crossbow strings cleaned and oiled. We still have plenty of bolts, spears, and swords aboard from our last load."

"How about our crew openings, Dippy?" Zale asked.

"We still lack a physicker, Captain ... and a chaplain, if we're concerned with tradition," Dippy replied. "Not essential needs, of course, so long as we have no sick or injured bodies."

"Or injured souls," Fump added.

"If our souls were perfect, would we be in this guild?" said Beep to a rumble of laughter.

Zale glared at the table. Whatever job they took, timeliness was more important than ever. Zale mentally assessed anything they could do now that might help.

"Beep, Fump ... let's have the berthing deck amidships cleared of all goods and chattels, and stow all extra supplies in the hold."

"Aye, sir, that's no problem," Beep said. "Is this to clear the benches?"

"Yes, Beep ... and please ensure the sweeps are in ready position."

"Are we ... rowing our next voyage?" Fump asked.

"Expediency's the word," Zale said. "If the wind betrays us, we must be ready to man the oars. That way we'll limit any becalming or tiding over as much as we can manage."

"We're a pretty light crew if we think much rowing will be involved," Chim said, "and we've not had a proper coxswain since losing Axel to the *Pilfer*."

"He'll get his reward for *that* treachery," Zale muttered. "Sailing a few months under that sot of a captain ought to do it."

"Sir," Dippy said, "I might have a notion for some additional crewmates, with your permission. Rowing or not, a few more hands on deck would not harm us."

"I'm inclined to agree," Zale replied. "Make it so."

"We could use a navigator for night-watch," said Beep.

Zale rubbed at his scratchy chin. "Take Jensen for that."

Beep's mouth fell open. "Jensen, sir? He's a little green, barely out of his vocational studies ... and more a carpenter at that."

"Gives the lad a good chance to prove his worth," Zale said. "Nothing like cutting a man's sleep to find out what he's really made of."

"Yes, sir," Beep said.

Zale leaned back. "Very good, crew. With that business out of the way ... I have some news of a potentially ... less-than-savory nature."

The room fell into the silence of anticipation. Zale's gruff sigh carried loudly. "Gentlemen ... the mastery bar has been raised."

Chairs slid and fists pounded the table.

"Can they do that?" asked Chim, his face suddenly grave.

"That's not supposed to happen *before* the deadline!" exclaimed Beep.

"That's harsh, man," said Wigglebelly. "That's real harsh. Hey, who can we pay off? There's always someone to pay off, man."

"You *pay off* the bar, addle-brain," Beep replied.

"*Huhuhuhuhuhu*," Wigglebelly erupted, looking to his comrades for support, finding none.

Zale rubbed the bridge of his nose, giving the initial shock time to settle. The one person who was still sitting quietly was Yancy. "What say you, Fump?"

Fump gave a light shrug. "How high have they raised it?"

"Over a million," he said.

The room again broke into a furious racket.

"It seems," Zale said once he could hear his own voice, "that the powers-that-be don't much relish the idea of granting their top crews quota flexibility and other such perks. Pratt says we should be *flattered* that we're still *relevant*."

"If they like us so much," said Chim, "maybe that could be to our advantage. Every crew in this guild knows enough about certain sanctioned cargo runs to stir hostilities abroad. I'm sure our good leaders would hate to have to answer for some of the jobs they've ordered."

"Aye, that's fair enough," Dippy said. "Still, I think we'd be wise to avoid a bout with the officials."

Zale liked Chim's thought process. True enough, many jobs over the years had been ordered by kingdom officials that involved less-than-friendly negotiations with other lands, if not outright theft. He agreed with Dippy, however, that tussling directly with kingdom officials would not bode well for them.

"An opportunity has presented itself," Zale said. "Dippy and I met a man at The Wench's Tavern, claiming to be within the inner circle of Brumm nobility."

Chim gave a low whistle. "That's no easy journey. At least one mountain pass, if not two, depending on which way you go."

"Oh, man." Wigglebelly shifted his girth and rubbed his hands together. "He must want something *really* expensive."

"He seeks an artifact known as the Grimstone," Zale said, "allegedly some piece of the celestial object that fell to Eliorin long ago and brought about the Shadow Age."

"The *Shadow* Age?" Beep asked. "Is this guy for real?"

"I was there," Dippy said. "This guy was real. Set the bloody table on fire with his hands."

"Not just fire," Zale added. "It flickered *purple*, and instead of heat came a completely unnatural chill."

"Sounds like a magician," said Chim.

"Maybe some kind of illusion," said Beep.

"The man knew of the raised bar," Zale said. "In fact, he's the one who told us about it. He promised that the pay from this job would more than cover the new goal."

The room fell into a contemplative stillness.

"It seems a little too convenient," Fump finally said. "Too

good to be true."

There were a few nods of assent around the table.

"I agree," said Chim. "It's your call, Captain ... but to speak of the Shadow Age ... and a parlor trick that was probably some kind of flamethyst ... and then he just happens to offer what we'll need to pass the goal .... I can't help feeling a little skeptical."

"That wasn't flamethyst," Dippy muttered.

"There's another interesting development," Zale said. "This gentleman also managed to approach ol' Puffypants."

"Seadread," Dippy added under his breath.

"Maybe he's trying to play the field," said Fump. "Stir us to action by mentioning our biggest rival."

"I got the distinct impression that he came to Warvonia seeking the best," Zale said. "And he found them: Seadread and us."

"If Seadread goes for it," Chim said, "he could beat us to the goal with this one job."

"Or," Beep said, "the guy's throwing *both* of us on a bootless errand. Think about it. They've raised the bar. The officials clearly don't want us to earn quota exemption. Instead of just blatantly doing away with the goal, they just sidetrack us with a bogus job—make us flap our rudder aimlessly until the deadline passes and they raise the bar even higher, perhaps this time so high that no one could reach it."

"And if it's *not* a misdirection?" Dippy asked. "Even aside from the goal, it could bring us more boodle than we've ever hauled in a single charge."

"Everyone know," Zale said, "that I don't consider this mission lightly. Aside from the uncertainty, it could be dangerous. It might even tangle us up with Gukhan."

"Aye, Captain," said Dippy, "but such a large bounty should be expected to carry some risk."

"I think you're all forgetting something," said Beep. "This is supposedly an object of the *Shadow Age*, and the Shadow Age is just a fable!"

"How can you be so sure?" Chim asked.

"Because I outgrew the children's stories about grimkins and umbramancers."

Wigglebelly's smile disappeared. "Some say that stuff's true, man."

Beep groaned. "*Why* is Jaxon here again?"

"It's a risky proposition." Zale projected his voice before the conversation veered further off track. "Do we have any other prospects?"

"Well, it could be a long-shot," Fump said, "but we might have first dibs to bring in a shipment of verdantium from Korangar. Tourism trade loves the stuff."

"Hey, that's promising," Chim said.

"Just one shipment of green moonstone isn't going to get us to over a million lyra," Dippy said.

"No, but it's such a short voyage, we should have enough time to pick up something else," Chim said.

Fump nodded. "Which brings me to job number two...."

Zale stared at Fump, impressed, finally feeling a glimmer of hope that they might have a real opportunity to sink their teeth into.

"It's a chancier run to Akkadia," Fump said. "The university down in Miskunn's after a cosmic mineral called heptalatticite for research, and they'll pay big for it. Apparently the grimkins haven't been willing to negotiate fairly and need some motivation. It'd be a small shipment. Even against the winds, we might get back faster than usual."

Zale rubbed feverishly at his stubbly beard. "This *does* seem promising, Fump."

The Korangarian capital of Vartu was only about a week's sail north of Warvonia, where they could retrieve the shipment and hurry back. Akkadia was a bit farther, across open waters to the east, but still doable. The feather-covered, beak-mouthed grimkins could be a sketchy bunch, but Zale's crew had dealt with their kind a few times over the years.

These jobs brought a certain comfort to Zale—a familiarity. He could imagine the cargo. He could trace their course in his mind's eye. Their outcome seemed inevitable. He saw none of that with the Grimstone job.

"What if the grimkins won't cooperate?" Beep asked.

"Those lightweight, flightless wonders are of little concern," Dippy said.

"Chances are they'd think twice before getting the Tuscaw-nese officials too upset," Fump said. "If not, we'll intervene—make those grimkins squawk like egg-laying hens until a favorable arrangement is struck."

"The grimkins can be a stubborn lot," said Beep.

"Aye," Zale agreed. "There'll be no time for shenanigans."

"Sounds perfect to me," Chim said. "Let Seadread chase the wind while we hurtle past the goal with *real* loads."

"Well, that settles it then, right?" Beep asked.

Dippy looked at Zale. "What do you say, Cap?"

Zale placed both hands upon the table with an air of finality. "To you, Fump Willigan, I say stow an extra ration of ale for yourself, and draw up the papers. We've got ourselves two jobs to the goal, men!"

CHAPTER 3

CHANCE MEETINGS

7/22/3203 P.A.

Zale's mind raced that night as he lay in bed, trying in vain to sleep. The clock in his bedroom had long passed the twenty-seventh hour, working its way steadily beyond midnight. Before he knew it, the third hour of morning was upon him.

He sat up with a grunt. The bed squeaked in protest as he gave himself a light spring and stood. Looking back, he was relieved to see that he hadn't woken Lola. He grabbed a robe and tied it over his shirtless gut, and stepped into a pair of padded slippers.

Throwing open a sliding door, he made his way out to their balcony, where spread before him was a gorgeous view of Warvonia below and the sea in the east. Eliorin's planetary rings cast a bright band in the sky, reflecting across the water and beyond the horizon. The moon shared the sky as a fading crescent, a meager showing in comparison.

Many a wayfarer had postulated how much more complex navigating the ocean would be without these rings as a guide. Such people, of course, were simpletons to Zale. To these comments, he'd often point out: "If the rings weren't there, the stars would be much brighter, and we'd learn to guide ourselves with them instead."

In fact several stars were still visible despite the rings, on clear enough nights. Enough stars to still pinpoint the cardinal directions, if one knew where and when to look.

But tonight Zale's mind was on much more than the rings, moon, and stars.

He knew seeking the Grimstone could be a fool's errand. Clearly his crew thought as much. Yet, he was unsettled. Had that man Vidimir truly come from the nobility class of Brumm? If so, and it was the Palace that sought this artifact, Zale and his crew might have been remiss to brush it off so quickly. Even worse, if Seadread's crew took the job and managed to succeed, it would reflect all the more poorly on Zale.

He needed some kind of verification. On the morrow his crew would be at work readying the *Queenie* for their short stint to Korangar. Zale, he decided, would be elsewhere, visiting one of his most trusted sources for obscure information, past and present.

It was time to see trusty old Tomescrubber.

Jira "Tomescrubber" Dunkeld was a spry, hunchbacked old gaffer with a thick thatch of white hair and more spring in his step than a marsupial. His shack was just beyond the westernmost fringes of Warvonia, at the edge of a dense forest full of corkscrew willows and curly-trunked, blue-leafed oaks, like wooden serpents emerged from the ground and frozen in time.

Arriving there took Zale all of three hours upon the back of his sturdy and stout pony named Rudy. Zale was naturally an early riser on even restful nights, often up with the first hint of sunlight creeping over the skyline, if not before. All he'd needed was a stein of black coffee, and by the fifth hour he was saddled up and on his way.

After three hard knocks the door swung open. The squat old man peered up at him, eyes widening with recognition. "Zale!" he laughed, giving his hand a hearty shake. "Things slowed down on the mercantile front?"

"Anything but," Zale said. "I have a bit of a quandary, Tomescrubber. I'm hoping you might know something about a certain artifact ... something of an *ethereal* nature."

"Oh?" Jira hopped aside. "Come in, come in. Have a seat."

Jira shut the door and scooted his way toward another room.

"How about some tea, huh? Or a glass of wine? Ruca Merlot—some of Sharm's finest!"

"Tea would be perfect, thanks."

Zale sat on a bentwood chair, sinking into its cushion. He gazed around the eccentric hut, enticed by the variety of scattered sundries throughout—half-melted candles upon tables, vials, bowls, chunks of rocks and gems, dried herbs hanging overhead.

Most of all his eyes scanned the shelves packed with dozens of old books. Old Tomescrubber had once been a student of Miskunn Vocational University under the most unusual discipline of historical arcana. Over the years he rose to the station of professor, and during that time he had been a keeper of annals, chronicles, and archived writings of the most esoteric sort. None of these he was allowed to keep for himself, of course, but he studied them voraciously. The volumes in this room were Tomescrubber's own personal notes—cherry-picked minutiae that he considered most relevant, most fascinating, most mysterious, and generally most worthy of further study.

Jira returned with a tray and two steaming teacups. "Here we are," he said, lowering the tray toward Zale.

He placed the tray upon a low table and sat in another chair, facing Zale. "So, within my humble abode, the great Zale 'the Gale' Murdoch . . . or *Macpherson*, I should rather."

Jira knew one thing about Zale known to no one else outside of his immediate family: Murdoch was not his birth name. Zale had been adopted at an early age, and he barely ever knew his real parents. It was Tomescrubber who later helped him track down his original family name, Macpherson, on a curious whim.

Murdoch took a sip of his tea. "*Zale* will be fine, good sir."

"And what is it that brings you here, my old friend? Have you taken up an interesting new quarry?"

"An opportunity has come up, but my crew and I haven't exactly jumped at the chance." Zale shifted in his seat to the sound of creaking wood. "I've been approached about an object known as the Grimstone."

Jira gave him a good, long stare. "Grimstone, you say? What about it?"

"A ... potential client is asking after it. He spoke of it as an item of great significance, although he associated it with the mythical Shadow Age."

Tomescrubber rubbed at a twitchy eye. "'Mythical,' you say? *Historical* would be more accurate, although who can trust half of the history we have on record, anyway?"

Zale nodded politely. Academics generally fell into one of two camps: some believed the Shadow Age occurred and some did not. Kingdom history tended to support the latter. Those who believed one way often scorned those who believed the other.

Zale, as many others, kept a mostly neutral stance on the matter. Although, if the Shadow Age came up in meaningful conversation, such as when discussing a job, he typically chose to side with kingdom history.

"What do you know about the Shadow Age?" Zale asked.

Jira shrugged. "Who knows much of anything, really? It's a relatively short period, as history goes—just over four centuries—characterized by a darkness so powerful that it could replace the life-sustaining energy of the sun, albeit in a very unnatural way. It was started by a great object which fell from the heavens, what we refer to as the Dark Entry. Its impact brought about the Darkness Cataclysm, which ended the Foudroyant Age."

Zale took another sip of tea. This was a refresher for him. Eliorin's history was marred by several cataclysmic ages that left gaping holes in the records of ancient history. Some suspected there were entire cataclysms that went unrecorded. It was easy to fathom how an age of evil sorcerers, cold fires, and other mystical elements could have found its way into the mix. Zale remembered Vidimir's strange fire in the tavern.

"It's how grimkins get such a bad rap, you know," Jira said. "They became associated with sorcerers and darkfires and energies of the Void, the use of which seemed to come quite easy for them. Even our children hear stories about grimkins and mages that are rooted in the Shadow Age."

"This man I met," Zale said. "I think he might have conjured some of this darkfire you speak of. It was a purple flame, from which I felt a chill rather than heat."

Jira bolted upright and nearly spilled his tea. "You don't say? That is an energy of the Void, specifically conjured by using the mineral known as *byrne*, something else which is believed to have its origins in the Shadow Age."

"And what of this Grimstone?"

"Now *that* is a thing of legend." He hopped up from his seat and made his way around to a shelf of his privately scribed books. He tapped at their spines, peering at each one, and finally stopped with a triumphant "Ah!" Jira pulled the volume and leafed through its pages. The old man grunted and hummed in thought, flipping page after page.

"Here we are! Grimstone!" He brought the book back to his seat. "As legend has it, when the Dark Entry arrived, it soared through the atmosphere as a ball of blackness. There was no fire—no light of any kind. It was as though a chunk of outer space itself had broken the sky. As it fell, and its darkness swept over the land, the Entry was struck."

"Struck in midair?" Zale asked. "By what?"

"Bursts of light, essentially—the ethereal power of Aether, the antithesis of Void. It was a counterattack—one that, unfortunately, failed."

Zale worked his mind to see if he could piece any of this together. In the more esoteric history, the Dark Entry's arrival marked both the start of the Shadow Age and the end of the Foudroyant Age, which had been characterized as a period of strange electrical turbulence throughout the land. Scientists and historians couldn't argue about the age's existence, but much disagreement existed about what actually happened. Ancient accounts included everything from random flashes of light in the air to bolts of lightning from the ground to fires so bright they were like looking directly at the sun.

"Would this be lightning still present from the Foudroyant Age?" Zale asked. "But a *counterattack*—by whom, the planet?"

"Some might say that," Jira replied. "But, if you give any credence to certain legends, the blasts came not from the planet but from a being. A being of the Ethereal Realm, to be exact."

This was not something Zale had ever gleaned from history. "An angel?" he asked.

Jira nodded. "An astral. An archastral ... formerly, that is. By the time this Dark Entry arrived, the archastral Zophiel had already given up her immortality to save the world from the deathly cold Albedo Age." Jira cleared his throat. "I should tell you, Zale, that this legend is generally ... *rejected* ... by kingdom officials. Our history—our *faith*—is to be placed in the Patriarch, Birqu Umis, who established the Throne of Light. The Throne channels the blessing of the divine through Metsada Palace, thus giving us the Light of the Land. So, what I'm about to tell you is according to certain *legend*. Don't stab the messenger."

"Fair enough," Zale replied.

"By this legend, the Throne is among the 'gifts of Zophiel,' and Birqu Umis was but a man chosen by this former archastral. Zophiel, after she became mortal, chose Birqu as a husband, and *this* is where the lineage of the Throne of Light began."

"What legend is this?"

"It's a legend of legends, really—the legend of the Heroes of Time."

"And how does this relate back to the Grimstone?" Zale asked.

"Oh, well, that's simple!" Jira said with a laugh. "When the blasts of light hit the Dark Entry, a piece of it broke off. *That* is what has come to be known as the Grimstone."

Zale scratched at his chin, seeing the parallel between this account and Vidimir's. The object Vidimir sought supposedly carried the power of this Dark Entry which had, according to legend, overpowered the Light in days past.

"You learned all this from the university, did you?" Zale asked.

Jira waved him off. "This is research of my own volition. The university course was always watered down. You should see the pale stalk of a man they've got running it now. Gives me the creeps!"

"Has anyone ever found this Grimstone before?" Zale asked.

"Never. That it exists in legend only makes it purely that … *legend.*" He spun the book to face Zale. "Look at this. 'Within the land where none may land, the Grimstone lies between what has been and what will be.' *That's* our only clue about where it might be located … and it's a load of gibberish!"

"My prospective client indicated it might be in Gukhan."

The old man paled at the name. "Well … as it's forbidden to outsiders, I suppose that *is* a 'land where none may land' … sort of … but I'd hardly call that conclusive."

With all this talk of legends, Zale agreed. This hardly seemed conclusive. "My crew thought as much," he said, "that it'd be a fool's errand. If I may ask, Tomescrubber, if someone wanted you to find this thing, would you do it?"

Jira sat still for long moments, staring into the space of his hut's living area. Finally, he answered, "I think you're right to avoid it. For one thing, it *could* be a fool's errand. And Gukhan …" He shivered. "Who wants to deal with *that*? I might believe that

Zophiel truly did attack the Dark Entry with the power of Aether as it fell, but there's no historical proof that the Grimstone—a broken shard of the *Ni'shan-qa Til'la-ni'tha*—actually exists."

This all seemed to support the decision Zale and his crew had made not to pursue the Grimstone. He still couldn't help but wonder...

"What if it *does* exist?"

Tomescrubber's eyes hardened. "Then it's a powerful relic of the Void, part of the thing which brought us the Shadow Age once before... and *that*, my friend, makes it very dangerous."

Starlina Murdoch sat in her nightgown within her Warvonia apartment, running a brush through the tangles in her long, straight hair. Its woody brown color shone in the light, high-lighted by strands of pale blue, a relatively unusual color combination known as sky-wood. It played delicately about her tall, oval face. Her skin was lightly tanned from ample time outdoors. She loved going to the beach, even though she despised the ocean.

"Guess what *I* heard," cooed Amira, Starlina's closest friend.

Starlina looked at Amira through her vanity mirror. "Are you going to torture me with secrets?"

"I'm torn," Amira said. "You might want to know this... but, then again, you might not." She flung her white-blonde hair back around her thin neck.

Starlina narrowed her eyes. Amira was her roommate and coworker, and naturally they shared much of life together. It had already been a long day for them at Friendly Oaf's Taproom serving meals, busing tables, and cleaning dishes.

Certainly the work was not glamorous, but it would suffice until the opportunity for better work. Starlina had worked there for nearly three years, Amira for just over one year, and the two of them became instant friends. The hope was that they could pursue their chosen career disciplines together at Rocknee Vocational.

Amira desired to run her own shop as a cobbler or tailor. Starlina long held that she would add beauty and appeal to Warvonia's inland scene as a designer. Then fewer of their citizens might turn so adamantly to the sea. She hadn't yet decided if she would focus on the ins and outs of buildings or landscaping or fashion—perhaps even a bit of each. She still had time to figure it out. Amira, assuming she earned final admittance, was set to head off at the start of Agust. Starlina wouldn't be able to join her until the next term, nearly eight months later, because of her seventeenth birthday occurring too late in the year.

Starlina gave a threatening wag of her hairbrush. "Then you'd better come out with it, or you might be off to Vocational with a teacup lodged in your throat."

"It's about your dear Jensen."

"Jensen? Well, he's already left university. I'm supposed to see him before his next departure with my father."

Another departure. Another long sea adventure far from home. In the past, she only had to bear such partings with her father, but now Jensen was part of the crew, just like he'd always dreamed. For Starlina, it was like a sucker punch to the heart.

Amira seemed fit to burst. "Oh, I can't tell you. I really shouldn't. His shipmates are far too loose of tongue."

Starlina glared at her. "Not telling me now might be quite hazardous to your health."

"This *could* be misreading the hearsays, mind you ... but, Starlina ... Jensen means to propose to you!"

Starlina felt a nervous flutter in her stomach. This was not something she felt prepared to deal with. "Oh ... I see."

"'I see.' *That's* your response?"

Starlina turned back to the mirror and resumed her brushing. "I don't suppose this rumor came with any intention on his part to change careers, did it?"

Amira scowled. "You've still not accepted that he's a seafarer, and yet you continue fawning over him. And why shouldn't you? Almost anyone else would kill for the chance to be married even before starting at university!"

She wasn't wrong. Sixteen was oft considered a prime age for marriage in Tuscawny. Then all the flirtations and courting and dating dramas were already out of the way, no longer a distraction from studies. Then, in theory, there was more support at home, a couple working as a team through the ups and downs of life.

Amira took the brush from her hair mid-stroke and slitted

her eyes in something of a scandalous, wolfish look. "Wait. Jensen has brothers, doesn't he?"

Starlina chortled. "Forget it, Amira. They're both in Stonehaven, and they're both spoken for." It was another port city in the north, much smaller in sea trade than Warvonia, and it was also where Jensen's parents lived.

"Ah well," Amira sighed. "Always hoped I'd find a good man before university. Since I haven't, Mother thinks I should wait until *after* graduating to even date anyone. I ask you, Starlina, where's the fun in that?"

Starlina shook her head. Sometimes she was glad her parents weren't around to nag her about such things. Although, other times she longed for the classic adversarial encounters that parents and daughters tend to have. They were cute, loving, not like the constant fights she'd had with her mother. That was over two years ago, before her mother left for Sharm. Starlina had not heard from her since.

Of course, her father was around for none of this. He was off chasing sea monsters and valuable bounties, and now Jensen was right there with him.

"I *do* love him, you know." She managed a wry smirk. "It's just that, if he really loved me back, he'd become a fisherman or a dockhand instead."

"Oh poor, poor, conflicted Starlina." Amira worked her hair into a loose braid above her neck. "I wouldn't half mind it if a sailor called on me. Their arms all contoured with muscle, their hands rough from the ropes ... and all that pluck and grit from their time at sea. That's not to mention the exotic gifts you might get from foreign lands."

Starlina picked up Jensen's lilac-colored gemstone from her nightstand. She ran her thumb across its smooth, glossy surface. "Yes, they do come with such gifts." She clenched her fingers around the stone. "But then they're gone again, missing your life ... missing your children's lives. At night a cold, empty bed awaits you, and the warm embrace you desire is an ocean's distance away. Is that really a life to be excited about, Amira?"

"You despise his occupation, and yet you keep his hopes alive. It seems you might finally have to make a choice, Starlina Murdoch."

Starlina opened a drawer and dropped the stone inside.

"I dearly hope you're wrong, Amira. Because if you're right, I fear I shall be forced to break his heart ... and mine in the process."

A steady breeze caressed the ships and sailors of Warvonia's harbor. Zale stood tall and proud in the morning air, sipping a fresh brew of coffee and overlooking the newly scrubbed hull of the *Queenie* with a deep feeling of satisfaction.

There she bobbed with a sense of calm, a single-masted beauty, her planks fashioned of deep, woody-red roastwood from the Monarch Mountains. Furled was her fresh, new sail, its yard wobbling lazily in the breeze, oozing with anxious anticipation to be drawn taut and absorb the wind's thrust. Soon its wish would be granted.

Zale harbored great excitement to be back on the water. He watched from the wharf as the men aboard the ship scurried about with their final preparations. All throughout the *Queenie*, provisions were being double- and triple-checked, ropes were being set, pumps were being tested, bolts were being tightened, and quarters were being readied by the ship's crew of nearly thirty men.

"Good morning, Captain," a man said.

Zale nearly choked on a sip of coffee. The man's voice was lilting and strong but not overpowering. Zale quickly wiped his mouth and turned to face a well-tanned, middle-aged man with a perfectly smooth head. He was lean and nearly a half-head taller than Zale, dressed in a long, black, double-breasted frock coat with patterned material and buttons from neck to waist.

This was the same bald man Zale had seen in the tavern the night he met Vidimir.

After a suppressed, sputtering cough, Zale managed to respond. "Yes?"

"I pray you'll forgive my intrusion. She is a beautiful ship."

"Much obliged, sir."

The man extended a hand. "My name is Fulgar Geth. It is my understanding that you are short some vital crewmen."

Dippy, Zale thought, believing his first mate must have arranged this meeting. He had also been there, in the tavern.

Zale shook Fulgar's hand. "Are you offering to fill a role?"

"I can fill many roles," Fulgar said, "but chief among them is healer and spiritual guide."

Zale frowned. "Then you're a physicker and a . . . chaplain?"

"If you prefer to title me as such, Captain."

"I have to admit," Zale said, "that neither charge is our top priority. Having a physicker onboard suits me well, but our upcoming voyages are expected to be short ones. Your share would be no more than our general deckhands. Should your services save anyone's life or limb, I suspect we could discuss further recompense. I offer no promises."

Fulgar gave a short bow. "I offer no expectations, Captain. The honor of sailing under the great Captain Murdoch is payment enough. Call it . . . a bolster to my career."

"I'll have nothing outlandish—no bizarre Dualist rituals or Zunist sun worship."

Fulgar stiffened his back. "No, Captain. I believe many religions have hints of truth, but my devotion is to Eloh."

"Do you also have a loblolly boy or some such assistant?"

"No, sir. I offer only myself."

"You must bring your own tools and supplies," Zale said. "We have some of the basics, but my quartermaster lacks the time to muster additional inventories."

"Exactly as I prefer it."

"Very well, sir. We'll add you to the ship's roster. Welcome to the crew of the *Queenie*."

Dippy had beckoned Captain Murdoch to Warvonia's canals, a few miles up the coast from the harbor, and to the calm-water docks a few miles inland. Long canoes sporting rowing teams darted up and down the canal with men standing at the helms, shouting commands. These canals were popular for watersport in Warvonia, as well as for seafaring professionals to stay fit and well-practiced between jobs.

When Dippy summoned him here, Zale had demanded to know why. His first mate insisted on waiting until Zale could see for himself. Their impending voyage in mind, Zale reluctantly obliged and tried to keep the detour from vexing him too much.

"What's all this about, Dippy? More than lollygagging, I should hope."

He left open the implication that Dippy should be with his crewmates, finalizing preparations aboard the *Queenie*.

Dippy squinted down the waterway. "With our talk of recruiting a coxswain, sir, I got to thinking. There's one such soul who happens to be between jobs—none better, I'd say, in the art of steersmanship. Been in my sights a good while now, actually."

Zale swelled at this good news. "Well, that's encouraging! A few able rowers would be a nice boost, but a skilled coxswain could prove especially advantageous. Is this gentleman known within the guild?"

Dippy cleared his throat. "Not exactly, sir. I shall have to pull some quick paperwork to transfer from the aquaculture guild, but I believe Chief Pratt's office will process forthwith the request."

"I suspect so. Aquaculture—that's intriguing. Leader of fishing boats, then?"

"Yes, sir."

"When can I meet this strapping new seadog?"

"Be along shortly, I expect," Dippy replied. He seemed quite determined not to look at Zale, still watching only the waterway.

As rowing teams glided by, Zale could tell the novices from the veterans. Whenever he saw a team struggle to synchronize their strokes or perform a smooth turn, he hoped that leader was not who Dippy had in mind.

He smirked upon sighting a shell of four rowers with a female standing at the helm, her voice blaring into the docks. Her mocha-colored skin seemed to shine in the sunlight. Wavy locks of chestnut-and-gold hair draped over a gray headband and played about the shoulder-straps of her sleeveless top.

By now they could hear the lady coxswain's commands, called out in a clear, well-enunciated voice with husky under-tones that demanded attention. "Easy on port!" They turned in toward the dock, her crew in perfect form.

Zale stiffened as the crew boat approached. *Surely not*, he thought.

"Check it down!" the woman shouted. The crew buried their oars in the water, bringing them to a stop beside the dock.

"Dippy..." Zale said under his breath.

Not twenty feet away, the lady coxswain was stepping onto the dock.

"Daubernoun," he continued in a low grumble, "what are you getting me into?"

"Captain Murdoch," Dippy spoke in a grand voice as the woman approached, "please meet Evette Caskmore."

Evette flashed white teeth, and her big, brown eyes focused sharply on Zale. She stood tall and extended a hand. "Captain Murdoch—I'm honored. I hear you have need of an able coxswain."

Zale was taken aback by the firmness of her handshake. "Pleasure to meet you." He leaned in to his first mate. "Dippy, a word with you, please."

Dippy hastily held up a finger to Evette and turned around with Zale.

"Dippy, what are you *doing*?" Zale muttered.

"Finding us a coxswain, sir. One of the best."

"You know we can't have *dames* aboard!" Zale hissed. "We're an all-male crew. A woman would throw our whole operation into a tailspin."

Women at sea were traditionally considered bad luck. In some ways this went back centuries to superstitions that women aboard ships caused turbulent waves and violent storms.

But Zale knew not all storms were the weather kind.

Some crews handled mixed genders with success. Zale had had no such luck in the past. In his experience, a woman with an otherwise all-male crew was a nearly unavoidable distraction.

Confined together for weeks, men could preoccupy themselves with their work, their crass jokes, their unadulterated banter, and the prize to be won. With even one woman aboard, most men became subject to an entirely different set of behaviors and instincts. An otherwise able crew might be thrown off its game.

"I've vetted this one, Captain," Dippy said. "Just speak with her. With time so short, she's worth at least a consideration."

Zale groaned. "You might be forgetting, Dippy. At sea, your first love is your ship, and she is a jealous lover. Bring a woman aboard, and the men forget themselves and their duty to the ship. It's tantamount to adultery!"

Dippy returned a wry smile. "Ironic, sir, coming from the only of us who is, in fact, married to a woman."

"I'm a lot more concerned about the crew than myself."

"It's not just her, sir." Dippy gestured at the four men who had been in Evette's boat and now stood upon the dock. "It's four more men to fill the gap in our rowing ranks. We'll have that many more hands to streamline our voyage."

Zale could hardly argue with that, despite his reservations. He turned back around to face Evette. He reverted to a more congenial persona. "I should tell you, just to be upfront, that we're an all-male crew."

Evette kept her shoulders back, maintaining eye contact. "I'm accustomed to male crews. As with your guild, Captain, women aboard fishing vessels are few and far between. That's just the way it is. I know how to handle it."

"Not to be presumptuous," Zale said, "but the sailors of our guild might be of a somewhat less refined class than your aqua-cultural charges. The seafaring merchant guild of Warvonia is filled with honest men, sure, but just as many sanctioned scally-wags, privateers, and looters."

"Captain... I've twisted many arms of quick-fingered gropers. I've kicked more balls than a provincial fieldblitz team. Aquafarmers might not be quite as *refined* as you think. With your reputation, I'm sure your crew is more professional than simple looters."

Zale rubbed fervently at his chin whiskers. *At least these are two short voyages,* he considered. *If the first one's a disaster, we'll just part ways before the second.*

Finally, he held out his right hand and shook with Evette. "Welcome to the crew of the *Queenie*. Today is Tunesday. With any luck, we'll set sail Flamsday morning. Preparations are underway now. Dippy here will give you the rundown about your share as coxswain and shares for your rowers, who when *not* rowing will slog alongside our other deckhands to do whatever is needed."

"Thank you, Captain," she replied. "We'll be ready."

She left them, returning to her fellow rowers with shouts of triumph.

"I hope to Eloh I don't regret this," Zale said to Dippy. "If this doesn't go well, it's on you." He managed a smirk. "If it *does* go well, it's on me."

"Aye, Captain," Dippy said. "I'm just glad that we're crewed enough to be on our way."

"On that note... very fortuitous how you found a man doubling as physicker *and* chaplain. Sublime work, Dippy."

"Sir?" Dippy replied with a slight tilt of his head, eyes blinking.

"He found me earlier at the wharf," Zale said. "The man named Fulgar."

"A fascinating notion, Captain, for which I'd love to take credit... but, I must confess, I know of no such man."

Zale frowned, now wondering how the man had come to know of their impending voyage.

"Curious case."

And, in thought, he departed from the canals.

Chapter 4

ALL ABOARD

7/25/3203 P.A.

"**W**ho's got a smooch-cake for ol' Pop-Pop?!"

"We do!" sang three eager voices.

Zale's granddaughters ran into his embrace and pecked his bristly cheeks with kisses. He shook hands with Dane, Haly's husband, and walked into their home exchanging greetings. Baby Hazel reached out from Haly's arms, and Zale gladly took her into his own.

"*Squeakle-Imp!*" he piped in his playful, higher-pitched voice.

Whenever possible, Zale made it a point to visit his grandchildren before setting sail. If things went well with their upcoming two voyages, fewer of his visits would be for the purpose of saying goodbye.

Tonight Zale and Lola were in for a treat: fresh pottage stew with boiled vegetables and roasted beef, followed by leftover marzipan cake from Nova's birthday. The broth's warm, savory smell set Zale's stomach to growling, a most welcome home-cooked meal before subjecting himself to Wigglebelly's cooking aboard the *Queenie*.

"This smells delicious, Haly," Lola said.

"Pop-Pop," started little Nova timidly, "could you say the 'Treasure of Mac'?"

Zale thought a moment. "The 'Treasure of Mac,' you say? You've got a prodigious memory there." He took a seat, his grand-daughters gathering round. "Now, girls, sailors hear a great many tales and stories over the years. This is one I've known most of my life, since I was just a lad, passed down from my parents."

He cleared his throat.

> "The Treasure of Mac is not very far;
> Once you know where to look, then you'll know
>   where you are!
> O dear Mac, if you're here, thy great name is alive;
> Thy back to the river, then ten paces five!
> O most brilliant Mac, the treasure is nigh;
> Your head must be spinning, from looking so high!
> O Mac, you great rascal, thy foundation is rock;
> It's dark water below, and below must ye hop!
> O wondrous Mac, if here faith do ye lack;
> Then ne'er shall ye claim the great Treasure of Mac!"

The girls cheered as soon as he finished. "What *is* the Treasure of Mac, Pop-Pop?" asked Fawn, oldest of the girls.

"It's just a fun old treasure hunting rhyme," Zale replied. "I like to think that ol' Mac, in the end, had enough faith to find the greatest treasure of all."

"What's the greatest treasure?" asked six-year-old Sage.

It seemed such a simple question, but even the best of treasure hunters would likely never know the answer. Whatever was the largest payout known, merchant sailors only dreamed of fetching an even higher number—a never-ending cycle. Still, Zale found himself imagining where the Grimstone might fit in the greater scheme of high-value cargoes.

"If I ever find out, I'll let you know," Zale said.

"Okay, I think everything's ready," Haly announced.

In short order they were gathered round a long, wooden table, breathing in the rising steam from bowls set before them.

"Bring on the eats!" cheered Fawn, a spoon already clutched in her hand.

"Wait," said Haly. "First we should say a blessing. Sage, would you like to?"

Sage hesitated but finally answered, "Okay." They bowed heads. "Thank you, Eloh, for this day. I hope I have a good day tomorrow, and I hope I like the food. Thank you for the stew. I like it, even though I didn't a few minutes ago. And let Pop-Pop have a safe trip. Selah."

"*Selah*," everyone repeated.

"Glad you came around on the stew, Sage," Zale said with a wry smile.

Haly sighed. "There was much drama involved earlier over the stew."

Dane gestured toward Sage. "I told you you'd like it." Sage mumbled something incoherent into her spoon.

"When do you have to leave, Pop-Pop?" Fawn asked.

"As soon as first light on Flamsday," Zale answered, "if our fortunes hold out. That's after staying overnight on the ship getting everything ready."

"And then you won't have to make quotas anymore, right?" Fawn's face lit up with hope. "You'll be home a lot more to come visit us!"

Zale gave her a doting smile. "I hope so, sweetie." He looked over at Nova, who was slurping away at her stew, much of it landing on the table. "Careful there, Nova. Some of that stew might end up in your mouth."

"Where are you sailing to this time, Pop-Pop?" Fawn asked.

"We've had a few prospects, actually," Zale replied. "One's a beautiful green stone from Korangar called verdantium. Another's a special kind of space-rock for the university in Miskunn."

"What's the other one?"

Zale's hand, holding a spoonful of stew, stopped halfway to his mouth. "How do you know there's another one?"

"You said 'a few' prospects. Usually that means more than two, or you would've said 'a couple.'" She bounced in her chair, pleased with herself.

"So happens there was another job someone approached me with. Something called the Grimstone. This man I met told me that it might somehow help the Light of the Land. I say two to one it doesn't exist."

"In co-op yesterday," said Fawn, "one of my friends said the Light is fading. It sounds kind of scary. Our land needs the Light to survive. It's holy light that the divine—Eloh, I think—gave our land when He used lightning to make Alpha Makutu." She referred to the kingdom's famous star-shaped plateau, upon which the king's Metsada Palace rested.

"Just because you heard it," Dane said, "doesn't make it true."

Fawn continued. "Some stories I've read talk about using powers of darkness to help the Light. Maybe the Grimstone is something like that."

"I don't really like you reading those stories," Haly said. "They've got too much about the Shadow Age and sorcery and grimkins—not something you kids need to read."

Dane stood from his chair. "I'm going to grab that marzipan cake."

"Yum!" Fawn cheered. She turned back to Zale, looking him straight in the eyes. "Pop-Pop, if you could really do something to help the Light, would you?"

Dane returned with the marzipan cake. Zale's mouth hung open as though frozen mid-breath, not because this was his favorite dessert. As the adults served cake to the children, Zale stared pensively into his bowl.

Lola's arm was linked in Zale's as they walked under the nightglow of the rings, navigating the maze of cobbled streets and alleys on their way home. Neither of them moved particularly fast, especially with their path going in a generally uphill direction. Zale didn't mind. The humid air was warm and pleasant, a light breeze streaming through the alleyways. Soon his next voyage would begin, and he wanted to enjoy this walk with Lola before departing.

"That meal was zesty sustenance, wasn't it, Dwoey?" said Zale. "Haly does whip up a mean batch of pottage."

Lola returned a delightful smile. "That she does. Of course, she learned from the best."

"You mean the café manager down the street, right?" He cackled, pushing playfully into Lola. She laughed, as she always did, at his goofiness. "Are you and she going to the theater while I'm gone?"

"I think we are. But those dancing men from Eidyn are just so hard to look at." She jokingly fanned at her face.

"Oh, just throw a bucket of water on yourself."

They conversed further about family, the destinations of Zale's upcoming voyages, home improvement ideas, and things they might want to do once they had more time. They were just discussing how they might start a small garden, when another voice stopped them short.

"Lovely night for a stroll, Captain." A pale-skinned man stepped out from a side-alley and into their path.

Zale squinted and took a step ahead of Lola. Already his hackles were up. He only wished he had his sword with him. His family had come to prefer that he not carry it when visiting the kids, which he'd begrudgingly obliged.

The man came closer, and the dim light from a streetlamp illuminated his face.

"Vidimir?"

Memory of a cold, purple fire ignited in Zale's mind. This man had known too much about Zale's family even back in the tavern, and here he was again, an encounter that Zale assumed to be more than coincidence.

"I'm glad you recognize me," Vidimir said. "I understand your ship is nearly ready to depart."

"I don't really think my ship is any of your concern," Zale said.

"No need to be defensive, Captain. I approach you merely as a man with much at stake."

"Those can be the worst," Zale replied. "What is it you want?"

"Merely to ask you a question. If you could really do something to save the Light, would you?"

Zale's heart skipped. Lola gasped. It was the exact question Fawn had asked earlier.

Vidimir gave an insidious half-smirk. "Kids do say the darnedest things, don't they?"

"You keep your smug, prying face *away* from my family!"

Vidimir laughed. "Don't worry. I have better things to be concerned with than your family. It is, however, a fantastic question. It is, in fact, a question I've already placed before you.

I do so hope, Captain, that when you set sail, it is the Grimstone you seek. It is a most urgent service to your kingdom."

"Turns out everyone tends to think their need is most urgent. I'll pursue what best suits me and my crew. Your particular curio is ethereal mythology. We could circumnavigate nations and wander islands for weeks and come up with nothing."

"Did I not point you in the right direction, Captain? Rest assured you can trust my information. The Grimstone is out there, ripe for the taking."

"I don't trust you as far as I can piss."

Vidimir adjusted his shirt collar. "Are you a gambling man, Captain?"

"I don't gamble, Vidimir. I calculate. That's why I'm the best."

"Nor do I," Vidimir said. "I hedge my commissions most carefully. For every man who claims he's the best, another stands eager to prove him wrong. It comes down to this: you will retrieve what I seek, or someone else will. And be assured that your kingdom will remember those who answered the call to service . . . and those who did not."

"Is that some sort of threat?" Zale growled.

"It is simple reality. The choice is yours, Captain Murdoch." Vidimir gave a curt nod. "Pleasant night to you both."

He spun on his heels and walked into the shadows of the side-alley.

Moments later, when Zale peered into the side-alley's length, the man was gone without a trace.

"Captain aboard!" cried Dippy upon the deck of the *Queenie*. As deckhands scurried about, he grabbed at the rope of a nearby bell to give it a hasty ringing. "I say, Captain aboard!"

Most of the crew turned in sudden realization.

"At attention, men!" bellowed Zale. Silence fell across the deck. "Officers, *repooorrrt*! Everyone else, as you were!"

Although not sailing until the next day, Zale was clothed in fine seafaring array. One of his best blue tunics covered a white shirt, V-necked over a field of chest hairs. A monocle rested within a small pocket of his tunic, secured to a button by a gold chain. Upon his shoulders rested a navy-blue captain's coat with brass buttons down the flaps, its long tail hanging to the knees of his sandy-colored trousers. Below his knees were the turned-down tops of his brown cavalier boots. His best brown leather tricorn hat, complete with white, red, and blue feathers, covered his head, routing the breeze cleanly across the sides of his face, and his favorite saber was sheathed at his side.

He drew in a deep breath of the salty air, observing the friendly white clouds across a perfect sky. "Ah, we can't cut the waves soon enough, Dippy. This wind is exactly where I want it."

"Yes, sir. I quite agree," Dippy replied.

Within moments Kasper "Beep" Gibbers, Yancy "Fump" Willigan, Rosh "Chim-Chum" Pureblood, and Evette Caskmore stood before Zale and Dippy.

Zale scanned the area and found the smooth-headed man he sought. "You too, Fulgar."

The plump form of Jaxon "Wigglebelly" Harper emerged from the galley, puffy chef's hat upon his head, grasping a large pot with oven mitts. He walked up to the other officers and stood in place.

Zale frowned. "Not you, Wigglebelly."

"Ah, yeah," Wigglebelly spoke in his light, airy voice. "Just passing through, man. Whole crew's here."

"That they are," Zale said. "As you all can see, we now have a full crew. Quick introductions would be appropriate. Mister Fulgar Geth will act as our onboard physicker and chaplain."

Fulgar bowed in greeting. "Healer and spiritual guide, sir. Thank you."

"Right," Zale mumbled. "Take your physical and psychological woes to him."

"Hey," Chim said, "our chaplain's name rhymes with *vulgar*."

"Well, that makes him a perfect fit for this crew," Beep said.

"Next," Zale said, "we have Miss Evette Caskmore. She is a seasoned coxswain and will lead our rowing team. In fact, she brings with her four able rowers and deckhands . . . because, after all, many hands make faster plunder." He took note of the shifty glances already darting around. "Yes, she's a female. I'll tolerate no shenanigans on that account. Fump, ready her a private space within the hold. Is all copasetic with your quartermaster's mate?"

"Aye, Captain," Fump replied. "All's well. He's a bland sort of fellow. If he were a spice, he'd be flour. But he gets the job done."

"*Huhuhuhuhu*," Wigglebelly chuckled. "Flour. That's good, man."

Beep turned to him with a scowl. "Why are you still here, Wigglebelly?"

Zale cleared his throat. "Alright, men—er, crew—sorry, Evette, you might have to answer alongside the men until I get used to that."

"No need to change your methods on my account, Captain," Evette said.

Zale nodded. "Back to your final preparations. Dippy and I will be about the ship to ensure all's well. *Dismissed!*"

The officers dispersed, and Zale turned to Evette. He wanted to personally drive home his support of her command as coxswain.

"Miss Caskmore, what do you say we set things to order with your team?"

"Sounds good, Captain," she replied.

"Dippy, assemble all who will act as oarsmen in the event of need."

"Yes, sir!" Dippy yanked at the bell pull. "Oarsmen, below deck, on the double!" Those not already below made their way down the staircase.

Zale, Dippy, and Evette descended to the main inner deck of the *Queenie*, which housed the oarsmen benches as well as the crew hammocks. Zale inhaled the stout, woody aroma of the ship's roastwood planks as they entered. It was something like the charred logs of a campfire, but he loved it.

The galley was just ahead from the bottom of the stairs and below Zale's cabin in the ship's aft. From here they turned the opposite direction. This was also known as the berthing deck, where rows of hammocks hung from the support beams. Positioned between the hammocks were the oarsmen benches. To landlubbers it might look like insufferable clutter, but to Zale it was pure function. Often the hammocks were removed and stored during daytime shifts, with only a few left out for those on nighttime watch. Beyond the benches, moving toward the bow, were the stairs down to the hold, officers' quarters, and sickbay.

Dippy stood board-straight, sucked in a deep breath, and called out, "Captain on deck!" The commotion of voices and movement dissipated.

Zale made his way toward the center aisle between the rowing benches, his boots clomping heavily upon the boards. He stopped briefly beside Dippy and counted eleven men among the benches. "Is this everyone? I thought we had a dozen assigned oarsmen."

"Uh ... yes, sir ... mostly. It seems we are missing one of our designated oarsmen at present. That would be our newly appointed navigator ... and carpenter, Jensen. Perhaps he's conducting a repair, sir."

"Jensen," Zale repeated in a low, growling voice, rolling his eyes. "Let's hope so."

Dippy remained like a sentry at the base of the stairs as Zale continued down the aisle. Evette planted herself at the start of the aisle, arms crossed and hard eyes scanning the area and the men she would command during any situation that required the use of oars.

"As you've no doubt heard, we have a new coxswain aboard for this voyage," Zale said, pacing the aisle. "I'm here to set her charge in order. She comes with four able-bodied coxswain's mates, who will also serve as deckhands where needed." He nodded in the direction of the new crewmembers. "Introduce yourselves, men."

"Archie Hunt," said the first, his skin like dark mahogany.

"Cal Norton," said the next, a strapping young man.

"Winston Clergy," said a middle-aged fellow.

"Fritz Flitter," said the last, a man of wild fire-orange and brown hair.

"Your proficiency as oarsmen could make all the difference in a pinch," Zale said. "We race not only to bring in a copious bounty but also against the mastery bar, of which we are very much within reach. Now, I turn your attention to Coxswain Evette Caskmore."

Murmurs and sneers filled the deck. Zale watched closely for anyone who dared insolence, and also how Evette would handle it.

Evette slung her arms behind her back and stepped forward, shoulders back and head held high. "Oarsmen of the *Queenie*, listen up! When we are called to the sweeps, my voice will be your guide, your light in the darkness. By its command will you make this ship soar through the waves like an arrow in the wind. By my direction will you bank us around sea stacks and turn us toward or away from enemy engagement. *I* am your eyes. *My* voice is your conscience. You will hear it during the day. You will hear it in your dreams at night."

"I expect we will," muttered one of the oarsmen, Jonas. He nudged a shipmate, who remained smartly rigid.

Evette cast the man a sharp glare. "I have on good authority that I'm the only one here to lack a certain male body part. Get on my bad side, and you might find yourself lacking the same. Whether gelding or stallion, I *will* motivate you to move this ship. Are we clear?"

She was met with silence.

"I said, *are we clear*?!"

The oarsmen gave a jolted "Aye," followed by a nearly incoherent mix of "sir" and "ma'am."

Evette gave a satisfied nod. "Captain, with your permission, I'd like to acquaint these men with my primary calls and commands."

For a moment Zale almost believed that she commanded him, too. He recovered, straightening his posture.

"The deck is yours, Madam Coxswain."

Zale's office chair creaked in protest as he sat back from the desk of his private quarters. He took the spectacles from his face and rubbed the bridge of his nose. He tossed his glasses lightly upon the stack of flaxsheets before him. This was his least favorite part of any voyage, the pre-departure paperwork—a mess of expenses, ship's logs, accounts and certificates of provisions, guild documents of crewmembers added and released, a slop-book with a meal-plan from Wigglebelly that might as well have been written in slop.

Zale stood and stared through the aft windows at the increasing brightness of Eliorin's planetary rings as the sky darkened to twilight. It was late into the day's twenty-second hour. Most of the crew had already supped aboard the ship, partaking of whatever manner of gruel Wigglebelly and his mates could throw together amongst final preparations.

Tonight everyone was to stay aboard the *Queenie*. At first light they were scheduled to leave port. Their destinations were set. First they would put their stern to the rings and sail north for Korangar. After that, they were bound for Akkadia in the east.

That's the right move, Zale continued telling himself. Vidimir's sudden appearance and persistence last night had been meant to scare him into racing off to find the Grimstone. To Zale it made things all the more suspicious. Still, as a cautionary measure, he paid off a couple of friendly soldiers in town to keep an eye on his family. One could never be too careful.

If Vidimir really was some off-color pawn of nobility, it seemed there was a coordinated effort to keep both Zale's and Seadread's crews from reaching the mastery bar. It could be the kingdom's underhanded effort to ensure they both stayed in active service. Zale was quite content to call their bluff.

A knock sounded on his door. "Come in," Zale called.

Fulgar entered. "You asked to see me, Captain?"

"Please, sir, have a seat." Zale gestured toward a small padded chair.

Zale landed within his own creaky chair, taking a moment to stare at the physicker. Fulgar was a bit too undefined for Zale's taste. He meant to learn more, find out his motivations.

"Have you been able to set your space in order?" Zale asked.

"Yes, Captain. The onboard supplies were admittedly lacking, but I have supplemented them, I think, sufficiently enough with my own cache of instruments and medicinals to handle most injuries and ailments."

"Good to hear," Zale said. "I can't help but wonder, er ... Doctor, Physicker ...?"

Fulgar smiled politely. "Healer—please, sir."

"Healer. I can't help but wonder how you came to know of the unoccupied stations of our crew. How did you know we lacked a physicker?"

"It's well-known, sir, that the famous Captain Murdoch can be found at The Wench's Tavern whenever he's between jobs. It's also known that much of his crew loiters about Friendly Oaf's Taproom. That is where I caught word of your openings, sir. I hope this does not displease you."

"Not at all," Zale answered dismissively. Of course, he knew that taproom well, being the place where his own daughter worked. "Then, these short voyages to Korangar and Akkadia were enough to entice you to seek me out?"

"To sail with the great Captain Murdoch? Of course!"

It wasn't the first time someone had sought to join his crew for such a reason, but Zale didn't feel entirely convinced. Fulgar seemed a man of experience, not the type so easily guided by the fame of his boss. He would keep a watchful eye on this one.

Zale rose from his chair, indicating an end to their meeting. "I trust you'll understand, Healer, that yours is one post I hope does *not* need to prove its worth."

Fulgar stood in turn. "I quite agree, sir." He made for the door, stopping just as he reached it. "However ... I must say, Captain, that I'd rather hoped you would pursue the other opportunity at hand."

Zale frowned with a blink of confusion.

Fulgar lowered his voice dramatically. "The Grimstone."

Ah, so there it is, Zale thought.

"So," Zale replied flatly, "it would seem there *is* more to you than the piously noble healer we see on the surface. You might as well sit back down." Zale walked past Fulgar, opening his door to shout at the nearest seaman. "You, there! See that I get a stein of ale straight away." He closed the door. "Not even yet at sea, Healer Fulgar, and you've already got me drinking."

It was a warm, breezy night in the harbor of Warvonia, Starlina's favorite kind of weather. She laughed and jogged with Jensen, hand in hand, their steps thumping against the wooden docks. They had enjoyed a picnic supper together along the waterfront, watching the sun disappear behind them. After they were done they took a stroll, with no particular aim, as they had done so many times since childhood.

So far the evening had been wonderful. She felt relaxed in his presence, free to just enjoy herself. She was comfortably dressed in a white, sleeveless top, a blue mini-skirt patterned with yellow suns and moons, and white sandals. She had painstakingly styled her hair in rope-like braids that coursed across the side parting, wrapped both ways around her head, and tied together in the back.

She had even had a pendant formed around the lilac kuntupite Jensen had given her. It dangled about her neck from a silver chain like a pinkish-purple teardrop.

Jensen was garbed in his sailing clothes—a loose gray shirt, tan pants, and a hooded jacket. It was a subtle reminder that he would be leaving soon, a reminder she tried to push out of her mind.

He was, by now, supposed to already be aboard the ship. "I want to spend every moment I can with you first," he had told her.

Then he led her toward the docks. She chose to believe it was just more aimless fun, more loitering about with different scenery.

Starlina frowned when she saw her father's ship, the *Queenie*. Before she knew it, Jensen was leading her up the gangway.

"*Jensen*, have you lost your mind?" Starlina hissed, although she couldn't help but chortle at the roguishness of it all.

"*Shh!*" He removed his hooded jacket and placed it upon her shoulders. "No sense making you *too* obvious."

"But what are we even doing here?" She tucked her long hair into the hood and pulled it taut. "You'll be in so much trouble if we're caught! You're supposed to be *working*, and I'm not supposed to be here at all!"

He waved her off. "They won't have even noticed I was gone."

"You *know* I don't like being aboard ships, Jensen."

"Yes, I know... but I thought you might at least fancy a quick tour of my home away from home. That, and the view of the rings across the water from the stern is absolutely stunning."

"This is my *father's* ship. I've seen it before!"

"You won't be disappointed," he replied. "I promise."

They stepped onto the main deck, the bustling crew paying them little heed in the darkening twilight. Jensen led her up the stairs to the short quarterdeck, location of the helm, where he gave the ship's wheel a pat. "Don't you find it special, Starlina, to be upon your father's ship just before sendoff?"

She puffed derisively. She wanted this time with Jensen, but he knew how she felt about ships and sailing. "Oh, please. I haven't so much as heard from Father in the last week. It's completely unknown to me where you're even going this time—just away from Warvonia... from home. I imagine he made certain to bid farewell to his wife's granddaughters. Darlings, all of them, but they're not even blood relations!"

They stepped up to the stern deck. Jensen led them toward the very end of the ship. The water stretched before them and away from the harbor, like liquid glass reflecting the soft whiteness of the moon and rings. Jensen spread his arms wide, his hair whipping in the breeze. "You see that, Starlina? What do you think?"

She stared into the beyond—the gateway to lands that were not for her. "It *is* beautiful," she conceded, "like a rippling tapestry."

"Now, imagine being completely surrounded by that view on all sides. Breathtaking, isn't it? It's the absolute perfect backdrop." She noticed his hand fiddling with something in his pocket. "I ... I have a question for you...."

No, not here! Starlina thought with alarm. She turned away, walking toward starboard. "And what's so great about it, really? It's just a massive field of water."

"Wh-what's so great?" Jensen followed her to the starboard taffrail. "It's what every sailor dreams of. Those open waters, the horizon laid out before you—it's like freedom."

She spun toward him with a severe look. "Freedom from what? From home? From commitment? From the family you leave behind?"

She turned back away, looking out toward the ships of the harbor stretching into the north. *Why have I fallen in love with such a dolt?* she thought. *Will he never understand?*

"N-no. No ... that's not what I mean."

"I really think I need to leave this place, Jensen," Starlina said.

"Starlina, please. This is what I'm made for. This is what I'm good at. I love nothing more than sharing it with you."

She wanted all the more to get away. On some level she knew that she chose to suppress the differences between Jensen and her, focusing only on the good. She had for years. Being here, aboard this ship, only brought those differences to the surface, making them impossible to ignore.

"What you *love* is the ocean," she said. "This ship. My father. I just can't...."

She stopped, squinting into the distance. A purplish flicker had caught her eye. "What is that?"

Jensen looked in the same direction. "Is that a... purple fire? How strange."

"I think maybe you should tell someone, Jensen."

He hesitated only a moment. "Yes... yes, I think maybe I should. Just stay up here, Starlina. I'll be right back."

CHAPTER 5

LEGEND BECKONS

7/26/3203 P.A.

Zale glared at Fulgar, saying nothing until his stein of ale arrived.

"What's your business with the Grimstone?" He took a mighty draft of his drink.

"As you might have already discerned, those who desire it are dangerous," Fulgar replied. "They will have what they seek, at any cost."

Zale half-shrugged. "Is this to say that they'll pay anything for it, that the reward is colossal ... or is your interest of some more pious nature?"

"Indeed, money is no obstacle for them."

"You didn't answer the second part of my question."

Fulgar gave a cool, wry smile. "If you're asking if your spiritual guide is pious, then of course I must say *yes.*"

"That's not what I meant. Put another way, are you playing at some scheme to convince me to go after the Grimstone so you'll have it for your purposes?"

Fulgar's expression softened, his mouth a thin line. "No schemes, Captain. As I said, I am but a guide."

"Let's just cut the charade and get to who you *really* are."

"All that I've told you is true, sir, but I have not told you everything. I am of the ancient Order of Aether Diamond, protectors of the Light of the Land and keepers of its secrets."

"I know nothing of this Order," Zale said. "How do you know I've been given any opportunity related to the Grimstone?"

"When Vidimir offered you the job to retrieve the Grimstone, back in the tavern, it was not altogether difficult for me to see and hear what was happening. He did, after all, cast darkfire upon your table."

"Yes . . . that he did."

"And he offered substantial reward, did he not?"

Zale frowned. "That's a little beyond your charge, Healer."

Fulgar raised a placating hand. "Forgive me, please. Then, may I ask, why not seek it?"

"It's an adjunct of Shadow Age myth." Zale shook his head, as if to shake away his doubts. "We've no reason to believe the thing even exists."

Fulgar arched an eyebrow. "You think Vidimir disingenuous, that he meant to lead you to something that isn't there . . . perhaps . . . so that you would miss the bar's deadline?"

"That cuts reasonably close." Zale took a gulp from his stein.

"The Grimstone is real, Captain. It is a piece of the Dark Entry, broken as Zophiel used the last of her power to attack it. After that, her mortal body gave up her soul. She died in the arms of Birqu Umis, the Patriarch. It was then, in the year 3021 of the Foudroyant Age, that the Shadow Age began."

Zale sighed deeply. "So you say, but you speak in legends. I can't verify any of this in actual recorded history."

"It is *real* history. How it's recorded depends very much on the source."

"Much like the Grimstone, I imagine."

"The Grimstone existed within the Grandtrilian continent during the Shadow Age. Some in the Order believe it was here in what is now Tuscawny."

Zale tried to assess whether or not this man should remain aboard his ship. He seemed to reek of ulterior motive.

"Your records sound inconsistent," Zale said. "Vidimir claimed the Grimstone to be elsewhere."

Fulgar tilted his head. "Can an object not move locations over millennia, Captain?"

Zale merely grunted in response.

"I believe Vidimir directed you toward Gukhan, yes?" Fulgar asked.

"I don't feel quite at liberty to discuss that," Zale replied. Now that Zale thought about it, Fulgar had not been that far from Vidimir's table, but he was still surprised Fulgar had been able to pick up so much of their conversation. His mind lingering on the name of Gukhan, Zale took another drink.

"There was a point at which the Dark Entry was under the ground," Fulgar said, "and the Grimstone above. With them in such proximity, all of Grandtrilia was in especially grave danger. Our land exists by way of the divine, and so it is by the Light of the Land that it is held together. For the land to be without the Light is akin to the body breaking down from the inside, like an evaporation of its very structure. You would cease to exist. Our land nearly succumbed to the darkness in those days, but certain heroes appeared, who fought for our land and drove the Grimstone away."

"These 'heroes'—were they also ethereal astrals?"

"Not astrals," Fulgar replied, "but they did possess *etheretics*. Genetics passed down from the linage of archastrals, such as Zophiel, who had become mortal for the sake of our world. With their divine powers, they overcame the forces of darkness and banished the Grimstone from our land. They became a chapter of legend—the heroes of their time."

Zale perked, remembering his conversation with Tomescrubber. "Heroes of Time. This is part of that legend? Who were these heroes?"

"Forgive me, I do not remember all their names, but I do know they were led by one of the name Macpherson."

Zale sat upright with a jolt. He felt chilled to the bone upon hearing his own birth name.

He gazed out a portside window, looking to the harbor south of the *Queenie's* berth. "On your word that it's real, you would have me go after this Grimstone?"

"I mean not to overstep my bounds, sir. You must pursue that which you are called to pursue. If you do not retrieve the

Grimstone, then another might, and the dangers of this artifact in the wrong hands are unspeakable."

"Dangers, such as . . .?"

Fulgar sat back, seeming to consider his answer. "Void energy is darkness, its very essence in opposition to Aether . . . to Light. Some would count Void as among the divine etheretical energies that have entered our world over the eons, but that is wrong. Void is anything but divine.

"Since the Shadow Age," he continued, "certain substances exist in our world which allow their users to connect with the Void and channel its power. Byrne, also known to some as the Dark Ethereal, is one of them. You witnessed Vidimir use this in the tavern."

Zale nodded.

"The destructive and manipulative forces of the Grimstone are much greater," Fulgar said. "If the Grimstone were ever reunited with the rest of the Dark Entry, we could see the land plunged into another Shadow Age, possibly one even fiercer than the first."

"The Dark Entry? You mean that thing still *exists*?"

Fulgar returned a deadpan look. "We don't know. It has never been found. Yet, we also have no evidence that it was eliminated. Our strongest confirmation of the Dark Entry's presence is the Grimstone itself. Even this small fragment was not something that Macpherson and the Heroes could destroy. Rather, it was cast away and hidden."

A hidden object of great power—the perfect formula for a

high-value catch, Zale thought. He still wasn't sure what to make of Fulgar. The man seemed to have a deep understanding of this legend from a source of information Zale had never heard of. For Zale, information was like having a sharpened sword at your side. You could never go wrong by having it, and it just might come in useful.

"Vidimir claimed the Light is weakening . . . that the Grimstone would help it," Zale said.

"Search your soul. Is it sensible that dark brightens light? Is white made brighter by black? No. They are not compatible. One must overpower the other. It is not to help the Light; it is to *replace* it. If someone strong enough controls the Grimstone, with its power can the entire land be transformed for the sole purpose of serving masters of the Void, such as the umbramancers of old. Perhaps you can see how *grim* is a good descriptor for this object."

"You do paint a rather bleak picture," Zale agreed.

"And, yet, there is an element of fate which is hard to ignore. These 'heroes' I spoke of—it was Augustus Macpherson, your ancestor, who took the greatest measures to safeguard it from ever falling into the wrong hands. Having befriended a grimkin shaman, he underwent a sacred ritual with the Grimstone, fusing his own blood with the object so that only he—or one of his bloodline—could again claim the Grimstone and free it from its hidden sanctum."

Zale turned away from the window. "The bloodline of Macpherson?"

"Indeed, Captain. For you, of course, this makes the Grimstone more than a mere bounty. It is nearly a birthright. You are the namesake of Macpherson, are you not?"

"How do you know that?" Zale shot back. He'd already had his fill of strangers inexplicably knowing the details of his personal business.

"I am of the Order, sir," Fulgar said calmly. "Our records are more complete than even those of your guilders."

"Ha!" Zale boomed in triumph. "If all this talk of bloodline is true, then why should I rush to retrieve this thing? I'm the only one who can!"

"*If* that is the only way—and there might yet be other powers which can break it—heed closely what I said: Macpherson's *bloodline*, not merely Zale Macpherson."

That brought Murdoch's face from flushed to blanched. "You imply my family, as well."

Fulgar nodded. "It could be that no others know of this. But, should others who seek the Grimstone eventually make these connections, then not only you but your children and grandchildren and all in your line are in certain danger."

Zale was gripped by sudden anger at his shortsighted ancestor. *How could he not know the danger heaped upon his descendants?* Then another thought rattled him. *Has anyone else made this connection with my family? Vidimir?*

He looked Fulgar over. "Why would you want me to retrieve it anyway? With the bloodline lock removed and my brood absolved, I would just bring it to Vidimir for the payoff. I owe that to my crew. Your Order and the kingdom can sort out the rest of this legendary gibberish. That is not my concern."

"Just so, Captain. Even simply releasing the Grimstone from its ancient hiding place in Gukhan would count as a success to the Order. No one can ascertain the intentions of that nation, which is in itself unsettling."

Zale puffed a derisive laugh. "If it's as powerful as you say, there are those who might say it's even more dangerous in my hands than Vidimir's. Does this not concern you?"

Fulgar took a moment to answer. "I think not."

"And why's that?"

"I believe you are a good, honorable man—a family man— with a good heart and a good soul."

Zale scowled at the notion that Fulgar presumed to know him. "Let's be clear, Healer. I am no *hero*. I don't save damsels in distress. I don't rescue helpless, furry little anthropods from oppression. I retrieve unique and valuable cargoes for this kingdom, and I bring them to the buyer for payment. We ask no questions; we question no motives. We expect only to be handsomely paid for our services—no more, no less."

"As you say, Captain."

Zale scratched at his chin. "Perhaps it's in Gukhan, but that's an entire *country*—not much of a lead."

Fulgar briefly felt inside his coat. "I believe I can help with that, Captain, and perhaps achieve a more targeted search."

Zale heard loud shuffles and shouts from the decks outside. It was a subtle shift in the bustle of readying the ship. This was more frantic . . . disturbed.

A strange flash reflected in the portside windowpanes. Zale strode toward starboard and looked out to the north. Fulgar joined him.

A sloop several berths away erupted into flame. It was not just fire.

It was purple fire. Darkfire.

"Hell's fury," Zale growled. "It's coming this way."

Fulgar's eyes were wide, his mouth half-open. "This is a most disconcerting development."

Zale snatched up his hat and made for the door. "It would seem, Healer, that your legend has come to taunt us."

Jensen skidded into such an abrupt stop that he almost slipped right over the starboard taffrail. He had just pointed out the strange inferno to Beep and others on deck, setting off a frenzy. Starlina, still by the taffrail, looked paralyzed with fear. The eerie purple flames were only about four berths removed from the *Queenie*, eating their way through the docks at an alarming rate.

"Starlina!" he gasped. "We need to get you out of sight." He spotted a bolt of sailcloth stowed against the inner railing. He grabbed it, unrolling part of the heavy canvas as he ran. "Stay under this until I come back for you."

He flung the sail over her and urged her to the deck before she could protest beyond a stifled yelp.

Jensen stood up straight and looked around. He smoothed out his shirt, both thankful and surprised that no one had taken notice.

"Men!" barked Captain Murdoch down on the main deck. "Make for the waves!" He nodded to his first mate.

Dippy rang the bell. "Cast off all lines!" he bellowed. "Ready the sweeps and shove off the dock!"

"Aye—on the lines, sir!" Beep replied, grabbing two men to assist.

A merchant cog two berths away exploded, shooting purple fireballs and enflamed timbers into the air. Jensen tumbled halfway down the staircase to the quarterdeck. The blast and sudden swells in the water bounced the *Queenie* violently.

Jensen pulled himself up by the rail and glanced overboard. Flaming debris from the explosion landed upon the berth beside them. The hungry flames spread instantly to the planks of the dock. Very soon, the fire would reach the *Queenie*.

"Sir!" Jensen pointed. "There might not be time to cast off!"

Beep and Dippy both ran to the starboard rail.

"Fire's coming this way!" shouted Beep.

"Hack the lines—*all* of them!" ordered the captain.

"I'll take care of the head line," said Fump, pulling an axe as though from nowhere. Their quartermaster had the placement of hidden objects on the ship down to an art.

"I'll take the stern!" A bald man Jensen had never before met ran nimbly up the stairs, passing by Jensen.

"You ever cut a dock line before, Physicker?" shouted

deckhand Miles on his way below deck.

"That'll take more than a scalpel!" Beep added as the man flew past quarterdeck.

Upon the afterdeck, the bald man drew something from within his coat and swung. The rope was thicker than a man's arm, yet one swing was all it took. There was a flash of white, and the line was free. Jensen stared with mouth agape.

"Time to shove off!" Captain Murdoch roared. "Keep a wary eye on the fire!"

"Fire, you call it," Jensen said with a shiver. "I've never seen fire like *this* before."

The captain looked back at him just as the bell rang out again.

"All oarsmen at the ready!" Dippy called.

That included Jensen. He started for the stairs.

"Beep!" yelled Murdoch. "Lash the wheel amidships to keep her straight. Stand ready to steer hard to larboard as soon as we're clear of the dock."

"Aye, sir!" Beep headed for the helm on quarterdeck.

Jensen was nearly bowled over as he made his way down the stairs to the inner deck. Evette and the other oarsmen already had the oars positioned and ready to extend outside the ship.

To his horror, he saw that the flames had already made their way around the dock, past the ship's bow and now at portside.

Jensen, along with several others, stumbled his way to a bench and grabbed an oar. Another crewmate sat next to him to assist.

Wigglebelly was somewhere behind him, his airy voice shouting over and over: "Don't touch the fire, man! Don't touch the fire!"

"Everyone to larboard!" Evette cried out. "Find a part of that dock that isn't burning!"

"Almost all of it's burning!" someone shouted.

"Ready!" Evette called. "*Push!*"

The crew gave a mighty shove into the dock. It was mighty enough, in fact, that the remainder of the dock gave way and several of the oars pushed right through into the inferno. When they emerged, flames engulfed them, as if they had just been dipped into burning pitch.

"Give way together!" Evette shouted. "Oars in the water—now! *Pull!*"

They plunged the oars in a frenzy of splashes, heaving to move the ship forward. Jensen watched his oar lift from the water, and his eyes bulged at the sight of fire still clinging to its blade. Mere water was not enough to quench the purple flames.

"*Pull!*" screamed Evette.

One of the oars snapped. The two rowers fell from their benches at the sudden loss of drag.

"It's on the boat!" cried a deckhand.

"Fire of the dead, man!" Wigglebelly gasped. "It'll bring us all straight to Gheol!"

Another deckhand, Clement, slapped Wigglebelly across the arm. "Shut up and row, fool!"

Grunts of strain and anguish filled the deck as they tried to row. Seconds later, another enflamed oar snapped just above the blade.

Evette shook her head in dismay. "It's no good! We're tangled up in the debris and losing oars fast!"

"Find a way to douse those flames!" Dippy bellowed from up above. "Man the pump!"

Feeling increasingly helpless, Jensen gave his all on the oar. He heard a sickening *crack*, and splinters erupted outside. The oar-shaft flew forward and whacked him in the forehead.

He fell, and the back of his head slammed into the bench behind him.

Then he felt nothing, as a deep, dark calm swept away his vision.

Zale pointed at the purple flames which now dared to touch his ship.

"Keep spraying the hull!" he roared.

Deckhands Redvers, Owen, and Bert manned the ship's pump, normally reserved for bringing water to clean the deck. Now they used it to hose down the outer hull.

Murdoch remained in utter disbelief over their state of affairs. Before a few days earlier, he had never even heard of darkfire. Now it was consuming everything in the Warvonia harbor.

"The water's freezing on contact!" Beep gestured wildly over the railing. "And the flames are still spreading!"

A plume of violet flame whipped over the larboard beam. Deckhands Sal and Elihu screamed and fell, their arms caught by the flames. Steam rolled from their arms, and any skin the flames had touched turned a frigid white. It was not steam from something hot, but rather the condensed air that surrounded extreme cold. Wind accompanied the flames like a winter blast.

Fulgar was upon Sal and Elihu in a flash. He pulled something small from within his coat, like a thorn, and jabbed each of their arms. A faint, brief orange glow spread from the site of impact through their frostbite-cold extremities, slightly restoring their natural color.

"Get these men below!" he shouted to the nearest deckhand.

He drew what appeared to be a long dagger or shortsword, double-edged and tapered to a sharp point. Its blade was black with tiny sparkles, like stars in a night sky. Soft-white light, like ringglow, emanated from every angle and edge of the blade.

Zale stared in wonderment. Yet another surprise from their new healer.

Fulgar reached over the railing and swung the blade back and forth in quick, short strokes. Its glow intensified and extended beyond the weapon's tip, like a mini-lighthouse emitting a white beam out to sea.

He aimed it at the nearest of the chilly inferno. The flames actually receded.

"Captain!" Fulgar shouted. "I can buy us but a little time . . .

but the darkfire ... it consumes with a will!"

Zale chanced a look over portside. Fulgar was right. This was not the combustion that fires normally destroy with. In these flames was a strange, monstrous hunger. What it consumed it simply *ate* away, leaving its deathly chill.

Zale's breath escaped as steam. The water below the dock was turning to ice. He backed up to midship, taking in his surroundings. He felt the natural wind in his face, knowing it fondly over the frigid gusts of the darkfire. It was blowing eastward, perhaps a point or two east-northeast, bow to stern. He inhaled, nodding to himself.

It was now or never.

"Full back the sail! The wind favors us, men! Beep, stay ready at the helm!"

Fump smirked. "Sailing backwards, Captain?"

"Work your magic, Fump. Drop the sail and prepare to backfill. Tail her out like we did back in the Whiteland haul."

Fump rolled up his sleeves and bit down on the blade of a dirk. "Aye!" he growled through his teeth. He took to the rigging with crewmates Ian and Rowan, their ascent as deft as spiders on a web.

Zale aimed his voice toward the lower deck and called out, "Evette, get oars up to stern! Four should do it."

"Haul up four spare oars from the hold!" she ordered down below. "Do it *now*!" Her head appeared from below a few moments later. "On it, Captain!"

Zale turned to Dippy. "We'll punch into the water behind

the ship on larboard to give our rudder support. Evette, all remaining oarsmen to starboard! We'll come hard about, lads!"

"Captain!" shouted Fulgar. "We must make our move!"

"Fump!" Zale shouted.

"All set, Captain!" He was already on his way back down.

"Haul sheets and braces!" In short order, the sail bellied full toward aft, a peculiar sight for any ship.

At long last, the ship started moving. Back at the helm, Beep held tight to the wheel as it wobbled awkwardly.

"Steady! Prepare to bring 'er about!" Zale bellowed. "Fump, slack sheets in the turn. We won't get far if we blow out the sail."

Fump tightened his grip on the line, his gaze focused and eager. "Aye, sir!"

"Oars at the ready, Captain!" Dippy shouted from the stern.

"Ready to hard port, sir!" cried Beep.

"Starboard oars ready, Captain!" called Evette from below.

"Ready on the braces!" yelled Fump from portside.

Zale watched... waiting... waiting... until, finally, the prow was clear of the dock.

"All hands *heave*!" he roared.

Like clockwork, every member of the crew performed their role in perfect unison. Most who didn't hold to something fell to the deck as the ship turned hard around, creaking all the way. Already they felt the relief of the warm late-Jovidor air sweeping the ship.

"Quarter-turn ought to do it," Zale said, mostly to himself. Once satisfied, he called, "Come about!"

"Oars to port!" Evette bellowed.

"Resetting the yard!" shouted Fump, pulling forward on portside. "Starboard full back!" he yelled to his mate across the ship.

Zale felt a rise of anxiety. The ship was not slowing enough. The last thing he wanted was to inadvertently spin right back into the dock. "Look alive, you grog-guzzling vermin! Pull those oars portside and steady 'er! Pull to the blood!"

Finally the ship steadied, and they faced away from the harbor. Cheers erupted all over the ship.

"We're not out of this yet!" yelled Chim, who had been helping with the yard braces.

Indeed, purple flames still licked at the hull of the ship. Fulgar worked to contain them with his bizarre weapon, but they spread faster than he could put them out. Zale heard a shriek from below that could only have come from Wigglebelly.

"Get those infernal fires off my ship!" Zale ordered, his voice getting a bit hoarse. "Hack off the boards if it comes to that."

Without tarry, several men took hold of ropes and chopped off the chunks of the ship's hull that Fulgar could not relieve of darkfire. Dippy and three deckhands ran their oars back to the deck below to help stabilize their course and make headway.

"Fump," said Zale, "let's get that sail reset. Capital work, sir."

"Doin' what I can with what I've got, Captain. On it!"

"*Beeeeeep!*" Zale called to his boatswain.

"Sir!" Kasper answered from the helm.

"Make use of this easterly wind and steer us to blue water."

"Aye, with pleasure, sir."

Zale thought they might finally be in the clear. Then, as if fate needed a good laugh, a shard of purple-enflamed wood flew into the air, directly into the sail. It caught like dry straw, as men screamed in shock.

Fulgar leapt upon the rigging and doused the fire with the soft-white glow of his blade, although not before the fire had left a gaping hole in the sail. Miraculously, the mast, ropes, and rigging all escaped unscathed.

Fump groaned. "I'll get the spare sail."

"Admirable teamwork, crew," Zale shouted. "All of you worthy to be Murdoch's Mates! Once we're trimmed out and underway, officers to my cabin. You too, Fulgar. Beep, steer us away from the harbor as fast as you can. I've had enough of docks for one day."

"Aye, sir. I couldn't agree more."

With that, Zale removed his hat, wiped his brow, and entered his cabin.

Tonight's events had jostled Zale to the core.

Sometime after they turned the ship away from the dock he had made a decision. Now he mulled it over quietly, allowing his officers the brief respite of conversation.

Following their roaring sendoff, he felt obliged to let the

men crack open enough rations of ale and wine to calm the crew. Never to the point of inebriation, however. Zale's tolerance for drunken sailors during an active expedition had been made clear. Anyone careless enough to become intoxicated would be tied naked to the prow until the sea spray rid them of their stupor.

"And this was going to be an *easy* voyage," Rosh mumbled.

"Chim, if it were too easy, it wouldn't be a Murdoch voyage," Fump said.

"Do *all* your jobs start with this much excitement?" asked Evette.

"Only the good ones." Beep took a large gulp from his mug.

Chim, the teetotal oddball of the crew, lifted his glass of water. His abstinent lifestyle kept him not only from alcohol but also tea and coffee and basically anything with flavor. "Highest marks to the captain for leading us out of that inferno!"

"Hear, hear!" cheered the others with a clink of glasses.

The violet hellstorm still flared in the distance, all too visible through the stern windows. Zale stood from his chair and pulled the window shades, one by one, until the nightmarish sight was obscured.

"No looking back," he spoke gruffly. "Too many fine vessels ruined tonight, none of which we can afford to have on our consciences. If we hadn't already been there with a full and capable crew, the *Queenie*'d be one of them."

Zale walked back to his chair. "Quick status update, please."

"I've got men on the sail now," Fump replied. "They'll have her hoisted in no time ... and by no time, I mean a little time."

"We're sweeping ahead, slow and steady," Evette said. "One man—Jensen, I'm told—was knocked unconscious after his oar broke."

Zale made a conspicuous eye-roll. "Of course he was. Where is he now?"

"Once we cleared the dock, I had him carried to his hammock. We couldn't be bothered with it before then," she replied.

"If it pleases you, sir, I'll give him an elixir to ease any aches he might have upon waking," said Fulgar in his gentle voice.

"Fine," said Zale.

"We didn't have to shoot anyone," Chim put in, "so I don't have much to report. I'll make sure the machetes and axes we used to hack the hull are nice and sharp next time we need to attack our own ship."

"I'm sure Fump'll have that repaired in short order," Zale said.

"You know me," Fump replied. "I'm a perfectionist. I'll oversee that work myself to make sure it's good and solid."

Beep stroked at his long beard. "Course set northward for Vartu, Captain. With Jensen down, I have Tate currently at the helm."

"And you, Fulgar," Zale said, "how do you explain this weapon of yours?"

Everyone stared at Fulgar. It was now openly clear that he was more than he had originally purported to be.

"It is a novidian anelace—a long, triangular sort of dagger," the healer answered simply.

Zale eyed him sharply. He'd expected more of an explanation than that, and he was certain Fulgar knew it. "How does a *healer* come to have such as this?"

Fulgar smiled, looking almost amused. "Let us say, Captain, that it is in my grasp by virtue of birthright."

Zale slanted his eyes at Fulgar. The comment hearkened back to their earlier conversation about the Grimstone and his ancestor, Macpherson.

Zale's mind was made up.

He stood and paced the semicircular end of his cabin. He felt his officers' eyes pinned on him like darts. "Men ... in light of recent events and information, I've come to a decision."

They all set their drinks down. Now he knew he had their rapt attention.

"Beep, we will require a slight change in course."

Their eyes became like saucers, all but Fulgar's, with his ingratiating tranquility. Zale was placing a lot of stock into the words of this man, but every instinct within him rang clear. His thoughts lingered on the object desired by the kingdom's elite ... the object his greatest rival hoped to shame him with ... the object of unspeakable power ... the object—the *birthright*—that he was uniquely positioned to acquire.

He was certain, and he spoke without the slightest hint of doubt.

"We're going after the Grimstone."

CHAPTER 6

BOUNTY OF BOUNTIES

7/27/3203 P.A.

Now they were bound for the Grimstone. Zale had declared it so. His officers' collective silence upon hearing this decision had spoken volumes. No one argued—perhaps they were too exhausted anyway—and no one voiced support.

Only Chim spoke, asking one simple question. "Why?"

"Tonight's darkfire event solidified for me just how real these powers are," Zale told them. He made brief eye contact with Fulgar. "And I've just learned there might be an advantage to getting it that we can exploit."

Further details could be discussed later. In truth, Zale was still processing his discussion with Fulgar. Zale knew one thing for certain. If his family could be tied to the Grimstone, now being sought by powerful, dangerous people, then he intended to get his hands on it before Seadread or anyone else. Then *he* could control the outcome.

Then the mastery bar would be as good as theirs.

At about the first hour of morning, Zale was at his desk, barely able to keep his eyes open. He was just about to climb into his hammock for much-needed slumber when someone knocked on his cabin door.

"What is it?" Zale answered.

"Sir," said Dippy from behind the door, "there's a... matter... which you'll appreciate knowing about right away."

Zale groaned. That sounded like the last thing he would appreciate right now. "Come in," he replied. He collected his crew log and scribbled journal of the night's events and stuffed them in a desk drawer, not even bothering to look toward the door as Dippy and whomever else he was with entered.

"Eventide, Captain," greeted Fump.

Zale spun around to face them. "Fump, it's the middle of the—" His breath caught in his throat at the sight of the third person standing with Dippy and Fump.

It was his daughter.

"*Starlina?*" Zale gasped, standing. "What in Gheol's blazes are you doing here?"

Dippy urged her to an armchair, looking thoroughly vexed.

"We found her crouched under the spare sailcloth," Fump said. "Gave the men a real fright."

Starlina scowled, her arms crossed, and she refused to make eye contact with anyone. She was a vault, Zale knew. If she would talk at all, it wouldn't be in front of these men.

"Thank you, gents," Zale said. "She'll be fine here. You two get some rest."

The men left without another word.

Zale remained quiet for many long moments, trying to blink away the fog of fatigue, hoping he was just imagining things. If a grimkin had rowed up to their ship, that would've fit right in with the weirdness from last night. If a teron had fallen from the sky, that they could deal with. If Wigglebelly had fallen overboard from fainting, standard procedure. But *this* . . . this flummoxed him completely.

"Starlina, why are you here? You don't even *like* sailing."

Her oval face appeared even longer than usual, her hair was frazzled, and her eyes appeared dark and puffy.

"I didn't *mean* to be here," she replied. "I despise my being here as much as you do."

"I don't despise . . . . I mean, I'm happy to see you, Starlina, but it's not safe for you to be here. We're on a dangerous mission. Sweet Eloh above, I'm just glad you're *okay*. You must've seen what we dealt with tonight."

"The purple flames? I only saw that from a distance before Jensen threw that giant sail over me."

"Jensen!"

Starlina looked at him directly for the first time since arriving. Zale could tell she hadn't meant to say that, but there was no denying that she had.

"We were seeing each other before the voyage," she said, "and he wanted to show me the ship. It was just after I got here that those ghostly-looking fires appeared." Her voice dropped to a whisper. "What *was* that?"

"It's called darkfire. We don't know how it started, or perhaps by whom, but it has injected a certain urgency into our quest."

"Darkfire," she repeated. "It was so ... cold."

Zale nodded sympathetically. "You shouldn't be here, darling. Perhaps it's safest if we let you off at Vartu along the way."

She frowned. "I thought you were already bound for Vartu, and then heading back home."

Well, that was *the intent*, he mused.

"There's been a change of plan. Now we're sailing well past Grandtrilia. I'm sure you don't want to stick around for that. It's not safe. If you can find passage home from Vartu, then great. If not, then keep near the harbor. We'll swing back through during our return."

"How long will that take?"

"Hard to say," Zale answered. "About a month, depending on how smoothly things go."

"A *month*?!"

"Better give us six or seven weeks to be sure. Things might get sketchy. If I didn't feel like he'd somehow get you in worse trouble, I'd be tempted to leave Jensen with you at port."

"Where is he now?" she asked quietly.

"In sickbay, after being banged unconscious by an oar. Maybe he'll wake up with a fully active brain for once, so I can beat it back out of him."

"Please don't be too hard on him," Starlina said. "You know he thinks the world of you."

"So did my cat, but she had twice the backbone and thrice the instinct of that lackwit. For the life of me, I don't know what you see in him." He paced his cabin aimlessly, fatigue getting the better of him. "It's late. We'll deal with this tomorrow. You can use my hammock. I've slept many a time in these chairs, anyway."

Her eyes were downcast, pain in her expression. "I'm sorry to trouble your mission."

"Ah, well, at least you finally get to experience life at sea with the greatest crew there is."

Starlina pulled herself into Zale's hammock, already looking seasick.

Zale breathed in the salty morning air as he looked out upon the open waters. This was the best part about sailing. Beyond the horizon in every direction were lands and treasures aplenty—known and undiscovered, settled and untouched, plundered and plundered to-be.

Amongst the salt in the air, he detected a hint of sour.

It had started even before his morning coffee arrived. Beep had entered his cabin looking sleepy-eyed and hot under the collar, a wad of folded charts tucked in his arms. He slapped the navigational pages upon Zale's desk, curtly reviewing their new course.

Their course had been altered from almost due north to a

few points northeast, where they would curve around beyond the shoals of Korangar and break due north for the southern coast of Gukhan. If the winds favored them, they would land in about two and a half weeks. This was before factoring their diversion to Vartu to drop off Starlina. It was a simple correction, requiring little review, although to do so was protocol, one that Beep performed so mechanically that his view on this impromptu, unilateral change was obvious.

Beep wasn't the only one. As soon as Zale stepped onto the deck, he heard Fump grumbling about how they'd provisioned for a voyage half as long, and now they'd have to be more careful with rations. Dippy called out, "Captain on deck," with such haste that the deckhands barely heard him. Starlina, who had left the cabin even before Zale awoke, still wasn't looking at him. Any of the men he encountered on deck gave no more than perfunctory nods and brusque greetings.

In itself, the Grimstone bounty was a no-brainer—one prize to set them for life, and, if Fulgar's words held true, Zale was uniquely positioned to retrieve it. Still, the crew had two major reservations. First was the destination: Gukhan, a mysterious land infamous for its aggression toward outsiders. Second was that the crew still wasn't convinced that the Grimstone even existed.

Zale knew it was a gamble. Then again, so was placing their fate in the hands of two simpler jobs. The fickle valuation for something as common as verdantium could quickly work against them, causing them to fall short of the goal at the last minute.

Heptalatticite, the other commodity, was not common and thus could command a steep price, but they would have to wrest it from a group of grimkins who had already been unwilling to negotiate. There were still things that could go wrong, risks that could still cost them the mastery bar, and every risk was an opportunity for Seadread to surpass them.

Thus, as Zale thought on it, the Grimstone job actually seemed more and more plausible.

He was content to let the crew stew over a decision they didn't like, so long as their work got done. Any act of insolence, however, would be dealt a swift blow.

That reminded him of a certain sailor whose name had come up the night before, the one responsible for bringing his daughter aboard the ship. Zale found him with crewmates Tate and Miles near the starboard rail on the main deck. Zale approached from behind.

"Good morning, Jensen."

The young man jumped, caught completely unawares, even though Tate and Miles had looked straight in Zale's direction.

"I see you're awake now," Zale said, "at least in the sense that your eyes are open."

Jensen's hands fluttered about his pockets, like a schoolboy caught with another student's homework. *Curious case*, Zale thought, scowling.

"G-good morning, sir!" Jensen replied.

"I trust you've familiarized yourself with our new bearings in preparation for the night watch."

"Yes, of course! Well, I mean, I'll be going over that with Kasper in advance of my charge. I'll keep us straight and steady, sir. You can count on that!"

Zale growled under his breath. "No doubt you will, sailor, or you'll be rowing your way back home after we bring my daughter to safety in Vartu. Even in ideal conditions, your ill-conceived little stunt will cost us three days of detour, if not five. I hope you're fonder of coffee than sleep, because that's about all you'll be getting."

Jensen's young face paled as Zale turned away.

Jensen had a feeling he would find Starlina upon the afterdeck.

"So, you enjoy the view after all," he said.

"Don't speak to me, Jensen."

He placed his elbows upon the railing beside her. "You know I didn't mean for this to happen, right?"

She kept her eyes toward the ocean. Knowing her, Jensen figured she was looking not at the water but rather for any sign of land. "I should've known better than to set foot on this boat. Nothing good could come from it."

Jensen bit at his lip, remembering his prior intentions. It felt like so much longer ago than last night. "Looking at the bright side, now you can finally experience the majesty of the open seas. You get to see your father's crew in action."

"I didn't *want* to sail the seas, Jensen! What am I going to tell my boss? Amira will be off to university by the time I get back. I won't even get to tell her goodbye!" Her tears sparkled in the sunlight.

Jensen sighed and inwardly cursed his recklessness. This was indeed an unmitigated disaster. "I'm so sorry, Starlina."

"I know it's not what you intended," she said. "No one could have foreseen that awful fire. How do you suppose that happened?"

"I think the biggest question is *who* made that happen? Whatever it was, word around the ship is that it's responsible for the captain changing our course."

"Such a dangerous, unpredictable profession this is."

Jensen almost laughed. He felt awful that Starlina had ended up on the ship, but there was also a glimmer of excitement. Never would there be a better chance for her to see for herself what it was like to sail. "That's part of the excitement. Although, I must say, usually we have some idea what it is we're actually bound for, *and* the amount of the expected payout."

Finally she looked at him, her face softer, more relaxed. "How's your head?"

"Much better, thanks. The headache comes and goes. Healer Fulgar says it should feel much better by tonight. Although, my impending lack of sleep might not help the recovery."

She ran a hand through his hair, caressing him gently. He closed his eyes at the touch, both soothing and exhilarating. Jensen suddenly wished she could be here with him on every voyage. She actually smiled, showing her perfect teeth.

"My father doesn't deserve so much loyalty from you," she said. "Oh! You've got a knot on your head."

He winced. "Ah, yes... it's still rather tender." He took her hand from his head and held it, relishing her skin's warm softness. "Well... I'd better find Beep and get ready for a long night keeping the ship on course." With another quick smile, he turned toward the stairs.

"You're right, you know," Starlina said.

Jensen turned.

"It is beautiful .... The ocean, I mean."

He came back to her, drawing even closer than before. "Before now I believed it to be the most beautiful thing I would ever see from this ship."

He inched closer, his heart beating faster as he neared her tanned face. There was no other person he'd rather see, no better time than now. *A sailor takes action*, he reminded himself.

He kissed her. At their lips' touch they drew breath, and his nostrils filled with an intoxicating blend of the salty air and the rosewater in which she'd last bathed.

He pulled away. "That was before today. I'll see you later, Starlina."

The midday Jovidor sun beat down upon the ship, making the

upper deck like a stovetop. Three days after leaving Warvonia, the *Queenie* breezed along through a mild chop in the water and full wind in the sail. Pleasant gusts of air pushed into the inner berthing deck, providing the comfort of the wind without the scorch of the sun.

Jensen sat with Starlina and several of his crewmates amongst the rowing benches, slurping Wigglebelly's latest batch of bean soup. Soon Wigglebelly joined with his own bowl, followed by Fump and Chim. They were gathered around the ever-intriguing Fulgar Geth, as he regaled them with tales of antiquity.

"... And so it was that Zophiel became the second archastral to enter our world to save it from cataclysmic doom. It is said that the brilliance of her atmospheric entry circled the entire world with golden flashes of light. Soon the deathly cold temperatures of the prior age started to rise, and our ancestors emerged from their caves to an unencumbered sun. All the ice and snow which had blanketed the land for nearly a millennium began to recede. There were those who emerged who had never before seen anything in the sky except for the clouds of snowstorms. The so-called Lightning Cataclysm, which brought about the Foudroyant Age—*Zophiel's* Age—was in fact not a cataclysm but rather an ethereal healing of the land.

"Men and women, grimkins and anthropods, all beings of Grandtrilia begged to worship Zophiel as a goddess. She wouldn't have it. Even as the fullness of her ethereal energy fed into the healing of this planet, even as immortality seeped from her body, she gave all the glory to Eloh.

"As a manifestation of her energy, an ethereal material was created."

Fulgar pulled the long dagger from the sheath at his side. There was no white glow around it, as there had been during their fight with the darkfire. The blade was solid black, like polished obsidian, with pinpoints of light that sparkled like stars.

Jensen imagined it was what the night sky might look like if there were no rings and moon.

"Novidian," Fulgar said. "In these days, any known traces of it are carefully guarded by the Order of Aether Diamond."

Their eyes followed the blade as he moved it slowly through the air, as if hypnotized.

"How's your knife black, man?" Wigglebelly asked. "Did you paint it that way?"

"It's not paint, Wiggles," Yancy said. "It's the mineral. How else would you explain the sparkles?"

Wigglebelly shrugged. "That's easy: tiny diamonds in the paint, man." He popped a large spoonful of beans into his mouth.

"Many weapons are forged with the intent to take life, or to overcome others," said Fulgar. "A weapon such as this is forged with the intent of *saving* life. The purpose with which one forms an ethereal material is highly significant."

"May I?" asked Chim, holding out his hand.

Fulgar nodded. He handed the dagger to Chim gently. Not out of fragility, it seemed to Jensen, but rather more like reverence.

Chim hefted the blade. "It seems light even for its small size.

Very durable, too, as far as I can tell." He gave the blade back to Fulgar. "How's this compare to steel or iron?"

Fulgar's eyes twinkled. It was a question he seemed eager to answer. "Nothing you have onboard this ship could stand against it."

Jensen had never met a physicker or chaplain like this. True, his devotion to Elohism seemed absolute, but this weapon... *novidian* ... was utterly unique. He wondered what the captain knew of this and if that had anything to do with their pursuit of the Grimstone.

"There was white light coming from it before," said Fump. "I've never seen any steel dagger do that."

Fulgar lifted the dagger, and the white glow appeared faintly all around it. "Ethereal materials grant their users certain powers, to widely varying degrees. Novidian is like a connection to the energies of Zophiel herself, to the divine life she poured into our world throughout the Foudroyant Age."

"So," laughed Tate, "it's like you're wielding angel's light!"

Fulgar tilted his head with an ironic smirk. "It is precisely like that."

Tate's mirth faded into something like awe-inspired terror. Jensen and Tate shared a glance, and he wondered if they were thinking the same thing. *Is this weapon in the hand of Fulgar an asset or a threat?*

"Will it shine for anyone else or just you?" Jensen asked.

"That depends," Fulgar answered. "For some, yes. For others perhaps it *could*, with time." He held it out to Jensen. "Please ..."

see how it feels to you."

Jensen reached out and took it by the grip. The white glow around it faded away. Even without its glow, the weapon was remarkably beautiful and comfortable to hold.

Starlina's gaze was fixed on the weapon, its starlight glimmer a solid match to the twinkling in her eyes. "May I hold it?" she asked.

"Of course," Fulgar answered. Jensen handed it to her.

As soon as it landed in Starlina's grasp, a nimbus of soft white surrounded the weapon and played about her hand. She turned it back and forth in examination, her expression dazzled.

"Hey, it's glowing again!" Chim exclaimed, pointing.

"So it is," Fulgar replied. "How does it feel?"

"It's like ... something fond ... like something familiar," Starlina said.

Jensen leaned toward her, his face alight. "Does it feel warm? Does it pulse or vibrate?"

"No, it's not like that," she replied. "It's more like holding something very dear to me, something so familiar that it's almost a part of me." She looked at Fulgar. "For something that indicates power, it seems remarkably ... welcoming."

Fulgar took it back from her. "There are some within the Order who say those with a strong connection to ethereal materials will achieve great purpose in life."

"This Order you speak of," Jensen said. "What is it? Where is it based?"

"We are sworn guardians of the Light and of the ethereals,

such as novidian," Fulgar answered. "Those of the Devotion are scattered, and our armories divided. No one member knows the location of every stronghold. Yet, if in need, we know how to call one another, to find one another, and gather."

Wigglebelly jittered with anticipation. "Hey, do you use that dagger to shave your head? That's like an angel rubbing you bald, man. *Huhuhuhuhu!*"

"I once had a full head of hair, actually. Black, with hints of white and blue."

Fump nodded with interest. "Three colors—nice!"

Tate jabbed at Jensen with a bony elbow. "Hey, your little lady's got a nice head of hair. Wish I'd have known we could bring along our own scrubbers on this trip."

"Now we have to detour to Korangar," grumbled the beady-eyed, often expressionless Kelvin in his monotone voice.

"Korangar's where we were supposed to be headed in the first place," said Chim. "I'm more concerned about this whole Grimstone search."

"Personally, I hope we find some pixies and munchkins along the way," Fump said with a chortle.

"Do you question the captain's judgment in this matter?" Fulgar asked.

The other men exchanged glances, hesitating. Starlina's eyes were fixed on Fulgar.

"Ah, screw it," Tate said. "It seems an awful rushed decision to me. Why'd he have to change his mind? If this was such a sure thing, we'd have left port knowing that was our bounty. That's what *I* think!"

"I've never doubted the captain before," Jensen said, "but this is very unlike him. We could take the short runs we planned and still beat Seadread."

Chim patted the empty sleeve on his left side, where normally there would be a second arm. "Sometimes one strong thing is better than two weaker ones."

Fump chuckled. "He's talking about arms and voyages at the same time. Love it!"

Heavy steps crept toward them from the stairs.

"Well, men, enjoying some glut and chatter, are we?" It was the unmistakable voice of Captain Murdoch. "It's some fine sustenance, Wigglebelly. Some of the best brew o' beans I can remember."

"*Huhuhuhuhu!* Brew o' beans. Sounds like bean beer, man!" chuckled Wigglebelly.

Shifty glances were aplenty. Jensen wondered how much of their conversation the captain had heard.

"Fine work victualling the crew on our modified rations," the captain said. "Gentlemen! We've a pleasant breeze chasing away the heat. Such a nice day to keep yourselves below deck."

"Yes, sir!" Tate piped, his voice unusually high. "As always, you couldn't be more right!"

"I wholeheartedly agree," said Fump. "I think we're all about to get back to work, sir."

"At ease, men," Murdoch said. "I've been considering things . . . and I believe I know just what our crew needs for a time like this."

Jensen grimaced and wondered if there was about to be punishment for too much lollygagging or, even worse, openly questioning the captain. He suddenly imagined being strung from the stern with his crewmates, dangling like lanterns.

"What's that?" Chim asked.

"It's time to clear the upper deck and bring out the extra ale."

Fump rubbed his auburn beard. "A deck party, Captain?"

"Aye, Fump. A deck party."

Deckhands hauled barrels and flagons and all the ship's most perishable foods to the main deck. Starlina watched them from beside the larboard railing, curious about this "deck party" that was about to take place. With any luck, she might even manage to enjoy herself.

The smooth head of Fulgar emerged from the tangle of crewmembers. He walked toward her, frock coat billowing and arms folded.

"Ah, Miss Starlina," Fulgar said.

She returned a cordial smile. "I'm not sure what's about to happen here will be chaplain appropriate."

"Probably all the more reason I should be on hand," he said. "How are you doing?"

"Trying to make the best of bad, I suppose. Perhaps some

drink will help." She flinched, remembering this was the chaplain. "And praying, of course. Is it wrong to drink and pray at once?"

Fulgar unfolded his arms, grinning. "Anyone with a drink probably has great reason to pray."

"Ah, of course."

She felt his eyes on her for a moment. "I merely joke, Starlina. Please, no need to prohibit yourself on my account. In fact, I pray you will enjoy the evening."

She relaxed against the rail. Fulgar really was rather charming. "And I you."

"Starlina." He leaned a bit closer. "Earlier, when you held the dagger, the novidian connected with you. That is why the glow remained in your grasp. You are, indeed, someone very special."

"I suppose next you're going to tell me that I'm here for a reason, to achieve some higher purpose."

He laughed. "Reason and purpose are Eloh's business, and whether they align with mine or anyone else's here is not for me to say."

"Indeed. I don't wish to be made any part of whatever is going on here." She was anxious to reach Vartu, where she would still need to find the fastest way back to Warvonia.

"Sometimes we find ourselves in precisely the last place we want to be. I don't envy you that hardship, Starlina, and I am sorry." He paused, casting a pensive look out to sea. "Yet sometimes, I have found, where we least want to be is actually what we need the most."

Starlina glared at the rail a moment, thinking on those

words. Then it was her turn to laugh. "Sounds like you're talking about purpose after all."

He turned back to her from the sea, looking amused. "Perhaps you're right. Purpose can be a tough thing to avoid."

She shook her head and stared at the water breaking away from the ship's hull below. "Any purpose for my being here is fulfilled. If there was ever a doubt that I belong on land and not aboard this ship, then that doubt is fully quenched."

Some quiet moments passed, with only the sounds of the water and crew's chatter filling the background.

"An interesting fact," said Fulgar. "Not everyone able to connect with novidian will ever come to realize it. It is believed that most with that potential live and die never even knowing it. I count myself fortunate—blessed." He turned back to her with a gentle smile. "And any others of the same affinity I consider a valuable ally. Should you ever perceive the Fielder's call, Starlina, I pray you'll come forth with confidence."

"Um … okay," she replied. "And a Fielder is …?"

"You and I!" he answered grandly. "One who connects with the ethereal energies which can be conducted by novidian." He folded his arms with a wink. "I should see if any of the men need assistance … with anything other than drink, of course. Thank you, Starlina."

She watched him walk away. She decidedly had no role to play in this quest of her father's. Yet, as Fulgar mixed in with the crew, she couldn't help but feel a part of something bigger than before.

Twilight glowed in the sky, flamethyst torches lined the ship, and the rich, reedy sounds of accordion chords filled the air. Wiggle-belly's thick fingers proved not only adept in the kitchen but also on the keys of the accordion. Jensen couldn't help but slap his thigh to the jovial tune.

Captain Murdoch stood upon the quarterdeck, over-looking the entire crew gathered below. He raised a tankard of ale overhead. "Alright, you scurvy gruel-mongers, cheer up your guzzle-pipes and strike up a tone pleasing to me ear!"

Wigglebelly played all the more fervently, swaying his girth to the tune as Fump, Chim, Dippy, and Beep clanged their tankards and erupted into song. Most of the crew joined in at the end of each verse, frothy drink splashing from their upraised mugs.

> "We're king o'er the seas; yeah, we bring the loot!
> To all other seadogs we give the boot!
> Our captain's name is Zale the Gale!
> *Hey! Ho! Lift up your ale!*"
>
> "*Queenie's* our ship; she's the greatest cat!
> In our crew we've got tall, thin, short, and fat!
> When a job's on the line we will never fail!
> *Hey! Ho! So let's set sail!*"

The captain's roaring laughter could've awoken the dead of the depths. Murdoch himself took up the next verse.

> "In all the guild, our crew is boss;
> Fump, Chim-Chum, and Wigglebelly sauce!
> Dippy and Beep and all the rest.
> *Hey! Ho! Zale's crew is best!*"

Starlina groaned loudly by Jensen's side. "Well, that settles it. My father is officially a madman."

"He's a riot!" Jensen yelled over the ruckus.

Murdoch held both arms high in the air, demanding the attention of all. "Gents! And ladies—" he motioned his drink in the general direction of Evette and Starlina "—already we've been tested to our wit's end. Many of you doubt my decision to change our course—"

"No! Of course not, Captain!" rang out shouts from the crew.

Murdoch held a hand forward, calming the masses. "I *know* of the chatter. Very little is said on ol' Pop-Pop's ship which he doesn't hear. But I tell you this—and hear me well—with the Grimstone in our grasp, the cargo will be simple, but the reward will be many times over the bounty we set out for—the bounty of bounties!"

"To the Gale!" roared Rolf "Hookknee" Cone, a brown-skinned, barrel-chested deckhand.

"*To the Gale!*" shouted the crew.

"Never doubted you for a second, Captain!" Tate shouted.

Wigglebelly set his fingers again to the accordion, prompting a flurry of dancing, stomping, and shouting.

A few men urged the jolly seaman along. "Faster! Play it faster! Wiggle that jiggle-bowl!"

Red-faced, Wigglebelly put his all into it, chuckling nearly in time with his music. Even Evette joined in the dance, hooking arms with the rowers who'd joined the crew with her.

Jensen looked around in wonderment. Here was this crew on a daring mission, going after some mythical object they weren't even sure existed, for a payoff they could scarcely imagine, and yet the entire ship was a festive uproar. Only one more thing could make this night complete.

He turned to Starlina and proffered an arm. She arched an eyebrow. "Come now, Starlina. We're here, under the stars and rings, and there's no more jolly a place on the entire ocean than this very ship. We can share at least one dance, can't we?"

After an eye roll, she took his arm. "Fine. One dance."

They started off easy, but that one dance seemed to shake the inhibitions from Starlina. A second dance followed, then a third, each more energetic than the last. Others of the crew gaped at them longingly, perhaps the first time there had ever been such jealousy of Jensen's position. Their options for female accompaniment at sea were extremely few—usually zero—and Evette was not to be trifled with.

Eventually the music died down, Wigglebelly barely able to breathe from being so winded, and Captain Murdoch strode throughout the deck.

"Evette!" Murdoch called. "I hear you've kept the men on edge and ready for action. That's well and good. This fair wind might not hold out much longer. I haven't seen a lady take such control of a group of men since the nuns of my boarding school days. Rancorous old shrews, the lot of 'em. But, if I hadn't had all their discipline, I might've ended up doing an honest man's work—bah ha! *Pop-Pop!*" His infectious laughter drew everyone around him.

"Shrew!" shouted Fump, snapping his fingers. "That should be Evette's nickname!"

"I'm down," Murdoch replied, "provided Miss Caskmore accepts, that is."

Evette clanked mugs with Fump. "With honor!"

"Ah, Jensen!" Murdoch turned his way. "Some nice dancing with my daughter out there. A fine display for this lot to sink their chops into, don't you think? Parade her around much longer, and I might have to get worried."

Jensen felt suddenly wary of those around him. "She's a terrific dancer, sir. Always has been. But point taken, sir. I'll be mindful of the crew."

"Oh, stop being such an animal," Starlina snapped.

Murdoch gave Jensen a hard nudge and leaned toward Starlina. "Relax, my dear. I'm merely joshing with the boy." He turned to Jensen. "We can't expect her to be used to the way we jab at each other, can we?"

"Ah . . . right, Captain," Jensen replied. Perhaps it was the ale, but Murdoch seemed a bit chummier than Jensen was accustomed to.

"Say, Jensen, I was thinking," Murdoch said, "how about we give you a little break from nighttime helms duty, just for a couple nights."

Jensen blinked in surprise. "Thank you, sir. Whatever pleases you, of course."

"Right, right," Murdoch said. "Beep! Over here!"

Kasper joined them.

"Let's get Jensen here off the helm the next two nights. I'm also thinking, keep the crow's nest clear."

Kasper frowned. "Sir, we need to keep a weathered eye for Vartu."

Murdoch waved him off. "Once Fump starts chasing butter-flies on deck, you'll know we're close to land. Right . . . no one *in* the crow's nest. Just hang Jensen here from it upside-down so I can hear him scream like a scalded-ass monkey! *Ah hahahaha!*"

Jensen was stunned, his eyes wide with concern.

Kasper flashed a glare at Jensen and walked off, leaving Murdoch to his mirthful chuckles.

The captain gave Jensen another nudge. "No hard feelings, Jensen. Might as well get used to a bit of subterfuge."

Starlina shook her head hopelessly. Captain Murdoch took off toward his cabin, clapping backs and bellowing wisecracks all the way.

CHAPTER 7

NEW BEARINGS

7/29/3203 P.A.

W hile Captain Murdoch may have been joking about Jensen being hung upside-down, he was in fact dead serious about assigning Jensen a post high up in the crow's nest. As most of the crew turned in for the night, Beep shoved a spyglass into his hand, and he was made to climb the rigging, all the way up to the crow's nest at some sixty-five feet into the air.

Every pitch and rock and heel gave him the sense that he was teetering from the edge of a cliff. The wind was completely unforgiving. For the first time ever, Jensen felt the onset of seasickness and nearly kecked up the prior day's bean soup.

It became easily the longest and most terrifying night of Jensen's young life.

Very little actual watching happened during the overnight hours. As dawn's light crept over the eastern horizon, however, his courage started to awaken. He stood up taller, held himself better against the wind, and began to relish the bird's-eye view.

Once over the fright, he realized how perfectly majestic the view was. He could see everything happening on the deck below him, more and more little figures scurrying to and fro as crewmen awoke. All around, for nearly ten miles in every direction, he saw blue skies, puffy clouds, and cerulean waters.

Except that something in the northeast caused him to double back. He spied hazy white shapes peeking up over the horizon. His eyes gave a dubious squint, struggling to make it out.

He grabbed the spyglass, fumbling as he tried to extend it. He nearly lost it over the edge but managed to catch it just before it fell.

Taking a breath, he swallowed, and he raised the spyglass to his eye. It took him a few moments to find the shapes again. When he did, he discovered more than just white. Dark shapes were there along with it. This could only be one thing: another ship.

It had very dark timbers—dark gray, perhaps, very nearly black—with two masts poking into the air. He saw no banner. If it was from Tuscawny, it was likely a vessel under private commission.

Jensen suddenly had a very bad feeling about whose ship that might be.

It can't be, he thought, glaring through the spyglass.

"*Captain!*" he called to the deck below.

He couldn't see Murdoch. Most likely he was in his cabin.

"*Captain!*" he called again.

A short time later Beep arrived at the mast. "What is it?"

"A ship, sir!"

Beep looked uncertain. He walked over to the railing and scanned the distance for good measure. "Come on down here with the spyglass! Meet me on the forecastle."

The climb down was about as unsettling as the climb up, perhaps even worse. When going up, he didn't have to look down, and at night he couldn't as well discern his height. In the daylight it was far more terrifying.

By the time he reached the main deck and made his way to the forecastle, both Beep and Captain Murdoch were waiting for him.

"Ah, Jensen—good morning!" greeted Murdoch. "Did you see something out there?"

"Yes, sir," Jensen replied. "I'd say nearly forty degrees to starboard—about four points northeast."

The captain and Beep exchanged a look.

"Hand me the bring-'em-closer," said Murdoch, reaching for the spyglass. Jensen handed it over and watched as the captain checked for himself. A very light sea fog drifted over the water, which Jensen hoped would not make a fool out of him.

Long moments passed as Murdoch scouted the horizon. Finally he lowered the spyglass, retracted it, and stowed it in his pocket.

"Did you see anything, Captain?" asked Beep.

Murdoch gave a slight nod. "Keen eye, Jensen. Well spotted.

It's another ship, alright. Beep, how far are we from Vartu?"

"Probably about two days, by my estimate. That's if this wind holds out."

Murdoch groaned. He aimed himself toward midship. "Dippy, *repooorrrt!*"

A few minutes later Dippy joined them. "Yes, Captain?"

"We've lost the luxury of lollygagging. Our detour is at an end. Set our course for Gukhan." He approached the taffrail and gazed into the east. "The race is on, gentlemen. Out there, with an ever-so-slight advantage, is the ship of old Puffypants, the *Iron Mermaiden.*"

"Seadread?" Dippy asked.

"That's what I was afraid of," Jensen muttered.

Murdoch gestured toward the elaborate wooden weaponry at the farthest aft railing. "Have our ballista at the ready, and bolts on standby for the crossbows. Better have the pitch and torches on hand, as well. Things could get dicey if we end up in close quarters."

"Aye, sir," Dippy said. "I'll get Chim and Fump on it straight away."

"I'll adjust our course," Beep said, walking off.

Seadread and Murdoch were rivals in the sense that they frequently traded places for top rank in the guild. Jensen had never seen them compete for the exact same prize at the same time. He wondered, with a gulp of angst, how the situation might escalate if they met face to face, crew to crew.

"Captain," said Jensen, "shall I keep the watchman's post?"

"No. You get some rest. Your job might be the hardest of all."
He looked upon Jensen with a grave expression. "You must try to
persuade my daughter to forgive us both."

The distant, hazy form of Seadread's ship remained in the eastern
horizon, its position changing very little. Zale watched it often,
his eye glaring through the spyglass.

"Looks like Vidimir got to Seadread after all," Dippy said
quietly.

"That's of no real surprise," Zale replied.

"Do you think they've noticed us?"

"Of course they have." He retracted his spyglass. "What's
more bothersome is that he was probably the first to notice our
proximity." He took a moment to feel the breeze. "This wind
won't hold our pace for long . . . but he'll face the same. Once we
start stalling, deploy the log-line and take note of our speed. For
Eloh's love, don't drag us. Signal Evette to have rowers stationed
and sweeps at the ready. If we get below three knots, plunge the
oars and pull with all we've got. That might be our best chance
to gain on him."

"Sure thing, Captain."

Zale made for his cabin, trying to sort out all the possible
maneuvers they might have to pull if they should find themselves going head to head against Seadread and his men. Captain

Rummy had a marginally larger crew for his slightly loftier ship. With two masts and more sails, Rummy could gain the advantage in full wind. The *Queenie*'s hull, however, was broad above the water and sharper below, tapering all the way to aft, a design of Zale's own order that made the ship rather heavy but fast despite it. Zale had also budgeted extra crew for proper rowing ranks, something Rummy was not known to do. Now he could only hope it would pay off.

He entered his cabin and found Starlina standing barefoot in an off-white top and pants that appeared to have been made of sailcloth. The clothes and sandals she'd arrived in were bunched in her arms. Her face exuded pure vexation at his arrival.

"Starlina, what are you doing?" Zale asked.

"You can set your course for hell," she snapped. "You and Jensen both."

He groaned. "I take it you're aware of our new bearings." He removed his hat and came a few steps closer, trying his best to look apologetic. "I know it's not what you'd hoped—"

"How can you expect me to remain on this wooden trap this *entire* voyage? I feel like a prisoner!"

"Try to understand . . . if we didn't change course immediately, we'd risk losing the prize altogether. I had no choice."

"Your *choices* seem to change on a whim." She threw up a hand. "I know it's of no use arguing with you. I'm going to bunk in the hold with Evette."

"In the *hold*? Darling, it's both safer and more comfortable here in my cabin."

"Don't *darling* me! I'll manage just fine. Mister Willigan is already putting up a hammock for me. Evette loaned me this ... outfit ... something she made herself. I couldn't stand wearing the same clothes another minute."

Zale didn't dare argue with her. She would already have to stay aboard the ship throughout their voyage. He wasn't about to dictate where she could or couldn't rest.

"Fine. Sleep wherever you're most comfortable. And I'm sorry, Starlina. I'll make it up to you."

"You want to make it up?" She breezed past him and took hold of the door handle. "Get me back *home!*"

She flung herself through the doorway and slammed it behind her.

"Man overboard!"

The call was muffled through Zale's cabin but nonetheless unmistakable. "This is a great way to start the morning," he grumbled, grabbing his hat.

Dippy was already bawling orders on the deck. "Throw out a lifebuoy! Haul him aboard!"

Fump, Jensen, and Evette stood by the rail, watching as the deckhands readied the lifebuoy. Evette scowled with tight lips, while Fump and Jensen looked rather amused.

Zale looked over the rail. Miles, one of the general deckhands, floundered about in the water. He looked more incensed than desperate. The lifebuoy landed on target, and in short order the man was hoisted back up.

"What happened?" Zale demanded.

Several eyeballs shifted toward Evette.

"Well?!" Zale shouted.

Evette leaned her hip against the rail and swept her hand toward the ocean. "He stumbled overboard."

"It was more of a cause-and-effect thing," Fump added. "He stumbled . . . because Shrew clobbered him in the face."

"I hit him middeck!" she shouted. "It was his own stupor that tripped him over the side."

"It was quite spectacular," Jensen said from the ropes.

Evette stood tall, rubbing absently at her nails and wearing a self-satisfied smirk.

"Explain yourself!" ordered Zale.

"Insubordination, Captain," Evette said with inarguable sureness. "He pretended to bump into me by accident and just *happened* to be ready for a two-handed squeeze in the process." She gestured at her breasts.

"It's true, Captain," Jensen said. "I saw the whole thing. Miles made a very blatant advance."

Moments later, Miles was brought over the rail, dripping. A nice, red welt had already formed on his left cheek.

"Crew, listen well!" Zale bellowed. "I don't care that we have two ladies aboard. They are a part of this crew. Any further uncouth advances, and I will personally ensure the offender is keelhauled from bow to stern and back again!"

"Yes, Captain," droned several of the crew in response.

"Show's over—back to work!"

As they began to scatter, Zale took note of the still air and their dramatically slowed speed. With this morning's excitement, he already figured Dippy hadn't yet run the log-line, but he knew well enough how slow they were going.

He turned to Evette. "Shrew, get those sweeps in the water. Let's keep our best pace until this wind picks back up."

"Yes, sir!" Evette said. She motioned for Jensen and a few of the deckhands to follow her below.

"I suppose something like that was bound to happen eventually," Zale groaned. He reached for his spyglass and aimed it northeast. "Puffypants is still out there."

"Aye, sir," Dippy said. "I've been watching."

Zale retracted his spyglass. "Stay abreast with Evette about the rowers, and have crewmen on rotation to keep from too much fatigue."

Dippy returned a lopsided smile. "I'll keep *abreast*, sir."

Zale frowned. "Maybe not the most stellar choice of words. *Up to speed*, Mister Doyle, so it's not *you* I'll have to throw overboard."

Dippy walked off, still smiling.

"Hen overboard!"

Zale burst out of his cabin. "What under the rings is happening?" he growled.

"Sorry, Cap," Fump said. "Just a bit of morbid humor. One of Wigglebelly's chickens went egg-bound and died overnight. We just cast it to sea. Of course, the bigger problem is that we've got one less egg-layer and already-stretched rations."

"Perfect," Zale said flatly.

Wigglebelly looked crestfallen. "I asked Fulgar to perform last rites on Flappy. It was beautiful, man."

"Yeah, it was already dead at that point," Fump muttered.

"Hey!" deckhand Jonas shouted from the quarterdeck. "A shark just snatched that hen!"

Wigglebelly gasped in horror.

Tate slapped him on the back. "It's just the food chain, Wigglebelly. Don't take it too hard. Say, what's for supper, anyway?"

"Chicken soup, man. My own mother's recipe, in honor of Flappy."

Zale walked off. He couldn't have made this stuff up if he'd tried.

The day droned on with low wind, more rowing, and an increasingly fatigued crew. They simply didn't have the manpower to run constant shifts on the sweeps. Whenever they could, however, they put two men on some of the oars to help lighten the burden and move the ship faster. With the sail up, any crew normally on the ropes stayed under Evette's command among the benches. Beep, Jensen, and Tate kept a regular rotation at the helm.

Later that afternoon, during Beep's turn at the helm, Zale noticed Jensen conversing with Tate and Kelvin on the forecastle. Curious what they were up to, he moseyed over in their direction. The young deckhand was showing something off to the others.

"...might look like rock," Zale heard Jensen say as he neared, "but if you pull it just so, it stretches. Now, watch this."

Jensen pulled at a grayish substance until it was almost straw-thin. It was vaguely familiar to Zale, something from a prior haul. He stayed behind Jensen's field of vision but remained within earshot.

"It seems very brittle, right, being so thin? But hold it firmly in place for a few moments, and it remains steadfast. Not only that, but at about this size and shape, it becomes an amazing cutting tool." He brandished a rusty old hinge, like something from a sea chest. "Found this in the hold. Tate, if you would. Hold it so it's fully open, and keep it in place."

He handed the hinge to Tate, who unbent the hinge and waited. Carefully, Jensen brought the straw-thin substance up to the hinge, moving it back and forth like a saw. Within seconds it broke right through. "You see? It cuts even metal!"

"Bloody blazes!" Tate exclaimed. "That's amazing!"

Kelvin nodded thoughtfully.

Zale felt hot under the collar. *Show's over*, he thought.

"So!" Zale boomed, stepping toward them. "You've got

resilite, do you? Extremely rare, that. In fact, I believe that was our haul on your first voyage, wasn't it?"

Jensen reared back. "Oh! Y-yes, sir. That it was."

"You're working very hard to get marooned, aren't you?"

"N-no! Not at all!"

Zale cornered them all toward the prow. "Listen to me, the three of you. *Every* part of *every* trip's bounty is cashed in and belongs in agreed shares to the crew. *No* exceptions!"

"Yes, of course!" Jensen sputtered.

"Stop sniveling and get out of my sight. We'll deal with this later." They scampered away, apparently with better sense than to test his temper any further.

Zale took a deep breath and looked out to the water. A steady fog rolled across the surface, like wispy clouds coming down for a visit. Out of what had become a rather impulsive habit, he took his spyglass and checked the distance, but not for long. With even a light fog there would be no sighting Seadread's ship.

Yet he sensed something strange in the tides, something which he couldn't quite put his finger on.

"Fine afternoon, Captain." Fulgar joined him at the prow.

"Only one week in," Zale said. "Already my daughter can't stand the sight of me, and I'm sorely tempted to toss the dolt she holds dear overboard. And, of course, I continue to hope I haven't doomed us all on this errand."

"I have noticed that you are indeed a thoughtful man. That's admirable in a captain, no doubt a large reason for your success."

"And how is your experience aboard the *Queenie* thus far?" Zale asked.

"You've a fascinating crew," Fulgar answered. "They are a headstrong, passionate bunch ... and they place much faith in your instincts."

But how much faith shall we place in you? Zale wondered. Fulgar had proven to be an able member of the crew, and the men seemed to trust him. He had played no small role in convincing Zale to go after the Grimstone, promising he could help achieve a more targeted search. It was time to find out what that meant.

"Let's hope they're right," Zale said. "And that reminds me. We need to speak on the matter of Gukhan. What's your lead on its location?"

Fulgar pulled a folded flaxsheet from within his frock coat. He smoothed it out against the ship's railing and held it close for Zale to see. Various wavy lines and shapes scattered the page, along with something like a spire coming to a very sharp point.

"I made a copy of this page from the Order's records," Fulgar said, "associated with the clues left behind by Macpherson. Along with this was the clue: 'As with decuple generosity, to those who give an inch, a mile is given in return.'"

"What does this mean?"

"We are not sure," Fulgar said. "However, *decuple* suggests tenfold, so we believe this might indicate a location ten miles away from something." He pointed to his flaxsheet. "It could be ten miles from this pointed structure, or that this structure is ten miles from something else. This snaking, uneven line could indicate a route or path which must be taken to or from the structure."

Zale felt a deep discomfort in the pit of his stomach. Some old sketch was not what he had hoped for. "I was under the impression you knew an actual location! We can't just roam some foreign land until we stumble upon this landmark and a path!"

"There is more within our records, which I believe will get us close. The legend indicates that this structure is visible from the water, accessible from the southern side of the island. It is not pinpoint accuracy, I admit, but at least we know it should be visible from somewhere along the southern shores."

It was a glimmer of hope, but this still sounded a little vague for Zale's comfort. "Seems rather easy; I mean, visible from their closest shore?"

"Just because you can see it doesn't make it easy, Captain. Gukhan ... there are many tales about that land. Many too fanciful to be true, I'm sure ... but, still ... there are often even hints of truth in tales. The 'Untouchable Society,' some call it."

"It's landlocked with Ska'ard, so clearly it's not *that* untouchable."

"The Ska'ardians won't go near their border. They don't even engage in trade. Few really know what that land is like, what secrets they harbor. Within the Order's ancient records, Gukhan is often said to be a 'tangible illusion.' Once we've arrived, there might yet be clues to unravel."

Hopefully they aren't clues that Seadread has already figured out, Zale thought.

"Whatever the case," said Zale, facing Fulgar, "the one thing that'd better *not* be an illusion is the Grimstone."

Starlina stood upon the stern deck, staring at the ship's wake. Somewhere back there were Grandtrilia and Tuscawny and Warvonia, where she wanted so badly to return. Instead, they were only going farther away.

"This proves my theory," said Jensen as he ascended from the quarterdeck. "Everyone needs fresh air eventually."

Starlina had taken to spending most of her time in the hold, away from the crew as much as possible. It seemed there wasn't a single one of them she could gain comfort with, as if they were all some alternate form of human with which she simply could not associate.

"Fresh air or not," she said, "I feel like I'm on a floating prison. I can't stop thinking about home. One week from today Amira starts at university. I can't imagine what she thinks has happened to me."

"Perhaps that you've run off with me on some romantic getaway," Jensen snickered.

Starlina's face pursed, not at all amused. "But that couldn't have happened, could it? You'd be out at sea, completely unreach-able . . . just as I am now."

"It won't always be this way. If we capture this Grimstone

and reach the mastery bar, everything could change. We'd have plenty to live on, and I wouldn't have to be on nearly as many voyages. Chasing that mastery bar would be a thing of the past."

"And that's an awfully big *if*, isn't it? We sail for Gukhan, the most mysterious land in all the Great Crescent, and my genius father doesn't even know where to look once we get there. It's like arriving to an unknown land—an entire country—expecting to stumble upon some rock that you heard about." She noticed Jensen's bemused expression. "I might spend most of my time in the hold, but I *do* pay attention to things."

"Most of us trust that Captain Murdoch has a plan. He has always pulled his crew through before."

Starlina threw her hands down upon the taffrail. "He's so hard on you, and yet you continue to have faith in him. It's remarkable, really. Just look at you, steering the ship all night. Your eyes are dark for lack of sleep."

"I just try to keep my sights on the goal. That's as much as any of us can do." Jensen shifted to and fro on his legs, his hand fingering about in his pocket. "You know," he said, "there was a reason why I brought you aboard this ship in the first place. Something more than showing you the view."

She stood bolt upright. "Jensen, we must stop this."

"What?"

Starlina painfully realized that out here, unlike on land, there was no ignoring what Jensen was. There was no suppressing the reality that he was a sailor, and he probably always would be.

"I'm sorry, Jensen. I should've told you long ago ... long

before you brought me here. You love ... *this* life. I do not. Our lives are on different paths. Next year, I'll be off to university, and we'll be apart, each with our own expectations of the years ahead."

"Starlina, please," he spoke softly. "Our love is stronger than any of these obstacles."

She wasn't sure she even knew what love was anymore. Jensen wanted a woman to return to between his voyages. She wanted—*needed*—much more than that.

"I'm afraid it's not," she said, her voice cracking. "I'm sorry."

She swept herself away and disappeared into the ship.

Two days later, on the first of Agust, Jensen stood alone upon the afterdeck, completely exhausted both physically and emotionally. His blank, enervated stare from the larboard stern was fixed upon the northeastern shores of Korangar, visible as a haze on the horizon's edge.

He had just completed another all-night shift of helms duty, and with the rising sun beaming into his eyes, his body felt locked in an awful state of wanting to be both asleep and awake, not quite able to achieve either.

Starlina had not spoken another word to him since ripping the heart from his chest. She no longer wore the kuntupite pendant. He saw her only from a distance, and even then it was mere moments before she'd retreat back into the hold. He languished in constant regret of having brought her aboard this ship, wondering how he could have been so foolish.

He wandered his way belowdecks and nearly bumped into Evette.

"You!" she said sharply, getting near Jensen's face. "Do something about this girl you brought aboard. All she does is mope. If she's not moping, she's crying. If she's not crying, she's talking about the self-centered pigheadedness of men... specifically *you*. It's just the two of us down in that hold, and if she weren't the captain's daughter I'd have already tossed her overboard tied to a millstone. Or, maybe getting rid of *you* would shut her up!"

Jensen was unable to form words before Evette had disappeared back into the berthing deck.

"That's why women on the ship is a bad idea," muttered Tate as he passed by.

By this point, Jensen was quite inclined to agree. He would not make that mistake again.

CHAPTER 8

GHOST SHIP

8/8/3203 P.A.

I t had been a frustrating week of sailing since putting the
Grandtrilia continent to their stern. Storms and unforgiving headwinds had forced many navigational errors and
adjustments. One morning Zale found that they had yawed too
far to the east, as though toward Ska'ard, a discovery that turned
him pink with rage.

"Are we helmed by Murdoch's Mates," he fumed, "or some
pack of slack-witted chowderheads?"

Typically their greatest variances occurred while the helm
was under the watch of Jensen or Tate.

Even seasoned sailors rarely stayed perfectly on course
when the elements got rough. Still, Zale found his patience with
Jensen running especially thin, as they made one course correction after another.

"Jensen!" he shouted just after sunup one day.

Jensen jolted such that Zale wondered if he'd been asleep

against the wheel.

"Are we sailing for Gukhan or Whiteland?" Zale asked.

"Stop blubberpotting around and sort your bearings!"

Part of the time they made great progress, catching the wind just right. Other times, with the crew simply too spent, they were forced to becalm for intervals that felt like an eternity. They plodded along via oars as much as they could, but it was slow going.

They hadn't spotted Seadread's ship, the *Iron Mermaiden*, for days. The notion that Rummy had out-maneuvered them galled at what few nerves Zale had remaining.

Zale emerged from his cabin that morning, coffee mug in hand, to a heavy covering of sea fog. "*Beeeeeeep!*"

"Morning, Captain," came the reply from quarterdeck.

"How long have we been in this fog?"

"Probably not even an hour yet."

Zale groaned and sipped his coffee. The closer they got to Gukhan, the more wary he became of changing conditions, no matter how mundane they might seem. "Taken any soundings as of yet?"

"Aye, sir, about half-hour ago. Lead line reported no bottom, as expected."

"Keep checking at least every hour." He went for another sip, his eyes glaring into the fog from over his coffee mug. Something felt off, his instincts on end. "You're absolutely certain of our position?"

Beep gave a curt nod. "I've been double-checking our—*ahh!*"

Timbers creaked and crewmates yelped as the entire ship listed toward larboard, groaning and vibrating until balancing back out.

Zale managed to grab a staircase railing but lost his coffee to the deck. "Oh, that's just *great!*"

"Maybe it's just me," said Fump, "but I think we hit something."

Zale met him along the starboard railing.

Fump pointed beyond. "I see land out there!"

Zale spun around to face Beep. "Quick, shift us larboard! Crew, watch for shoals and sandbanks! Frequent soundings starboard and port. Reef the sail and slow ahead! We'll not run her aground, men!" Yet, they had grazed land once already. "And check for any damage and leaks!"

Dippy appointed several deckhands for the ordered tasks, after which he rejoined the captain.

"Did we catch a massive tailwind throughout the night?" Zale asked.

"Not that much," Dippy said. "By our reckoning, we should still be at least a day or two away from Gukhan's shores."

Zale rubbed at his chin whiskers. "Vidimir told us he'd lost ships among islets near their destination. Best we review this situation. Officers, including Fulgar, to my cabin." He started off but turned on one final thought. "Except for Chim. See that the ship's weapons are loaded and ready for quick action."

"Aye, Cap'n," Chim replied.

Zale lingered on the deck a little while longer, glaring

past the ship with wary eyes and awaiting the damage report. Crewmen Archie, Bert, and Chester, their pursed-lipped purser, returned on deck to confirm no water in the bilge and no leaks in the hull. They had gotten by lucky on that encounter—*very* lucky.

Minutes later Dippy, Fump, Beep, Evette, and Fulgar gathered in Zale's cabin. Beep spread one of his maps out across the table and pressed his finger upon an area of water south of Gukhan. "We should be right about *here*. If we're seeing land, it's uncharted."

"Vidimir mentioned this to us in the tavern," said Zale. "Now's the time to be sharp and ready. We're in hostile waters, and enemy ships could spring at any...." He trailed off, his attention caught by a set of usually-unobtrusive numbers in the map's corner.

"Any... *time*?" ventured Fump.

Zale's eyes had shifted to the scale of the map. *One inch equals ten miles.*

"What is it, Captain?" Evette asked.

"Fulgar, that clue from your Order. 'To those who give an inch, a mile is given in return' ...."

"That's correct, 'as with decuple generosity.'"

Zale tapped the scale of the map. "Tenfold. Give one inch and receive ten miles."

Fulgar's mouth went agape. "A map scale!"

The others in the room exchanged uncertain glances. "A map scale?" Dippy asked. "Sir, I don't think we're following you."

Zale reached toward Fulgar. "Give me your drawing."

Fulgar handed it over, and Zale took it with the map over to the nearest windowpane. "Our most efficacious spiritual guide happens to have information from his ancient order pertaining to the Grimstone." He laid the map against the window. The sunlight shining through was dim from the fog but still enough. He carefully lined Fulgar's drawings up over the map. "It was still only a vague clue . . . until now."

Fulgar rushed toward Zale. "The drawing overlays your map perfectly! The pointed structure lies about fifteen miles inland. This irregular line on the drawing isn't a path at all. It's a river!"

Zale nodded. "It's a river flowing from the southern coast. Thus, accessible from the southern side of the island."

"And visible from the water. Not the ocean, but rather this river! Amazing!"

Beep stepped toward the map. "And these other shapes down below—these must be the islets."

"Charted after mainland Gukhan," Fulgar said. He met eyes with Zale. "Charted only by those of legend."

"So, now we know where the Grimstone is located?" asked Fump. "That's awesome!"

Zale rubbed his hands together, pleased with his discovery. Not only that, but Fulgar had contributed a valuable resource. Zale remained wary of the man's intentions, but this was a good step toward Fulgar proving his sincerity.

"Sir, may I?" Beep stepped up and reversed the pages, so that his map was on top. Using a pencil, he traced the shapes onto his map. "I'd better get this out there. If I'm seeing this right, we're bound to plow headfirst into a strip of land."

Someone frantically rang the bell outside. "*Captain!*" shouted one of the men.

Everyone rushed outside. Zale was surprised to see Jensen at the bell.

"Sir!" Jensen yelled. "Seadread's ship is upon us!"

Zale looked into the thick veil of fog. A dark form loomed ahead, turning his eyes to saucers. It was indeed the ship of Captain Rummy, emerging from the fog like a great, wooden kraken.

"Sweet Holy Realm," he muttered.

It was dangerously close, a clear sign of aggression under normal circumstances, coming toward them alongside larboard. Given the lack of visibility, there was an off chance that Seadread's crew had gotten lost in the fog and was just as surprised at their sudden proximity.

Zale wasn't about to give their fate to chance.

"Hands to the crossbows and ballista!"

"On it, Captain!" shouted Chim, who was already dashing to and fro about the deck, dropping extra bolts to the wood with a clatter.

"Everyone take up arms!" Zale roared. "Take cover where you can and prepare to shoot if they make hostile!"

If the approach was indeed hostile, Zale fully expected Captain Rummy to take the first shot of dishonor at another Tuscawnese vessel, and he was all too willing to return the favor.

On a whim, he turned to Jensen.

"Jensen . . . please see that my daughter is safe and protected."

"Of course, sir!" Jensen grabbed a sword and went below.

Seadread's dark, two-masted ship was now almost right beside them.

"At the ready, men!" Zale shouted, expecting an onslaught.

Everything went quiet, utterly still. Zale watched from midship, already certain his eyes were playing tricks.

The deck of Seadread's ship was completely empty. There was not a soul to be seen—not on the rigging, not at the rails, not upon the forecastle or stern, not even at the wheel. From the horrid-faced, screaming, bare-chested mermaid prow all the way to aft, the *Iron Mermaiden* was as a ghost ship. Ropes from the ship's sailyards, unlike lines of the standard rigging, flung unnaturally back and forth overhead, even reaching out above the *Queenie*'s deck.

Bolstered by long-seasoned instinct, Zale drew his saber.

"Captain, keep low," Fulgar whispered urgently. "Something here is much afoul."

No truer statement could've been spoken. In the muffled, foggy daylight, Zale saw the nervous shuffling of his crew. There was a disturbance about the fog that made his hackles rise, and subtle whispers of movement that didn't match with the men he saw. He looked again at Seadread's ship—the swinging ropes, the taut, steady sheets and braces keeping its sails under control . . . and the wheel. Deftly, he aimed his glass at the ship's helm.

"By the Light," he muttered. "Their wheel is not lashed, yet the ship is holding steady."

A few men at the rails shuffled, the sort of move a person might make when another is passing close behind. Soft thumps resounded throughout the deck. Zale's instinct swelled like an alarm. His eyes flicked again to the swinging ropes.

"Look alive, men! *We're being boarded!*"

Zale shed his coat and dropped it before his cabin door. His sword arm would have greater freedom of movement without it.

Crewmen spun about, swinging and flailing into the disturbed air around them, and soon found it to be more than wispy fog.

Cries rang out across the deck. "*Grimkins!*"

Grapnels launched from the other ship, snagging in the ratlines of the *Queenie*. Several of the black-feathered humanoids known as grimkins swung across, screeching through their beaked mouths like deranged eagles.

"We've got more incoming!" shouted Chim, hacking away one of the hooks.

"They've disguised themselves using byrne light absorption!" shouted Fulgar, pulling his novidian anelace.

Screams of pain pierced the air from men stabbed. As though shedding invisible cloaks, one by one the grimkins showed themselves, like feathered demons dressed in dark tunics. There were perhaps twenty of them. Angry screeches trilled from their beaks as they wielded curved, wicked blades. Steely clangs and shouts of battle replaced the stillness of moments before.

Murdoch's Mates sprang into action, parrying with swords

and axes Fump had furnished throughout the deck. Fump himself was a two-fisted, devilish fighter. With a sharp roar, he launched a hatchet into the skull of one grimkin and turned to crack the beak of another with a mace. He plunged a hand into a pocket of his trousers and flung a handful of sand into the face of another grimkin. As it screeched, holding its eyes, Fump drew a dirk. A flash of silver later, the feathered cretin fell to the deck.

Fulgar confounded his foes with the blazing white light of the novidian anelace, but his counterattacks became more than mere dueling. Zale did a double-take as Fulgar pointed his dagger toward the sky. With a flare of white energy, he drew several of the enemy weapons into his own like a magnet and cast them overboard. He turned another grimkin's weapon against it, jabbing it through the chest with only subtle movements of his own.

Evette and her oarsmen had taken up swords. She grunted and yelled with each strike. She was strong, deft, and surefooted, indeed one of the more capable fighters Zale had ever crewed. Even Wigglebelly was caught in the action, swinging a heavy bludgeon with the sort of proficiency only a master of the rolling pin could muster.

Zale laid into one assailant with swift, powerful blows. Rather than fancy footwork, Zale was known for the accuracy and strength of his saber handling. He was ambidextrous, typically drawing from his left hip and fighting with his right hand, although he was naturally stronger in the left. He backed his opponent into the larboard rail, eventually whacking away the grimkin's sword. He lunged forward and pushed into the grimkin with all his girth, sending it to the depths with a panicked screech.

Somewhere just behind, Beep reeled a captive grimkin over the quarterdeck balustrade with a grappling hook, preparing to heave it overboard like a bad catch.

"Captain!" Fulgar dragged Zale back by the arm.

"I'll have these curs mounted for decoration!" Zale spat in a fervor. He shook Fulgar off. "Every one of their vile heads on a pike!"

"Captain, you must get out of sight!" Fulgar shouted.

"Are you mad? I won't leave my crew in a fight!"

"Sir, it might be *you* they're after. The ancestor of Macpherson . . . the key to the Grimstone!"

"I'm not going anywhere," Zale growled.

Fulgar pointed his dagger toward a fallen grimkin's sword and guided it through the air straight into another enemy across the deck. "Then we shall do everything to protect you."

"There's more of 'em!" Dippy shouted.

More grimkins were now visible aboard the deck of Seadread's ship, a fresh swarm making for the ropes before the ship passed out of range.

"Get on those crossbows!" Zale ordered. "Beep! For Eloh's sake, all available hands to lines and sweeps! We need some speed!"

Chim's hand was already on one of the four larboard crossbow triggers. He took aim with his one arm, pulled, and launched the bolt straight into a grimkin on the other ship. He snatched up another bolt from the deck, loaded, aimed, and fired, felling another foe. It was a fluid motion, the sort of moment he was born for.

"Downright near a form of art, him at that," said Fump, a grimkin feather stuck in his fiery hair.

"Hookknee!" Chim called to one of his mates. "Hands on the aft ballista! We'll send 'em a final sting after they pass by!"

Even though all four crossbows were now in use, and feathery carcasses were filling the sea between them, there were too many grimkins that remained. They flung themselves to the ropes, at least ten per group.

Zale snatched a handheld crossbow from the deck, took aim, and speared one of the grimkins midair. Still, by his best guess, at least seven landed successfully.

All of them turned toward Zale. They sprinted his direction with earsplitting squawks. Several from his crew tried to intercept them, successfully taking down one here and another there. Most of his men, however, were still dealing with other grimkins already aboard the ship.

Zale stamped the deck defiantly and stood his ground. "Challenge me, will you! *Aaaahhhh!*"

He lashed out with the fury of many men, parrying and dodging their blades. It seemed they were taking some care in their strikes.

Fulgar might be right, he realized. *They don't want to damage their quarry.*

One swung low, thumping against his graphenite leg ineffectually. That one Zale kicked in the head with concussive force.

Three of the grimkins managed to grapple him from behind. He struggled against them, his hat falling to the deck. They forced away his saber and dragged him toward the rail.

"Unhand me, you quill-headed twits!"

Two more grimkins landed from Seadread's ship and gave their ropes to Zale's captors.

"Captain!" shouted Fump.

"No!" cried Chim.

"The birds, man! The birds!" squealed Wigglebelly.

It was the last thing Zale heard before the grimkins leapt and swung him from his ship.

Zale stumbled backwards to the dark timbers of Seadread's deck after a rough landing with his grimkin captors. All around him grimkins shuffled about and chittered in their strange native language. "What happened here? Did you animals overtake Captain Rummy's crew?"

A door slammed. He turned toward the captain's cabin and saw none other than Garrick Rummy himself. The pockmarked, pale-faced captain approached with long, unhurried steps, his churchwarden's pipe hanging loosely from his lips. He fitted a black, shabby hat upon the black hair of his head and stroked at his white, scraggly beard.

"*You!*" Zale shouted. "You treacherous ratbag! You'll have much to answer for after attacking a fellow vessel of Tuscawny."

"Zale... always the one for honor and decorum. Where's the honor in defeat, hmm?"

"*Fool!* My crew will stop at nothing to retrieve me."

Seadread shrugged, maintaining a smug grin. "Oh, yer crew will be dead. An unfortunate hazard o' the job, I'm afraid." He nodded to one of the grimkins. "Time for lights out."

The grimkin raised its arm with a series of squawking sounds, and easily a dozen of the creatures lined up against the larboard rail. They made strange motions with their hands, something Zale counted as faintly familiar. Purple flames appeared in the air before them. Once kindled, the grimkins shot the death-cold fireballs straight for the *Queenie*.

"Darkfire!" Zale roared.

He pushed his way toward the attacking grimkins but was immediately clotheslined by another one standing nearby. The hard fall knocked the air from his lungs.

He sat back up, gasping, and heard the anguished cries from his ship. The gap between them had widened, such that no one could swing across, and Seadread's grapnels had been cut loose. He felt some brief solace when two grimkins fell to crossbow fire. Then a particularly long bolt, unmistakably from their aft ballista, speared three grimkins at once. They fell overboard, a feathery skewer for the sharks. He faintly saw the light of Fulgar's dagger as he scrambled to deal with the darkfire attacks.

"Now, Zale," spoke Rummy, "I think ye know what we

be needin' ye for. Retrieve us the Grimstone, and we'll give ye quarter. That is, we'll spare yer life. All the bounty... and the mastery bar... go t' me."

"How stupid do you think I am?" Zale shot back. "I'm not helping you with anything!"

Seadread scowled deeply. "Don't be meddlin' with me, Murdoch. Ye be the most convenient solution, t' be sure, but you're plenty expendable. Yer bloodline be all we really need."

Zale's widened eyes betrayed him, his worst fear confirmed. Somehow, Seadread knew that all he needed was the bloodline of Macpherson, which included his daughter. Fulgar had been right.

"Yes, we know," Seadread said with a grin through his grungy teeth.

"Stop the attack on my crew, and swear to spare them."

Seadread reared back his head. "I really don't think so."

"Listen to me! I don't know where the Grimstone is located. I never knew about *any* of this until recently. But we might have just discovered how to map it, and that information is still aboard my ship."

"What am I t' do, Zale? Just swing ye back t' yer deck all friendly like, hopin' we all be in this together now, hmm?"

"You'll have to get us within shouting range under colors of ceasefire," Zale said. "I'll order my men to stand down. You'll do the same. Send one of your minions over to retrieve the map, and I'll order my ship to put Gukhan to its rudder, no looking back. Once we've won you the Grimstone, Rummy, you'll deliver me safely back to Warvonia."

Seadread stared back at Zale for long moments. Finally, he called out, "Belay yer fire!" He stomped hard upon the deck, and a man down below opened a hatch. "Moorland, raise the white and bring us back around."

Zale was relieved to see the grimkins forego their onslaught, although he was distraught to see large purple flames still licking up the side of his ship. He could only hope Fulgar and his mates would be able to deal with it as they had after leaving Warvonia's harbor, before it was too late.

Men—Seadread's actual human crew, slovenly as they were—ascended from the deck below to follow their captain's orders. Zale watched as they worked to turn the ship, chewing his lip nervously. He had bought them some time, but Rummy still had the upper hand, and the survival of everyone, including his daughter, now hung in an extremely delicate balance.

Suddenly, the ship lurched from starboard.

"What be that?" Seadread demanded.

Zale chanced a peek over the edge. A black longship filled with oarsmen had rammed them from below. So well had the fog concealed it that even Rummy's lookouts hadn't noticed the oncoming vessel. There were easily three dozen men in the boat, uniformed all in black with conical hats.

"*We are Gukhan!*" boomed a voice from below, amplified as though through a large megastone funnel. "*You will surrender or be destroyed!*"

If the Gukhanians boarded the ship, Zale would likely be

treated the same as Seadread's crew, despite being their prisoner. To the Gukhanians, they were all outsiders, and outsiders were not welcome. Still, Zale wondered if he could take advantage of the distraction.

Seadread snarled at the intrusion. "Sink that ship and send 'em all t' the fathoms, or they might alert the mainland! Set the oil t' boilin'! Ready pitch and torches!"

The orders were brutal and largely faithful to Seadread's present course of aggression. Zale had much preferred the approach of stealth, rather than waging battle in hostile, foreign waters. All the blood shed this night was on the hands of Captain Rummy.

Seadread's deck became a flurry of men and grimkins as they moved to deal swiftly with this new threat. Zale suspected the Gukhanians would not be so easy to subdue as Seadread hoped. Glancing toward the *Queenie*, it seemed the darkfire was being contained. As far as he could tell, there were no other ships of Gukhan about.

His chance was now or never.

He made for the larboard beam and practically threw himself into one of the jollyboats. He landed awkwardly between the rowing benches, his girth nearly crushing his arm. Ignoring the pain, he moved as fast as he could to pulley the boat downward. As soon as he hit the water, he set to the oars and heaved toward his ship, pushing through heavily belabored breaths and the sweat of exertion.

Leaving Seadread's ship undetected, in one of the captain's

own boats no less, had been nothing short of a miracle. He relished this with a smile as he motivated his loath, stubborn body to push toward the goal. He dared to believe he just might make it.

Another black longship crossed in front of his jollyboat, as though materializing out of the fog, and turned him aside. Without so much as a grunt, the sailors of Gukhan pulled him into their boat and opened a small wooden box right before his nose.

A thick steam puffed into his face, sparking a hint of recognition—narcotic mist-stones—before his body wavered into unconsciousness.

CHAPTER 9

CHILL OF NIGHT

8/8/3203 P.A.

J ensen and Starlina, along with others of the crew, nearly flung themselves over the port beam at what they'd just witnessed.

"They took the captain!" called Jensen, pointing beyond the rail.

"*Father!*" screamed Starlina.

Shouts of rage echoed all about the ship.

"Quiet, you fools!" hissed Beep. "You want them to attack our ship next?"

Completely silent, the Gukhanians sailed away in their black longship. They barely made so much as a ripple in the water. It wasn't long before the ship was gone from view, lost to the fog and maze of tiny islands.

"Demons, man," Wigglebelly said. "They're like giant sea serpents, all sneaky and black. I'm telling you, man, it's not right!"

Jensen and Starlina had dashed to the main deck as soon

176

as they realized the captain was taken by Seadread's grimkins. The situation had gone from bad to worse. Being held captive by Gukhan was far more terrifying.

Starlina stood middeck among the crew, silent and pallid, her father's coat draped over her arm.

"I'm so sorry," Jensen said. "We *will* retrieve your father."

Three seamen had also been slain in the battle: Tate and deckhands Elihu and Redvers. Their bodies were carefully wrapped in their hammocks by fellow deckhands Jonas, Clement, and Bert.

Jensen saw the captain's saber lying upon the deck and stooped to pick it up.

A boot stomped down in front of him. "No," said Fump. "Nobody but the captain touches that blade, as soon as he's back among us."

Jensen nodded and backed away. "Aye, and haste the moment that he is."

Starlina stepped between them and grabbed the saber. Fump and Jensen stared at her with mouths agape. "You sailors and your *codes*," she spat. The scowls of the surrounding crew deepened. She groaned loudly. "You really mean to leave my father's sword lying upon the deck, where it may be trampled upon or allowed to slide off the ship? I shall stow it safely in his cabin."

After a long silence, Fump shrugged. "That was my backup plan."

"Milady," Jensen said with a light bow, "you might yet make a fine captain yourself one day."

"Shut it, Jensen," she replied. She entered the cabin,

slamming the door behind her.

"What now, Dippy?" asked Miles. "Looks like you're the man in charge."

Dippy straightened his tricorn. "Make full the sail and get us underway," he ordered. "We've still got tailwind. It's high time we used it. Those devils will be headed for their berth in Gukhan, and we'll be behind them."

"Aye," Fump agreed. "Make our exit while Rummy's crew is still preoccupied."

"Keep a sharp eye all around us and men to the weapons," Chim said. "We're not out in the clear yet."

Taking stock of their increasingly dire situation, Jensen felt within himself a swelling sense of duty. "Sir," he said, "as we're down a boatswain's mate, I should very much like to steer us through these islets."

Hookknee gave a deep grunt. "Why, so we can turn up on the south side of Holbrook?"

"I can pull us through here," Jensen said.

"Beep, your call," Dippy replied.

"Could be useful, sir," Beep said. "With us this close to land all around, we'll need frequent soundings and eyes over both sides of the ship."

Fump turned to Jensen. "Looks like you're back at the helm. My only request: if you're gonna muck it up, just go ahead and warn us."

"I won't muck it up," Jensen said. It was the most certain he'd felt of anything since leaving Warvonia.

"We'll also keep watch from below," said Evette, "and we'll have two oars at the ready, one at each side, to help with any quick maneuvers."

Dippy nodded. "Very good, crew. Now, everyone, on the move! Captain Murdoch is depending on us!"

Much valuable time had passed when the last of the interfering Gukhanian scum finally screamed his last. To Garrick Rummy, defending his ship was not unlike protecting a castle. Try scaling his outer walls, and you might find yourself scalded to death by boiling oil, or water, or fire-hot sand. He was called "Seadread" for good reason.

He'd lost many of his hired grimkin army in the process. He'd be sure compensation for that got figured into his final price ... or perhaps he'd find a way to wring it from Murdoch ... or perhaps both.

The soldiers of Gukhan proved very proficient with their bows and arrows. It was not enough, however, for the flaming, pitch-dipped spears and arrows Seadread's crew used to return fire. Despite their fierce reputation, the Gukhanians clearly had not expected this merchant ship to be so heavily militarized. They died just as well as any other man, screaming all the way.

Garrick spat over the side toward their incinerated enemy. As he turned, he was sorely vexed to find that the *Queenie* had managed to set sail and disappear into the fog. After a moment, he chuckled to himself. "Craven maggots! They've sailed off without their captain!" He looked about the deck, frowning. "Bring me Murdoch! It's time we be on our way."

The men of his standard crew scurried around, looking clueless.

"Well, ye stumblin', grog-soaked cockroaches, where is he?!"

His eyes snapped to larboard, where there should've been stowed one of their rowboats. He ran to the side, looking to the water. All was calm and empty.

He spun around, apoplectic with rage. "Ye useless, mangy swabs! Murdoch's escaped!"

He turned back to the water, squinting into the fog. In spite of himself, he marveled at the possibility that fat old Murdoch had managed to row himself all the way back to his ship without being detected.

"Let out the reefs, square the yards, and bring us about!" he ordered his crew.

Loving a good chase, he smiled to himself, the fury already wearing off.

This might end up even better than I'd expected, he thought, feeling quite satisfied indeed.

Something poked delicately at Zale's face. *A finger? A claw? A*

talon? He wasn't sure at first if it was real or imaginary. Groaning, cognizance seemed to return like a fog slowly lifting.

Another poke at his cheek, like something inquisitive. His body ached in a dozen places, begging his mind not to make it move.

His eyes fluttered open and he gasped, sitting up. Something to his right scurried away into the shadows. He realized that he was in a barred cell, not so unlike the brig of his ship, except that this place was made of dark-gray stone. Even the surface upon which he'd been laid was just an upraised slab of rock. Whatever had been prodding at his face through the bars had gone into the neighboring cell, now out of sight.

"Insolent Seadread," he grumbled. "No, *traitorous* Seadread. Now you've got ol' Pop-Pop locked in a prison. You'll get your reward for this...."

A Gukhanian guard approached from outside, dressed in a uniform that appeared like black reptilian scales and a flattish, conical, chinstrapped hat. The man's face was square-shaped and pale but held an aura of darkness as he looked upon Zale with extremely hard and unfriendly eyes.

The guard thrust a metal spear halfway into the cell. "*Shti'qu-ta!*"

"Hey!" Zale hopped back and held his hands up. "I don't know your language."

Scowling, the guard held a finger to his lips. "*Shh!*"

Zale sat slowly upon the stone bench, and the guard walked off.

It was nighttime. He could tell by the soft glow of ringlight coming through the thin slit of a window on the back wall of his cell. His breath steamed in the chilly air.

He rubbed his arms for warmth and looked into the neighboring cell, where a bunk was mounted above the floor. He felt certain something was hiding underneath.

"Hello?" he called softly. "Is someone there?"

A small, furry, raccoon-like creature slowly crawled out from under the bunk. Most of its fur was the color of rust, with white streaks in its face and a handsome ringed pattern in its bushy tail. As it stood upon its hind legs and walked closer to the bars, Zale saw that it was dressed in a white, sleeveless tunic and dark, grayish-blue trousers, with a utility belt around its waist. Its ears poked through a dark-red bandana, and a golden earring dangled from its left ear. At full height, its head came up to about Zale's midsection.

"You're an anthropod, then?" Zale said.

There weren't many anthropods in Grandtrilia, although there was known to be a decent concentration of them in Holbrook and some of the Crescent's lesser islands. Anthropods came in a large variety of animal species, differentiated from their feral counterparts by traits such as bipedal walking, wearing of clothes, and the ability to speak.

"Re-re-re pa-pa-re-pa-da," the creature chittered.

Great, Zale thought. The ability to speak intelligibly varied greatly between anthropods. Some spoke with perfect clarity. True to Zale's current streak of luck, this appeared to be one that spoke gibberish.

"What was that?" Zale asked. "Slowly, now."

The critter rubbed at his rust-colored fur. "Re-re...."
Then he gestured more broadly to his entire body, adding, "...
pa-pan...."

"Re...pan...? Red panda?"

The creature nodded. "Yee! Pa-pan...DA!"

"What's your name?"

"Rakakeetacha!"

"Well...I had to ask, didn't I? Been here long?"

Rakakeetacha held up two claws.

"Two... days?" Zale guessed. The red panda shook his
head, holding up his two claws again, more forceful this time.
"Two...months?"

Agitated, the creature stomped the floor. "Wee!
Rakakaka...!"

"Okay, okay!" Zale said. He lifted his hands to calm the beast.
"You'll attract the guards wigging out like that. Two *weeks*?"

"Yee!"

"You must be quite the adventurous little fella to be in
Gukhan all by yourself."

He shrugged his furry shoulders.

"Or, perhaps, you didn't *come* alone."

Rakakeetacha shook his head sadly.

Zale heard a hinged door swing somewhere beyond. The
red panda scurried back into the shadow of his bunk. Two men
approached, including the guard he had previously encountered.

They stopped in front of his cell.

"*You!*" snapped the additional man. His face was also squarish and hard, like it could've been chiseled from a block of stone. "Where from?" His words were fast and choppy.

Zale sized up the guard and wondered just how heavily fortified this place was.

"What is this place?" Zale asked.

"I ask questions, not you!" the man snapped. "Where from?!"

"Grandtrilia."

The man drew an angry breath. "Which nation?"

"Tuscawny."

"Why have you come to Gukhan?"

"My family lost something valuable in these islands on a prior voyage. I came looking for it. I did not mean to get so close to your mainland."

The man hissed through his teeth. "Nothing of your family is here! Tuscawny—*bah*! Your blood is a tainted, filthy stain to our land."

Zale gave a light shrug. "For what it's worth, my father was from Korangar."

"Your father was a dog!"

"Anatomically speaking, I would probably look much different if that were true."

"*Quiet*, dog! Your fate will be decided by our judge. All men die." His mouth stretched into a wicked grin. "Some men die sooner—some more fun to watch."

The two men walked away.

As the night deepened, so did the cold, and Zale found himself shivering upon the stone slab. He glanced into the neighboring cell and saw that the anthro-panda was asleep, curled into a ball upon the bunk. *The little fuzzball actually has a blanket*, he realized.

"*Psst!*" Zale said.

Rakakeetacha drowsily lifted his head.

"Hey, buddy. You wouldn't mind lending ol' Pop-Pop that blanket, would you?"

Zale flinched as the red panda bared his teeth and unleashed a series of irate, high-pitched chatters that could easily have been curse words in some animalistic language.

"Okay!" Zale whispered. "Cool your kettle. I was just asking."

Knowing there'd be no sleep for him, he kept himself upright.

"Right fine mess I've got myself into. Two swift bounties to the goal—that's what we'd decided. One quick stint to Korangar, one quick stint to Akkadia. Done. But I brought us here instead. Got myself worked up over a prize of legend, you might say."

He was met with silence, but the sound of his own voice was soothing, so he continued. "So close to that mastery bar. All I really wanted was to spend more time with my wife. She's more patient than I've ever deserved. I wanted to spend more time with my grandchildren ... be a better father ... maybe even find some kind of higher purpose for my life than just retrieving valuables for high-paying clients." He half-smirked. "Although, don't get me wrong, I *do* like the high-paying clients. They want to spend the cash, I'll find the stash. That's me—always helping others."

Still, there was not a sound from the other cell. "I'm not even that worried about getting out of here, to be honest. It's more a matter of *when*. The Gale always finds an opening to breeze through. If not really soon, though, that ratbag Rummy will beat me to the bar. Or, we'll neither one reach it before the deadline, and the kingdom will make it that much more unreachable." He sighed. "In the end, it's all about serving the kingdom until you're too feeble to do any more. Then you just hobble along till you're dead."

More silence. He looked sidelong in the other cell and saw that Rakakeetacha was staring at him.

"Ah, you probably don't even know what I'm saying," Zale said. "Not that you'd care any—."

He looked again at the narrow window, forgetting the rest of his sentence. He sprang from the slab and stared at it. "The Gale always finds an opening..." he repeated. The slit was just large enough to get his forearm through.

A sly grin formed on his face.

He dug into a pocket of his trousers. His fingers found it—a trinket no bigger than a five-lat coin. In fact, it had been fashioned to look exactly like that, like a thing of inconsequential value.

It was a gift from a friendly contact—as friendly as a thief could be, that is—just outside of Zebarb. Maybe it wasn't really a gift, come to think of it, as Zale was supposed to have given it back after their job of mutual interest was completed, but to each their own.

The thing had a hint of flocalcite crafted into it. There was also a unique compound on one side to activate it. All he'd need to do was spit on one side of it, and it would stick to anything whilst shining a small light. That light could then act as a beacon for his crew.

Flocalcite of the kind used throughout Grandtrilia was relatively rare in other lands, making it great for bargaining and trade. Here in Gukhan, seeing this light should really get the attention of Zale's crew . . . assuming, of course, that they had managed to evade the longboats and sail the rest of the way to the mainland.

Zale scratched at his chin, considering the object. He'd already used it before. Hopefully it would work again.

With a shrug, he lifted it to his mouth and gave one side a spray of spittle. The other side lit up within seconds, faster than he'd expected. He fumbled over it for a moment, blinding himself in one eye, and staggered to the window. Putting the light in his palm, he thrust his arm through the window and slapped the object just below.

It fell as soon as Zale lifted his palm.

"Oh *perfect!*" he hissed.

For a while he just stood there, staring at the window. Eventually his body remembered the cold and shivered again. He glanced at the anthro-panda, whose head was turned aside, no longer even bothering to watch, and went back to his cold slab feeling heavy and deflated.

Zale allowed himself to lie down, uncomfortable as it was. Occasionally he drifted off to sleep, only to shiver and jolt awake. At some point, while straddling that line between sleep and consciousness, he felt an increase of warmth around him.

He opened his eyes and realized that the tattered, woolen, yet wonderfully comfortable blanket had been laid over him.

He smiled, warmed by more than the blanket, and closed his eyes to find rest.

Jensen was just beside Fump when the ginger-haired quarter-master nearly swallowed his spyglass in excitement.

"There!" Fump called. "Did anyone else see that?"

"What did you see?" Jensen asked. Starlina hovered nearby.

Fump pointed emphatically beyond portside toward a target that, in the nightglow, looked faintly like a huge rock. It was distanced from the shore, at the top of a hill gradually sloping from the river. "A light! Out there! It just flickered and fell like a drunken firefly!"

Beep groaned from the helm. "Some of us have been busy trying to sail a river upstream!"

"Well you can stop here, Beep. I'd say *you're welcome*, but I'm not a smartass."

"What makes you think that's from the captain?" Jensen asked.

"Only bonafide Grandtrilian flocalcite shines like that," replied Fump.

Fulgar joined them. "That is not something you'd expect to see flash in the night of Gukhan."

"Exactly!"

Dippy had overheard and wasted no time issuing commands. "Take us in larboard, close enough for the gangplank, and drop anchor!" He came up beside Fump. "Do you know where it came from?"

Fump nodded. "I wager that thing's more than a rock, maybe a stronghold. Looked like the light fell from an opening."

"I do believe you're right about that, Yancy," replied Fulgar.

"Could be a trap," ventured Chim.

"If the Gukhanians are out there," said Dippy, "best we lure them outside while a small group moves on the fort."

"Do you really think he's there?" asked Starlina.

Jensen stood tall. "There's only one way to find out. Sir, permission to join the rescue team."

Fump came up next to him. "You won't crash this party without me."

"Fine," said Dippy. He looked about the deck and soon found their tallest, strongest crewman. "Hookknee, you accompany them. Chim, let's ready some bolts and projectiles to draw them out."

Fulgar had the novidian anelace in his hand. "I can help to

get their attention."

Beep grunted as he worked to keep the wheel steady. "Maybe try not to start a war in the process."

"This is Gukhan," said Dippy. "If there's one thing we can expect, it's war."

Zale sprang awake, the blanket sliding to the floor of his cell.

"Boomer!" Zale said with a snap of his fingers.

Rakakeetacha gave him a sideways look, chittering in tones that Zale took for grumbling.

"That's what I'm calling you," Zale said. "I'm sure, where you come from, your 'Raka' name is the norm. It's not just you. I make new names for lots of people. That's just part of the charm of Pop-Pop."

Boomer fisted one of his paws, scowling. It was hard to tell if he was actually angry or just making a show. "Boo-Boo-Boom!" He hissed with laughter, something borderline maniacal. "Yee!"

"*Ha!* I daresay you like that."

Zale jumped at the sound of impact. It came from underneath the floor. Having no idea what was happening, he reasoned the safest place was atop the raised stone slab and flung himself upon it.

Moments later, pieces of the floor crumbled away around the front and middle part of the cell. The head of a large hammer pounded through. Fump's familiar face popped up from the hole, white dust from the floor in his ginger hair.

"Fump!" Zale shouted.

"Ah, I told you guys this was the right place!" Fump shouted below. "What's up, Captain? We were just passing through. Thought you might like to join us."

"You thought right, sir! How in blazes did you get here?" Zale peered through the hole and saw that Fump was propped up by Jensen and Hookknee.

"*Fump!*" Jensen called from below. "Hurry up!"

"C'mon, Cap, we'll help you down," said Fump. "Hope you don't mind making this a quick getaway."

"That's the best kind," Zale replied, lowering himself into the hole.

He looked back. Boomer was holding the bars of his cell and chittering softly, a longing look in those dark, beady eyes.

Zale turned to the others. "Men, the anthropod is coming with us!"

"We don't have any way to get under that cell, sir," Fump said. "This place is very strangely built, like it was just carved out of a massive outcrop. We just barely got to yours. Do you want to try the hammer?"

"That'd be lots of noisy bangin'," Hookknee said.

"Captain!" Jensen dug in his pockets. "Here—try this!"

He tossed Zale something small, round, and gray. It was the resilite Zale had reprimanded him for having.

"Stand back, Boomer." Zale stretched out the substance

until it was much thinner. "This about right?"

"Pull it a bit more, sir," Jensen said. "Then hold it steady a few moments."

Zale followed the instruction and soon sawed away at the bars. It took agonizing minutes to finally clear a large enough space for Boomer to fit through. The anthro-panda twittered in triumph and jumped into the hole. Fump caught him. Zale promptly followed, carefully lowered by his crew.

"I can't believe we haven't been discovered by now," Zale said as they made their way through some rocky, winding passages.

"Fulgar and the rest of the crew have most of the fort's forces preoccupied outside," Jensen said.

"That man's got some wild sorcery in his bones," Fump said. "Comes in useful."

Boomer halted, staring into a room off the passageway. "Raka-Raka bo-*kakaka*!" He made a peculiar aiming motion with his arms before darting into the room.

"Um . . . what's he doing?" Jensen asked.

"Boomer!" Zale called. "We've got to move!"

A minute later the critter returned, bearing the smallest crossbow Zale had ever seen and wearing a bandolier loaded with tiny bolts. He had also stuffed a small cutlass into his belt.

"Boo-Boom, Boo-Boom! *Kakaka!*" Boomer cackled with a riotous grin.

"The little blighter's armed to the teeth!" Fump said with a laugh. "And *with* teeth!"

"This way!" Hookknee bellowed, leading them onward.

Some winding passages later, they finally emerged at the ground level of what indeed appeared to be a towering rock formation.

"Fulgar's map was tried and true," Jensen said.

The fort behind them was at the top of a gently sloping hill covered in feathery reed grass. To their right was a small grove of trees, and to their left a broad expanse of land which leveled off along the bank of a river.

They jogged downhill toward the open land. In the field ahead of them, about a dozen men were locked in combat. Zale saw the occasional burst of light, knowing it came from Fulgar's dagger. The *Queenie* was anchored in the river beyond, close enough to the bank that a gangway had been lowered from portside.

"We went full sail," Jensen said, "me at the helm. Beep and Miles watched from the beams, Evette from below, and we navigated those islets as if we'd known them our whole lives. Beep took over after we entered the river."

"Wasn't long before we spotted the mainland and the river mouth," Fump said. "We didn't really know if that's where they'd gone with you, Captain... but we also didn't know that they hadn't. Plus, that's where we needed to go per the map."

"*You* piloted through the islets, Jensen?" Zale asked. "I admit... I'm pleasantly surprised."

"Thank you, sir!" Jensen replied, beaming. "Once we got close enough, it was Fump who spotted the light from your cell."

"*Ha!* Excellent work, men!" Zale replied. "What about

Starlina? Is she okay?"

"Safe aboard the ship, sir."

They broke southward, toward a scraggly forest of evergreens, intending to give the battle a wide berth. That way they could get closer without being seen and join their comrades along the riverbank.

"That fortress must've been lightly manned," Zale said, breathing heavy. "But, if we keep this up for long, the might of their army will be upon us. Grimstone or not, we need to put this land to our backs."

Zale and the others emerged from the small forest and moved along the river. Zale knew that he was the slow one of their group, and he felt much inner gratitude as they remained close, matching their pace to his.

Three of the Gukhanian soldiers spotted them, bellowing aggressive gabble.

Jensen, Fump, and Hookknee drew steel as the soldiers sprinted toward them. To Zale, the soldiers' conical hats made them appear something like running tent stakes, and their black, scale-like armor looked uniquely unbreathable.

The cries of Zale's battletested crew dominated the air.

"For the *Queenie!*" shouted Fump.

"For Murdoch!" yelled Jensen.

Fump glanced at Jensen, then to Zale. "Well, naturally, by extension." With the composure of someone in a training exercise, he lifted his blade against a soldier.

Zale felt utterly exposed with no weapon. Moving with

deft agility, the Gukhanians wielded short one-handed, double-edged swords.

He heard a bizarre, high-pitched sort of gurgling sound from behind. Boomer darted ahead of him in a blur and leapt into the battle with blinding, animalistic aggression. He sunk his claws into the face of one Gukhanian, causing the man to scream and flail. With surprising strength, he whipped the man's neck sideways with a *crack* and jumped, spinning the soldier limply to the ground. Boomer whirled into another soldier like a flying squirrel soaring between tree limbs, drawing his cutlass in midair and slashing the man's throat. Before that man hit the ground, Boomer had pulled himself onto the soldier's conical helmet, drew his mini-crossbow, and aimed a bolt directly between the remaining soldier's eyes. The anthro-panda had subdued all three soldiers without ever touching the ground.

"*Rakakakakaka!* Boo-Boo-Boom, *kakaka!*" he cackled upon landing, reloading his crossbow.

"Holy hell," breathed Fump.

"He's a spritely little fella," said Zale. He bent slightly forward, as though speaking to a favored pet. "Who's gonna help ol' Pop-Pop kick some ass?"

"*Rakakeetacha, kakaka!* Yee! Yee!" Boomer cheered, Zale chuckling with delight.

"*Captain!*" Fulgar shouted from down the riverbank.

"Capital rescue, crew!" Zale called out.

All of Zale's officers and most of his crew had disembarked to fight the battle. The *Queenie* was right beside them along the river. Just to be in its presence again gave Zale a profound feeling of relief.

It was short-lived solace.

Fulgar and Dippy motioned toward the fortress, where a platoon of easily fifty soldiers marched out in a perfect square formation, their black uniforms glinting in the sunlight.

Zale could practically feel the steps of the Gukhanians marching toward them. His crew had beaten the odds on many a mission, but he feared pushing their luck too far.

"Hell's fury is upon us!" Zale said. "I say let the Grimstone wait for another day. Let's turn from this place! Quickly, now!"

The crew exchanged glances. Dippy stepped up. "With all the greatest respect, sir, we came for the Grimstone, and we want to leave with the Grimstone."

"We found the pointed structure on Fulgar's map," said Beep. "There is a riddle on it *he* says only you can solve."

"It is more of a monument," Fulgar said, "and it is not the location of the Grimstone as we thought might be the case. It is more of a starting point."

Beep pointed northward. "It's just within that forest."

"Fulgar explained it to us," said Evette—*Shrew*, he had nick-named her, "how the Grimstone's filled with power against the Light, how it's rightfully yours to claim . . . . It seems only you can retrieve it, Captain."

"Not to mention," Fulgar said, "that Gukhan is a haven of the Void. I can feel it everywhere in this land, stronger than I ever anticipated. It is safer anywhere other than here, even if it must be with Vidimir. At least then it's where the Order can keep careful watch."

Zale marveled at the apparent calm of his healer, given the horde of soldiers drawing nearer by the second. "I hope you have a real ripper of a trick up your sleeves, Fulgar," Zale said.

Fulgar pulled back his shoulders and rolled his neck, looking fully confident. "I've been known to play a trick or two, sir."

"Father!" Starlina shouted.

Zale turned toward the *Queenie*, where she stood by the rail.

"Starlina, get to safety within the ship!" Zale shouted.

"Take this first!" She picked up his coat from the deck, wrapped it around his hat and saber, and tossed them over the rail. They flew home to their target, right into Zale's awaiting arms.

When he donned his coat and feathered tricorn he was suddenly more than the man he'd been moments before. He was Zale "the Gale" Murdoch, captain of Murdoch's Mates and scourge of the seas.

He drew his saber and pointed it aloft. "*Aaahhh!*" he roared, charging forward.

Steely clangs sang in the air. Zale quickly took down two enemies with the strength and precision of his upper body. Chim wielded a battleaxe in broad circles with his one arm, always an amazing sight. Fump gave up the last of his pocket-sand, stinging several eyes before taking men down with the sword. Beep and Shrew were back to back, Beep pummeling with a mace and Shrew swiping with a cutlass. Boomer sprang from face to face, slashing with his claws and shooting his tiny arrows. From the deck of the *Queenie,* crossbow and ballista bolts speared the opposition who were not too close to crewmates.

Zale knew they could not keep this up for long. There were simply too many soldiers, and they fought with militant discipline that would soon outlast his scrappy crew.

A fallen sword suddenly sprung up and jabbed into the ground. It was an utterly baffling sight. Out of Zale's periphery, he saw another...then another...and another. He turned to see Fulgar directing them with his arms. *What the devil is he up to now?* Zale wondered.

A bright, electrical ball of energy formed in midair ahead of Fulgar, confounding those soldiers nearby. Jagged tines of energy, like miniature lightning bolts, zapped from the ball, guided by Fulgar. One by one, soldiers were struck down by the bolts, causing an epic stir amongst the Gukhanians.

Then the energy extended out to the upraised swords like lightning rods, expanding the electrical field. From each sword hilt shot additional zaps of lightning. Soldiers screamed all around them. Zale's crew steadily backed away, some even dropping to the ground to stay clear of the attack.

By the time this maneuver settled down, there were fewer than a dozen soldiers remaining, all of them looking frazzled. Zale's crew sprang forth to take them down.

"Where was *that* move earlier?" Zale asked Fulgar.

Fulgar flashed a tired smile. "If I am not careful, the overuse of power will expend a feeble, mortal body like mine. Such electrical and magnetic forces take much to conjure, as you yourself might yet come to realize, Captain."

"Ha! If I could do half of something like that, I truly would be a legend."

"A similar etheretical affinity is within you. Augustus Macpherson was a renowned Fielder in his day."

Zale's brow furrowed. "Are you saying that my forefather had powers the same as yours?"

"That and more. So you see, it is in your ancestry ... in your blood." He held out his novidian dagger, keeping it still until its white light pulsated around it. In battle it was a thing to be awed and feared. But here, as it rested in Fulgar's palm, it seemed to Zale more like something heavenly ... something ethereal.

"Please, Captain," Fulgar said, "now you take hold of it."

Zale narrowed his eyes slightly. "Why?"

"It is perfectly safe."

Zale reached for it cautiously, finally curling his fingers around the anelace's grip. There was nothing all that unusual about its touch. It was light and easy to wield, very efficient as a weapon, and undoubtedly sharp. Yet, there was a strange sort of warmth which flowed into his body.

"It feels..." Zale considered the sensation. "... almost familiar, in some way, like closeness or something intimate."

"And its glow," Fulgar said, "see how it remains within your grasp. The novidian, it seems, is connecting with you."

"Curious case." Zale felt awestruck. "This, then, grants your powers?"

Fulgar tapped his chest. "The power, ultimately, resides

within the being. For many it is dormant, locked away. Novidian might awaken it, and certainly it is a helpful conduit to direct and strengthen the output, but even without it there is power."

Zale offered the dagger back to Fulgar, feeling a strange reluctance to do so. "That is very unlike anything I've experienced."

Fulgar took the blade and glanced at Zale's new anthropanda companion. "I see you have managed to rescue a helpless, furry little anthropod."

"Well," Zale chuckled, "I wouldn't exactly call him *helpless*. Turns out that resilite Jensen had did just the trick to set him free."

Fulgar placed a hand on Zale's shoulder, leaning in. "Captain . . . I feel I should tell you something. I know you believed that the resilite in Jensen's possession was due spoils to you and your crew, and you reprimanded the young man for having it. What you might not know—what he later confided to me—was that he had purchased the material back from your past client with his own share of that voyage's payout. It was not stolen."

Zale felt lost for words. "That . . . is very good to know. Thank you for telling me, Fulgar."

Fulgar gave Zale's shoulder a firm pat. "The time for you to go is now. We will hold any further opposition. Go forth to the monument and retrieve the Grimstone entrusted to your name. I am sure that Eloh goes with you."

Zale adjusted his hat and walked off, Boomer following close behind.

CHAPTER 10

THE TREASURE OF MAC

8/9/3203 P.A.

"S o," said Zale as he entered the forest with Boomer, "how many soldiers did you take down, anyway?" Boomer held up both paws, revealing ten claws.

"*Ten?* Wow."

Boomer shook his head. "Nah-nah rakaka." He held up two paws again, closed them, and opened them again.

"*Twenty?* Now you're just fibbing."

This time the anthro-panda opened his paws three times. "Rakaka yee-yee kakaka!"

"Stop it! You lie worse than a Rocknee spear-fisher." They were notorious for claiming the sort of game brought in by deep-sea fishermen as their own, when everyone knew better.

Boomer hissed, his fur standing on end.

"Okay, okay! Whatever the case, you're quite the little hellion."

They came upon a glade minutes later, where rays of sunlight poked through the tree canopy and thinly spotlighted the forest floor. Here they found the monument, which Zale could tell had been cleared of vines and brush by his crew. Imperfectly black, like raw augite, the monument stood slightly taller than Zale. It had four corners, wider at the base and tapering all the way to a sphere at its apex.

Zale brushed his hand across the monument, looking closely at its surfaces. Kasper had spoken of some sort of riddle. As he perused, he started to hear a quiet pattering sound and looked to the ground.

Boomer was urinating on the monument like a small boy might against a tree, were that boy covered in fur and a bushy tail.

Zale cocked his fist. "*Boomer!* You knock that off. That's a family monument!"

Boomer scurried back, unleashing a series of agitated sounds.

"Go eat some leaves or bamboo or something," Zale said.

Back at the monument, Zale found the words he was looking for on the face of the sphere.

It said, quite simply:

> "*The one who succeeds will be in the know;*
> *Passed down and in memory the way you must go.*
> *Don't dare seek to enter that which no one can find;*
> *Unless the Treasure of Mac is locked in thy mind.*"

"The Treasure of Mac," he whispered. The words made him shiver. Here, upon this ancient surface, was a direct reference to the rhyme he'd grown up hearing as a child, one of the few memories he carried from his birthparents—a rhyme he now spoke to his own grandchildren, firmly planted within his brain.

Quietly he recited it.

"The Treasure of Mac is not very far;
Once you know where to look, then you'll know
    where you are!
O dear Mac, if you're here, thy great name is alive;
Thy back to the river, then ten paces five!
O most brilliant Mac, the treasure is nigh;
Your head must be spinning, from looking so high!
O Mac, you great rascal, thy foundation is rock;
It's dark water below, and below must ye hop!
O wondrous Mac, if here faith do ye lack;
Then ne'er shall ye claim the great Treasure of Mac!"

"Mac," he said. "All along, that was actually short for *Macpherson*."

He stood for long moments, staring at the monument in disbelief and trying to process this realization. He wondered if his birth parents had known the significance of this rhyme, or if it had been simply a blithe recitation passed down for generations.

Boomer zipped up his pants and stood, elbow against a tree, watching.

"Back to the river, then ten paces five," Zale finally said. "The river is that way." He pointed toward the east. "The monument is the starting point. So, with my back to the river—facing west— ten paces five." He turned to his anthro-panda companion. "Come along, Boomer. Fifty paces for me; probably not for you."

Taking what he thought to be normal steps, he counted to fifty. The forest thinned out, with fewer trees, and a beautiful view stretched before them—the peak of a small mountain miles away, heathery foothills, evergreens in full spruce dappling the downs.

"Head spinning from looking so high," he murmured.

His eyes started up high and worked their way down, where, more to their level, Zale spotted a distinct rock formation just beyond a grassy knoll.

It started from the ground and rose in gradually ascending tiers. Near the top a massive flat section of rock jutted out parallel with the land, perhaps ten feet aboveground. It reminded Zale of a ship's plank.

"Thy foundation is rock," he said with a deep sigh. "Okay, Boomer, looks like we'll have to climb onto this thing."

Zale grunted and groaned as he worked his way up the tiers of rock. Boomer, of course, had no trouble at all, deftly hopping from one tier to the next.

"This is a young man's game," Zale wheezed.

Finally they reached the flat section of rock that stretched out over the ground. Zale carefully worked his way toward the end of it. His gut wrenched as he reflected on the next words of the rhyme. He slid slowly toward the edge, to where he could see well enough below.

"'Dark water below,' the rhyme says. I don't see water."

The ground below did look darker than typical grass. Indeed, it seemed darker than even the surrounding grass.

"By 'dark,' I suppose it could mean something more sorcerous, perhaps this Void that Fulgar speaks of... but, still. *I'm* not hopping down into grass just because it's darker!"

Then, of course, he couldn't help but hear more of the rhyme in his head. *If here faith do ye lack.*

A gust of wind rustled the trees and the plants below, and he thought he noticed the faintest hint of distortion in the darker grass below.

"But it's not *water!*" he protested.

Even Boomer looked nervous. "Rakaka nah hop-hop," he chittered softly.

"Yeah," Zale muttered.

He stared and stared, the words of the rhyme and its warning about lack of faith playing over and over in his head. *Then ne'er shall ye claim the great Treasure of Mac.*

"*Oh!*" he cried. "This had better be worth it."

His hop from the rock was meager, but it was enough for him to meet the "dark water" target and, as though the grass had been an illusion, he disappeared through the ground completely.

A light, comfortable breeze swept through the field, swaying the reed grass and adding some relief to what had already been a very long day for Jensen and his crewmates. Beside them the *Queenie* rocked gently with the river's current, like an overseer of her crew.

Jensen watched as Fump led a parade of crewmates toward the ship with armloads of black Gukhanian armor and weaponry.

"Someone'll pay good money for this stuff," Fump said proudly. "Not sure who, but someone. And we might manage to score some extra barrels of food and drink from the fort before we shove off."

"Yeah, man," Wigglebelly said, dragging a bound-up mass of conical hats behind him. "I hope they have some cheese. I'm in the mood for a good pot of cheese soup, man!"

Fump groaned and continued walking toward the ship.

Jensen shook his head, clapping Fump on the shoulder as he went. Fump was a scallywag through and through, but his resourceful antics never hurt anyone. At least, not intentionally.

"Get what you can, mates!" Dippy's voice carried throughout the field. "Let's have the ship ready to weigh anchor as soon as the captain returns!"

Jensen scoured the field to collect weapons and anything else of interest from the fallen enemies. The task brought him a wave of sadness over the loss of Tate, his fallen shipmate. He lamented all the crewmembers who'd fallen, but he had come to know Tate the best. They had often worked the ship side by side and traded shifts at the helm. Collecting enemy belongings seemed to Jensen like something Tate would have especially delighted in.

When Jensen thought he had all the armaments he could carry, he managed to pile on one more small, double-edged sword before making his way to the ship.

Moments later he stopped.

He saw Starlina's familiar sky-wood hair, ruggedly feminine and enticing. It streamed in the wind like a stunning banner that Jensen would proudly raise any day.

"Starlina!" He left his plunder of swords in a pile and jogged up to her. "You came off the ship!"

She wavered a bit as she stepped off the ramp. "I had to take this chance to be on land. Although, I admit, it feels a bit funny to walk, almost like after having too much to drink at one of my father's homecoming socials."

Jensen chuckled. "You've still got your sea-legs."

Starlina scowled. "I've got nothing of the sort. That is a sailor's malady."

"You're well on your way to becoming a sailor, I think."

"Jensen Karrack, have I smacked you lately? Because I rather think I should . . . ."

Healer Fulgar approached with a cordial nod. "Nice to see you, Jensen."

"Always a pleasure, sir," he nodded back.

"Starlina, how pleased I am to see you emerging from the ship's hold. Some sunshine and free movement can be highly therapeutic."

"That's very much what I thought," Starlina replied. She took in a deep breath of the fresh air. "Ah! So much better than aboard the ship."

"Sir!" Ian Hopper shouted from the afterdeck. The deckhand pointed southward, down the river, trying to catch Dippy's attention on the shore. "Sir, you'd better have a look at this!"

Jensen and Fulgar squinted into the distance. Dippy pulled his spyglass. Moments later, he lowered it, looking displeased.

"Eloh have mercy," Dippy muttered.

"What is it?" Jensen asked.

"It's Seadread's ship, tacking its way up the river."

Beep approached from the field, abandoning a bundle of armor. "They'll block our exit to sea for sure. It'll take them a good while yet to make it here against the current. I can check if any of our maps show another way around, although finding much detail about the layout of Gukhan might be farfetched."

Dippy shook his head. "It's of little use, I think."

Fulgar's gaze was still aimed afar. "Daubernoun, please look to the land aside their ship."

Frowning, Dippy aimed his glass just off the western riverbank. When he lowered it, he looked pale. "His army of grimkins has already disembarked. They're charging this way! *All hands ready with arms!*"

"Or *arm*," Chim muttered as he shoved a Gukhanian blade beneath his belt. He drew his own saber and held it ready in his one hand.

Fump ran down the gangplank, having just stowed a load of

their plunder. "What's all the hullaballoo?"

"We've got incoming!" Dippy shouted. "Ground assault approaching, crew! We'll have to fend them off!"

Fump adjusted his cap, scowling to the south. "We'll whip up some surprises for these buggers." He turned back to the ship, shouting as he ran, "Tonight we stuff our pillows with grimkin feathers!"

Fulgar turned with urgency to Starlina. "Starlina, we cannot allow them to discover you are here. You are an especially valuable target, and therefore in great danger."

Starlina furrowed her brow. "What are you talking about? Do you mean because I'm the captain's daughter?"

"Yes, but much more than that. You descend from the line of Macpherson from ancient legend—the one who sealed away the Grimstone. Only one of his bloodline can claim it."

Jensen tensed, taking a step toward Starlina. "They might try to use Starlina to retrieve it before Captain Murdoch does... or if he fails."

"Precisely," Fulgar said. "You should go back to the ship and stay hidden."

Jensen placed a hand on her shoulder. "We won't let them near you, Starlina."

Her immaculate blue eyes looked directly into his. "Jensen," she said, "*please* be careful." She hugged him and returned to the ship.

Jensen readied a sword. "I hope you have some more tricks for us, Healer Fulgar."

"I yet might," Fulgar ran a hand down his smooth head. "So long as this body of mine can endure, I yet might...."

Zale's breath rose into the air. Some hazy semblance of sunlight attempted in vain to pierce a vast blanket of unnaturally dark clouds, as if ink blotted the sky.

It had taken him a few moments to recover from the shock of jumping into what appeared to be shadowed grass. Yet, true to the rhyme, it was like landing in water, except he was unable to bob or tread or swim. He only sank, feeling like he might drown in darkness.

Then he and Boomer were swept by a current, and moments later they emerged from the surface of a black pool. When they pulled themselves out, they were completely dry.

Under the strained, subdued light, the trees before them appeared as charred rampikes, like black, skeletal fingers poking into the air. The ground around them carried an almost violet tint that Zale couldn't explain via any biotic or botanical reasoning he knew of.

From the pool they followed a beaten path. They were outside, but their steps echoed, as if they were inside a vast, empty room of marble. All the plant life around them had full leaves and fronds and stems but also completely lacked in color, as if alive yet also dead.

They walked slowly forward and soon heard trickling water up ahead. Boomer bounded down the path, lulled by the refreshing sound.

Zale thought back to the few clues he had heard about the Grimstone's hiding place.

"Within the land where none may land, the Grimstone lies between what has been and what will be." He remembered Tome-scrubber's notes. "The land where none may land now makes sense. But what *has been* . . . ?" Boomer moved back and forth on the path ahead, exploring and sniffing about. "The past?"

Boomer suddenly leapt into the air with a high-pitched shriek. A great plume of purple fire erupted from the ground ahead of them, just off the path. A freezing gust of air blasted through them, a sensation now all too familiar to Zale.

Zale felt like his very blood was going cold, and not just because of the darkfire. "Is it even remotely possible that we're somehow witnessing a glimpse of the Shadow Age?"

"Sha-sha dee rakaka. Mu-mu dar . . . ."

"Much-much dark," said Zale, somehow catching Boomer's meaning.

Just ahead they saw the stream, which flowed with drab, grayish water. Boomer trotted toward it and leaned forward, about to take a drink.

"Boomer, no!" Zale shouted. He picked up a stick from the ground, half-wondering if it would crumble into ash or some toxic dust in his hand. Fortunately it held together, and he tossed it into the flowing water.

White steam surrounded the stick. Moments later it became frozen, encased in a layer of ice. Zale and Boomer watched it in stunned silence as it floated away.

"Assume absolutely nothing is safe," Zale said. "Just stay to the path."

Peals of thunder rumbled in the air. Jagged forks of lightning stabbed through the layers of clouds above them. Darkfire bursts continued at random, but never on the path. If they did not stray from the path, Zale reasoned, they would be safe.

Eventually the path passed through a copse of lifeless trees and came to an end at the entrance to an old stone building, like an ancient temple. Three steps led into its gaping mouth, which was as a black vacuum of lightless air. Zale looked around for any hint of flamethyst that could be struck for fire, but he knew it would be a lost cause. In this land, any agent of natural light was banished.

He slowly walked up the three steps, Boomer by his side. As he passed the threshold, a large torch burst into life with the bright purple flame of darkfire. Warily, Zale took hold the torch, feeling an enormous sense of discomfort that he now must rely on the deathly fire for his source of light. He continued into the rectangular corridor.

"*The Treasure of Mac is not very far . . . .*"

The words slithered through the air and straight into his ears. Zale froze.

His torch went out. Such a thick blackness surrounded him that he felt near to suffocating.

"*The Treasure of Mac is not very far ....*"

Zale's breathing was loud in the stillness. Boomer's rapid breaths were even louder.

"Once you know where to look," Zale spoke into the darkness, "then you'll know where you are."

Another torch mounted upon the wall ignited. Zale grabbed it and kept going.

"*O wondrous Mac, if here faith do ye lack ...*" the voice said.

"Then ne'er shall ye claim the great Treasure of Mac," Zale said.

A circle of darkfire flames within small buckets came to life, one by one, until they completely encircled a stone pedestal with a small, cylindrical object on top. It hovered just above the stone, encased within a translucent-purple orb.

"The Grimstone," Zale whispered. "To be honest, it's smaller than I expected."

Words were engraved in the floor before the pedestal. Zale read them aloud:

> "*I now reveal—to this rhyme there is more;*
> *Ye've passed through the dark days of centuries four.*
> *Behold the pedestal of ancestral fame;*
> *A power such that none can contain.*
> *Before thy quest can finally end;*
> *With the treasure let us see what thou dost intend.*"

He approached cautiously, glancing around the room. Images on the wall to his left showed a man standing before this very pedestal, placing his hand over the top of the orb.

"I take it this is a pictograph—an instruction," Zale said. "According to the last part of that rhyme, it wants to see my intentions. Hmm. It'd be nice to know what happens if it doesn't approve."

The next picture showed the man with closed eyes and rays shooting from his head.

"Apparently light's going to beam out of ol' Pop-Pop's head. Should be quite the show."

Boomer pointed at the rays in the last picture. With a cackle he said, "Heh-heh boo-boo-boom! *Kakaka!*"

"Well, that's comforting—thanks."

Zale rolled back his shoulders. He took a deep breath. He held his hand, which trembled, above the orb.

"Okay . . . let's get this done."

He rested his hand fully upon the orb.

His body seized for a moment as the energy took hold of him, and his eyes closed. He saw visions of handing the Grimstone to Vidimir, Fulgar watching from afar with folded arms. His crew received the single greatest payout in the history of the entire guild, shattering the mastery bar with fanfare and joyous celebration.

Zale opened his eyes. A flamethyst torch ignited on the wall to his right, where he saw more words:

> "To reach this place, thou hast walked in the past . . . .
> Before ye can leave, must ye see what comes last."

A wall in the darkness beyond the pedestal slowly raised, the stone grinding loudly with its movement.

Zale swallowed through a dry throat. "It seems we must first see what's beyond here."

Boomer chittered softly by his side, and together they walked into the darkness.

Jensen stood firm among the rest of Murdoch's crew beside the river as the feathery horde charged toward them with their dark, curved blades held high. Grimkin squawks and screeches blended with the steely clangs of weaponry, forming the chaotic chorus of battle. A few of the deckhands had pulled away the gangway to make boarding the *Queenie* less convenient, should any of the enemies get near enough.

Seadread's actual crew of humans had not deigned to risk their own skins in battle. That's what these hired grimkin goons were for. Ruthless as Seadread's reputation might have been, he was not one to play all his cards too soon.

Armed with one of the Gukhanian swords, Jensen swung with all his might against an opposing grimkin. The birdlike cretin was quick and agile, but Jensen's swings were stronger. He backed his opponent down toward the edge of the riverbank. It stumbled, and Jensen slashed its torso, with a final kick into the water.

Meanwhile, Fump and Chim, who were aboard the ship, had found the pieces of an old catapult and rigged it together just enough to be usable.

"Look out below!" Fump called.

Small barrels launched from the ship—extra barrels of pitch that Fump was notorious for loading prior to any voyage. "It's for sticky situations," he was known to say.

Most of the barrels shattered upon the ground, confounding several grimkins who stumbled into the gummy tar. Other barrels crashed directly upon enemy heads with sundered timbers and splashes of black goop.

"*Fire!*" Chim shouted.

Flaming arrows soared from the ship, aimed wherever the pitch had fallen, dappling the battlefield with fiery patches and enflamed grimkins, who flailed and squawked in panic. Fump and Chim cackled with glee.

Shortly after, Hookknee fired a six-foot whaling harpoon from the ship's ballista, impaling the heads of two grimkins and the arm of a third, pinning them to the ground.

Wigglebelly chuckled from behind one of the ship's cross-bows. "*Huhuhuhuhu!* I got one, man!"

Evette had both hands upon a club and yelled out with every swing, bludgeoning skulls and cracking limbs. Her four oarsmen held their own with Gukhanian swords.

Fulgar was nimble and deadly with his novidian dagger, striking down three foes within seconds. The fallen cutlasses of those grimkins flew through the air, directed by Fulgar, and slew three more.

The crew of Murdoch seemed to have the upper hand in this battle, with minimal injuries and most of the grimkins subdued.

As Jensen took down another opponent with a fist and a pommel to its beaked jaw, he realized that a small wave of grimkins had stayed back. He glimpsed a particularly hard-eyed grimkin with armored shins and talons, dressed in a uniform of dark red, tall and burly, holding a sword in the air and speaking orders to its comrades. They lined up, moving their arms in a most peculiar pattern, as though drawing rectangles in the air.

When the violet light hit his eyes, he knew what was coming. "*Darkfire!*" he shouted.

"Everyone stay behind me!" Fulgar ordered, bounding forward.

Fulgar's dagger was surrounded in ghostly, pulsating light, brighter than before. He stooped low, pointing his dagger at the ground to his left. Standing, he swept it through the air above his head, like the path of a rising and setting sun. He lowered himself again, completing the dagger's path at the ground to his right.

Purple fireballs shot out from the line of grimkins, soaring in their direction.

An odd ripple emitted from where Fulgar stood, like the momentary shudder of a filmy wall between the crew and the grimkins. Then Fulgar pointed his novidian toward the incoming fireballs, as many as he could catch. One by one, a barely visible field of energy surrounded the darkfire bursts, suspending them in midair. Shaking with exertion, Fulgar turned them in different directions, away from the crew, and some right back into the grimkins.

Fulgar dropped to his knees, breathing heavily. The return-fire had taken down only a few of the remaining grimkins. The twenty or so that remained charged ahead at the order of their commander.

Jensen readied himself for more combat, eyeing one of the grimkins coming his way.

That grimkin suddenly became invisible.

Fulgar stood back up, shouting, "Look out, crew of Murdoch! These foes are channeling powers of the Void using byrne!"

Zaps of electric energy shot out from Fulgar's dagger, striking several of the grimkins despite their invisibility. With each successful strike came a puff of black and purple dust. Jensen stared at Fulgar, stupefied by what was happening, his mouth hanging agape.

Fulgar glanced back at him. "I strike for their byrne," he said.

Jensen's crewmates flailed about and swung weapons against unseen foes. His heart racing, Jensen shuffled backwards, step by step, wondering if something he couldn't perceive was about to pounce. Sword pointed out, he turned wild circles, desperately hoping to thwart any surprise attack.

"Cal and Fritz just disappeared!" screamed Evette.

She kicked at the air before her and was rewarded by the sharp squawk of a winded grimkin. It lost its invisibility and raised its downy hands in defense, but it was too late to stop Evette's club from rapping it across the beak. Despite this, her coxswain's mates did not reappear.

In fact, to Jensen's horror, he saw more of their crew disappearing all around. Miles ... Kelvin ... deckhands Abel and Jonas ... more and more just gone in an instant. The rest of Evette's oarsmen vanished, soon followed by Evette herself.

All over the battlefield small clouds of dirt rose into the air, kicked up by crewmates being dragged away.

"What in Gheol's blazes is happening here?" shouted Beep.

Moments later he, too, vanished, his strangled shouts and curses diminishing with unseen distance.

Jensen gulped and kept his blade high. There was nothing left to do but fight and pray for a miracle to help them before they all succumbed to Seadread's grimkins.

CHAPTER 11

ONE STEP AWAY

8/9/3203 P.A.

One step into darkness, then another, and then more, until the darkness had so enveloped Zale that he had no notion how far into it he had gone.

"Stay close, Boomer," he spoke into the stillness.

There was no answer.

"Boomer?"

Still no answer. Zale gave the emptiness a deep, hard frown, his hackles fully raised.

Footsteps approached from somewhere ahead, an unhurried yet steady pace. It wasn't Boomer. These were the steps of someone taller, perhaps wearing boots, although the sound was muffled, more like footfalls landing on packed terrain.

The blackness before him brightened ever so slightly into dark gray. He squinted, hoping to see the source of the incoming steps.

Zale sucked in a breath when he realized a tall, thin figure of blackness itself walked toward him. Zale drew his saber, the scrape of its steel like a scream in the night.

"Who are you?" Zale asked, trying to sound firm and unafraid.

The figure stopped, perhaps about ten paces away. It looked like a man, a bit taller than Zale.

Zale adjusted an increasingly sweaty hold on the grip of his saber. "Are you . . . Augustus Macpherson?"

Whiteness surrounded the figure, like a solar eclipse in the form of a man. The sudden light stung Zale's eyes, forcing a series of blinks. No details about the man's appearance were revealed. It remained simply a black silhouette glowing in white.

The figure raised a sword of its own, a single-edged blade from which the brightness seemed to radiate.

"Only the bloodline of Macpherson may proceed," it said in resonant words distorted by echo. "Do you wish to turn back?"

"I am of the bloodline," Zale replied.

The figure centered its blade in a stance of readiness. Zale was unsure if this meant he could now walk right past or if it meant some further test.

"We shall see," it responded.

Zale took a step forward, hesitating. "Then, does this—? *Whoa!*" He lifted his blade just in time to block an attack from the figure. It was like striking a piece of wood. There was only dull impact and no metallic clang.

"Are you of the blood?" it asked.

"Yes!"

The silhouette thrust a jab, which Zale blocked. It slashed again, and Zale met the swing, following with his own counterstrike. An active duel ensued, each foe parrying the other with precision. Zale began to wonder if this is what it might feel like to duel against himself.

"Are you of the blood?"

"Yes!" Zale growled, teeth clenched as he swung again. "Didn't you hear me before?"

More dueling. Zale's steps shuffled about in an arena of unknown size, having no idea which way was forward or backward or how far he could go in any direction without falling into an abyss.

The silhouette swung hard at the tip of Zale's saber, causing his right wrist to buckle sideways. Before Zale could compensate to his stronger left hand, the silhouette stabbed its black, glowing sword into Zale's left bicep.

Zale felt frozen and numb as it held the tip of the blade in his arm.

The spectral figure leaned closer, asking the same question again in slow, deliberate words. "Are you of the blood?"

Yes, you undead lackwit! Zale thought, but he was unable to speak it.

Instead, the light vanished, he fell back, and he was once again surrounded by darkness. As it took him, two words echoed in the vacuum.

"*You are.*"

It was all happening so fast, crewmen disappearing all over the battlefield. All Jensen could do was swing aimlessly, hoping to strike one of their invisible foes before it struck him.

Fulgar tackled one grimkin to the ground, its visibility faltering. He ripped away a black stone from around its neck and electrocuted the grimkin with his dagger. His smooth head glistened with sweat. He frantically looked around at the ever-worsening scene.

Fump, Chim, and mates Ian and Rowan clung to ropes and swung from the ship's deck into the fray below. It wasn't long before Ian and Rowan also disappeared.

Chim spun neatly around and clobbered a grimkin behind its head with the blunt end of his sword. As he raised it for another strike, he was hit from behind. He yelled in pain, dropped the sword, and disappeared a second later.

Fump fought with a stylistic fervor rarely seen in merchants or sailors. He swung wide with a spear and turned to pin it into the chest of a grimkin like a javelin in a throwing tournament. Tiny dirks seemed to materialize in his hands, pulled from concealed areas all around his clothing.

Jensen squinted at the slightest distortion careening toward Fump. He charged forward into its path. He slammed into the form, eliciting an angered squawk of surprise. The impact was a shock to his senses. He saw the grass mash down where the creature landed and tumbled over the riverbank.

"Look at you, surviving and being brave!" said Fump. Then he also disappeared into a shouting distortion of air.

Jensen stumbled back and swung his sword wildly. He heard splashes from the river behind him and realized that the grimkin he'd just charged was coming back for vengeance. "Stay back, devil!" he yelled.

Suddenly a crossbow bolt struck it, and the wet anomaly gave an undignified death-screech. The bolt stayed in midair, its front half crimsoned with blood. Then it swayed and fell, with a now-visible grimkin, back into the water.

Jensen looked up at the ship. Starlina stood behind one of the crossbows.

"Wonderful shot, milady!" Jensen called.

"Oh, I got it!" she cheered. She loaded another bolt.

Most of the crew had vanished. The dozen or so remaining grimkins shed their invisibility, most of them preoccupied with a group of deckhands who had stayed close together throughout the fight.

Fulgar sprinted up to Jensen and waved madly up at the ship. "Starlina, you must get to safety!"

"You clearly need some help!" she called back.

This was enough to redirect the grimkins' attention. Their commander shouted out in their chittering language. A half-dozen of the cretins raised the gangway into position and rushed toward the deck.

"*No!*" Jensen cried out, dashing after them.

Fulgar followed, moving much slower than before.

In his frenzy, Jensen flung the first grimkin he reached into the river with only his hands. With the next one he locked blades, striking up, down, side to side. The grimkin struggled despite having the higher position upon the gangway. Jensen won a slash to its arm and gave it a hard push, so that it pounded into the hull before splashing into the water.

Fulgar zapped the next one, but it was a much weaker jolt than what Jensen had witnessed earlier. It was still enough for Fulgar to finish the job with a stab to the chest. The glow of his novidian anelace, however, had faded.

Starlina's scream pierced the air. One of the grimkins had grappled her from behind.

BONG!

A giant soup pot flew from the steps of the quarterdeck and into the head of the grimkin holding Starlina. It loosened its grip and crumpled down the stairs to the lower deck. Wigglebelly approached, wiping his hands together. "Take that, man! Grimy, grisly, feather-noggins!"

Another grimkin was right there to grab Starlina before she could get away. One of them kicked Wigglebelly in the gut. He bent over and was knocked to the deck.

"*Jaxon!*" called Starlina, looking with concern upon Wigglebelly, who moaned under the three grimkins working to heave him up.

The remaining three grimkins tackled Jensen and Fulgar and held them firmly to the planks, Jensen shouting obscenities into the wood. Before they knew it, Jensen, Fulgar, Jaxon, and Starlina—the last standing of Murdoch's crew—were firmly bound in rope and fishing net. As the rope was tightened, Fulgar dropped his dagger to the deck.

"Let us go!" screamed Starlina.

"Release us!" Jensen shouted.

"This will not end well for you, my feathered friends," said Fulgar.

Wigglebelly only wheezed and whimpered.

The grimkin commander circled them, its dark eyes narrowed and its beaked mouth stretched in grim amusement. As he passed by Fulgar, he snatched the anelace from the deck and gazed over it curiously.

The commander retrieved a parchment from within its dark-red tunic. He unfolded it, laid it against the mast, and pinned it with the anelace. His wicked eyes seemed to laugh at their plight.

He twittered further orders to his subordinates before the last of Murdoch's crew, including Starlina, were dragged away from the deck of the *Queenie*.

Zale stood upon a cobblestone surface under the light of day. He dropped his saber with a clang and immediately gripped his left arm, where the silhouetted figure had stabbed him. His arm felt perfectly normal. There was no rip in his coat.

"*That* was the test," he muttered. "It must have ... tested my blood."

"Capee rakaka!"

Zale turned with a start. "Boomer!" His anthro-panda accompaniment was standing just to his right. "By the sails, am I glad to see you!"

Zale looked at their new environs. He recognized this place: it was the market square of Warvonia, completely empty and utterly quiet. He picked up his saber and stowed it back in its scabbard.

"What is the meaning of this?" he asked quietly.

The ground rumbled, the onset of a tremor. Boomer chattered in alarm. Zale stumbled from the shock, and then took off down one of the connecting streets.

There were establishments he recognized, others he did not. Some he expected to find, only to see that it was something else entirely. Where he expected a cobbler he found a blacksmith. Where he expected an eatery he found a grimy-looking candle shop. The Wench's Tavern sign was where he expected, but the front entrance was boarded shut.

The entire street rippled underneath, the old stones welling like a tidal wave, knocking Zale to his back, a black sky in his sight overhead.

When he stood, he was elsewhere. Grassy knolls surrounded him, and as the hills contoured toward sea level, a dilapidated town spanned the view below. The land was ruptured, as though meteors had been raining down in droves. The air was extremely quiet—the sound of desertion.

Something erupted from the ground. Boomer screamed and Zale yelped. It appeared as a black mist, rising up and fading into the sky. Moments later, wails pierced the air. Whitish, wispy apparitions flew above them and throughout the streets of the town below. A black mist burst from the ground where he stood. It flew through his face and gave him a strong sensation of oncoming death.

His vision flashed, and a moment later they viewed a different plaza. He identified this as Sharm Square, built within a massive crater and the center of the kingdom's capital city of Miskunn. Their view was from a distance and up high, as though from the outer edge of the crater, although the expansive plaza was all he could see clearly. All around a towering central rostrum were thousands of stone-faced citizens. Humans, mostly, but also with a scattering of grimkins and anthropods . . . and one thing more.

Gathered amongst these civilian races were the white, wispy apparitions, this time with a bit more form. It signified, to Zale, that they had gained status in the civilization—a greater acceptance of sorts, perhaps a legitimization—as something undead now gaining vitality. It was horrific in every sense, like their vitality had come at the expense of the people and would for all generations to come.

A single figure stood upon the central rostrum, dressed in the full splendor of royalty and riches untold. The person's face was concealed within the darkness of a cowl.

All the populace revered this person. All hung on his every word. "Is this the king?" Zale asked.

Boomer shrugged. "Dunno rakaka."

The man in the center spoke, raising his arms up high.

"Amidst your certain doom, *I* am your savior! Where the lineage of kings has failed, *I* shall prevail! Even as the Light weakens like a guttering candle, fear not!—for I bring a new light... a light of the beyond... an Antilight, and with it shall be a greatness of purpose such as the Light of Eloh, who has forgotten you, could never achieve...!"

And the masses, their faces devoid of all emotion, were made to bow to him in reverence.

Zale's mind spun as he found himself back within the chamber of the Grimstone. He felt cold all the way to his bones, and a shiver crawled up his spine because of the visions he had just seen.

"The writing said we had walked in the past," he said quietly. Boomer watched him with wide eyes. "That was the Shadow Age we walked through to get here—the past. What we just saw... it said that was what comes last. Could that be... the future? A possible future because of the Grimstone?"

The wall to his left let out a great rumble, like the turning of millstones. The words that had been there before were gone, replaced by something different:

"Now, Macpherson, thy namesake may ye claim;
The Grimstone sought for virtue, fortune, or fame.
Is this my true treasure, this thing they call mine;
Or is there one greater that we've left to find?
Untold riches and power now can ye take;
My greatest treasure I must no longer forsake.
Unto thy hands the Grimstone we entrust;
Knowing its potential, do with it what ye must...."

Another torch kindled on the wall, this time showing a rather crude picture of an adult man holding the hand of a young girl. Beneath it were the words: *"Behold, the Treasure of Macpherson."*

Zale cracked a smile. "It seems old Macpherson was also a family man. With the Grimstone secured away, perhaps he went on to retire."

"Yee," said Boomer thoughtfully. "Hu-hum kaka pup rakaka."

"Yeah," Zale replied gently, "a human pup."

The translucent orb faded. Remaining atop the pedestal was the cylindrical object, the protection of Zale's ancestor now removed.

He approached the pedestal and looked down at the cylinder, which was about the size of a common building brick. The scenes he'd just lived replayed in his mind.

"If what we saw can be considered reliable, then this object could shake the very foundations of my kingdom ... maybe even far beyond that."

Boomer looked back at him and gave a slow nod.

"But if the Light of the Land is truly fading, and this can save it, then it seems this thing is not only valuable but *essential*."

He thought back to the crowd gathered in the capital city, bowing to their new ruler. "And yet, if by saving the Light civilization is turned into subservient zombies, what kind of a future is that for my daughter, or my grandkids, or anyone?"

Zale had never felt so morally conflicted over a bounty during the entirety of his long, successful career. For any other job, it was at this point that he would have just grabbed it and run, making haste back to their client for delivery and payment. This job, by now—and really right from the start—had become more personal for him than any before.

"Old Macpherson probably intended this," Zale said. "Make you question your motives for taking it, and maybe you'll think twice about proceeding."

He grabbed the cylinder, looked it over, and gave it a shake. "This is just a casing," he said. "There are words here underneath: 'DARK OPENS DARK.'"

Zale scowled. "All this way, and I *still* can't get to the actual Grimstone. It's always one more step away."

He didn't dare try opening it by force, assuming that could only make things worse. After a moment, though, he couldn't help but smirk.

"This must really be my ancestor's doing," Zale said. "Only a true Macpherson would pile on failsafe upon failsafe in such maddening layers."

He found a secure pocket for the cylinder within his coat and stuffed it inside. "Come on, Boomer. Let's get out of here."

Even though they knew what to expect, their walk back through the Shadow Age manifestation was just as unsettling as before. They jumped at every plume of darkfire off the path. They flinched at the flashes of lightning against the inky clouds. That still didn't prepare them for the icy remains of a human skeleton that floated down the stream just as they arrived.

Likely yet another deterrent of Macpherson's, Zale told himself.

It was disturbing just the same. They crossed that stream all the more carefully and continued down the path with quickened steps.

Soon they were back at the pond of dark water through which they had first arrived. Zale moaned about having to enter it, but he also didn't want to remain in this place another minute. They jumped into the pond, sinking into its blackness, and the undercurrent took them.

As hoped, they emerged back into the sweet, wonderful, natural light of day. They climbed out of the shadowy grass, as though it were water, and pulled themselves onto solid ground.

Boomer immediately rolled about in the grass and dirt like a dustbathing dog, chittering in ecstasy.

"Boomer! We don't have time for that! Quickly, now, back to the ship!" Boomer stared up at Zale from the dirt, seeming in no particular hurry to move. "Boomer!"

"*Rakakaka!*" Boomer spat, springing to his feet. He bounded to a nearby tree and peed on it.

"By the Light, I swear you're more a feral critter than an anthropod," Zale grumbled. They moved on, Boomer cackling from behind.

Upon emerging from the woods, he first felt a wave of relief at the sight of his ship, still bobbing peacefully in the river. Further observance led him to frown. The land outside the ship—a previous battlefield—was quiet and desolate. He couldn't help the sense of foreboding that grated at his nerves.

"Hmm," he grunted. "I suppose they're all onboard and ready to go. Well and good, as we need to put this land to our backs posthaste." He looked down at Boomer. "You're sure you want to stay with us, right? We're bound straight for Tuscawny."

Boomer nodded fervently. "Yee, yee. Tuskee, rakaka!"

Zale saw a great many burnt and exploded patches in the ground all around the riverbank. The evidence of significant action here was only more intense the closer he got. Much to his relief, he saw only the bodies of grimkins and Gukhanians scattered about and none from his crew. Of course, it was possible that any casualties had already been taken aboard the ship.

It seemed that most of the cadavers, particularly the grimkin ones, had been gathered and lined up in a rather strange fashion. There just wasn't any order to it that he could discern, perhaps the result of haste.

"Things definitely got hairy out here," Zale mumbled.

He looked up at the *Queenie* and scratched his chin. All of the upper decks were completely empty. He felt a great sinking feeling in the pit of his stomach. "Something seems amiss here."

Cautiously they walked up the gangplank. The ship itself didn't appear damaged in any way. It was quiet... eerily quiet. His boots clomped loudly upon the planks of the deserted deck. He drew the saber from his side.

His cabin was empty. The galley and officer's cabins were empty.

"Dear Eloh," he gasped. "Starlina!"

He moved as fast as his legs would take him into the deck below. The berthing deck, with all the rowing benches and crew hammocks, was totally unoccupied.

He continued farther, into the hold, to the makeshift quarters of Evette and his daughter. It was, as the rest of the ship, completely empty.

"*No!*" He slammed his fist into a support beam.

They returned to the main deck, hoping for some clue of what had happened. It didn't take long for Zale to notice Fulgar's dagger stuck in the mast with a parchment pinned to the wood. He pulled it free—the dagger in his left hand, the parchment in his right. The words of the page read:

Captain Murdoch, for you to see this letter, you must've returned to the ship. I know you hold the key to retrieving the Grimstone, if you don't have it already. I wish to reach a settlement with you. Pull the cord.

— *Captain Rummy*

Then he saw it, small with distance but unmistakable. Seadread's ship, moored down the river.

Zale found a thin rope draped over the portside railing. He yanked it. A tiny plume of black and purple smoke rose from beneath the rail, and then a sudden brightness filled his eyes from the land below.

The violet flames of darkfire were unmistakable. The corpses that had been arranged below ignited, and their arrangement became instantly clear. Amongst the death below, words came alive. They were like a fire in his retinas, kindling the rage that stirred within.

"CREW OR GRIMSTONE," the words spelled.

Shortly after, more words appeared below this, not out of bodies but upon the ground.

"MURDOCH'S CHOICE."

From these words more flames erupted, creating a trail of fire going away from the ship and into the west, in the direction of the mountains.

"If Seadread thinks my crew will be held easily against their will, the old fool's got another think coming."

He glanced at the weapon in his hand, and the novidian anelace greeted him with a faint white glow.

Beyond the ship, his eyes followed the darkfire trail as far as they could see. With one last look at the luminous dagger, he stowed it in his belt. He drew a deep breath and smacked the rail, knowing what had to be done next.

"Come on, Boomer. Let's go get our crew back."

As the grimkins dragged Jensen and his mates roughly along, the brightness that had been sunlight eventually faded into darkness. The ground beneath became rockier and bumpier. The sacks they had been captured in were of a strange stretchy substance, which could not be simply ripped or broken. He was surprised the grimkins could tug them so easily without any beasts of burden. Perhaps it was something about these strange sacks that made it tenable.

Jensen was yanked from his sack to the sound of much yelling and cursing from his crewmates. They had been taken into the large, cavernous expanse of a cave with a ledge high above an underground lake.

Jensen emerged ready to fight, but that urge evaporated at what he saw. Three grimkins each held a captive member of the crew: Evette, Chim, and Starlina. Cutlasses were pressed threateningly against their throats.

"Try escapee," one of them hissed, "and we killee."

"Starlina, it'll be okay," Jensen told her.

The grimkin holding Starlina screeched at him, its horrible sound echoing throughout the cave. It pointed up to the ledge above the lake. "*Go!*"

There the entire crew was bound together from their shoulders to the ground in lengths and layers of netting and rope, so tightly that they could barely move their arms and legs. Even worse, the grimkins tied more rope around each of them individually, binding their arms to their sides. Evette, Chim, and Starlina were added last.

Starlina was placed beside Jensen. "Are you all right?" he asked.

"I'm okay," she said. "Just a little flustered."

Seadread strutted toward them. "Well, well ... all o' Murdoch's crew in a nice package. What a position I be findin' meself in, hahaha!"

"Rummy!" shouted Dippy. "You've gone utterly mad! The guild will not take lightly to the disappearance of an entire crew!"

"You'll be the prime suspect," said Fump. "I'd lop off your head, if I were them."

"Ah," said Seadread, "but yer not, and as far as the guild be concerned, the unfortunate crew o' Murdoch sailed through fog int' a mess of sea stacks, ne'er t' be heard from again."

"Sea stacks?" asked Chim. "We'd never make *that* mistake, not after the Korangar shipwreck of last year."

"Why are you *debating* this?" hissed Evette. "He wants to drop us into an underground lake!"

Seadread cackled with his dry voice. "Here I was all prepared with an army, while Murdoch's got none other than his usual bunch o' crook-kneed barnacle munchers! And two females t' boot!" He came around the netting until Starlina was in his view. "What's this young poppet for, a bit o' entertainment? Come now, lassie, do ye sing? Do ye dance? Might be I'd have a place for a nice wench aboard the *Iron Mermaiden*."

Jensen swelled with wrath. "Back away, you black-hearted traitor!"

Starlina stared directly into Seadread's eyes with a look of pure loathing. "Not even in your dreams, you wretched filth."

Seadread shrugged. "Suit yerself. What happens next will all depend on yer ever-so-cunning captain."

"Captain Rummy," said Fulgar, "you have no idea what you're dealing with in the Grimstone. Even to hold it is a danger to you, your ship, our land, and any other land in which it dwells. Its evil is unfathomable."

"Yer words mean nothin' t' me. All we've t' do now is wait for yer dear captain. Please, do stick around for when he arrives." Cackling all the more, Rummy descended the ledge.

Beep, who was situated between Evette and Starlina, struggled about to move his arms. "Evette," he whispered urgently, "there's a tiny dirk in my beard. Can you get to it?"

"You mean that's for *real*? I thought that was just a rumor!" said Fump.

"It's for real, tied up under my chin. Can you get to it, Evette?"

"And just how am I supposed to do that?" Evette asked.

Chim made a chomping motion with his teeth. "Try biting it."

"Are you *crazy*?" Evette hissed.

"Anyone *else* have any way to cut us out of here?" Beep asked.

Negative mutterings answered him from throughout the crew.

Evette groaned. "Ooh, I should've stayed in the fishing guild. Where is it exactly?"

Beep tilted back his head. "In the backside of my beard, just below my chin, one slipknot tied around the hilt. It should come out with a firm enough tug."

Starlina pressed herself tighter into Jensen, a disgusted look on her face. "I'm glad he didn't ask *me* to do that."

"Light's bane," said Jensen with a quiet laugh, "that must've been difficult to get in there."

"Well, go on!" urged Miles.

"Yeah, I want to move my arms again," added Fump.

"Okay, I'm going!" Evette spat. She tried to position herself around the underside of Beep's beard. "You *do* wash under here, right?"

A few moments passed. Evette's mouth groped awkwardly within the thick black and yellow hairs. "I think I've found it," she said.

"Well, can you bite it?" asked Jensen.

"What do you *think* I'm trying to do?" she spat. "Do I . . . do I smell *flowers*?"

Beep shifted uncomfortably. "I comb my beard with oils."

"You mean, like, rose oil?" asked Chim.

"Lavender," Beep said, "most recently."

A wave of hushed snickers chorused throughout the crew.

"Oh, the things you're forced to admit in captivity," Fump said.

"That's... nice," said Evette, still from under Beep's chin. "But this thing is tiny, and... *ugh*... there's so much hair!"

"You've gotta really chomp it," Chim encouraged, "but also real carefully, so you don't lose it."

"Hey, just kiss her already, man!" Wigglebelly said from somewhere behind them. "*Huhuhu!*"

"All of you just shut *up!*" Evette said from within the beard. "I think I've almost got it."

Evette grunted with effort, while Beep clenched his teeth in pain. Finally, Evette emerged. The smallest dirk Jensen had ever seen dangled from her mouth. She let it go and caught it in her hand.

"There." She slapped it into Beep's hand. "Now, you finish the job."

Wigglebelly chuckled.

Somebody nudged the great oaf. "Ow, what?" he yelped. "I'm just glad she found the little thing, man."

"A pyre out of their own dead comrades—that's messed up," said Zale.

He and Boomer followed the trail of darkfire, careful not to touch it. It led them in a mostly northwest direction, toward the mountain range in the distance.

"I've heard stories about certain grimkins of Akkadia who believe it's an honor to receive cremation by shadowy flames. Before now I never would've taken that so literally."

"Yee kaka. Sha-sha fir *burrr*," said Boomer, mock-shivering.

Zale nodded. "Yes, shadow fires *are* cold." He smirked. "Despite your best efforts, I'm actually starting to understand you."

They arrived at the mouth of a cave just as the landscape transitioned into rolling foothills. The burning trail continued inside. Their path was covered in the darkfire's eerie, flickering purple light.

"Keep alert," Zale said quietly. "They could be waiting to spring a trap."

Soon the cave broadened, getting wider and wider, until it was downright cavernous. It was here that the trail of darkfire ended.

He saw a large, crystal-clear lake. He saw the rocky ramp leading to a ledge high above the water . . . and he saw his crew, bound together like an oversized bundle of firewood.

"Captain!" several members of his crew shouted.

"Is everyone okay?" he called back, his voice reverberating in the cavern.

"We're here, Captain!" Dippy said.

"Yes, we're *all* here!" spoke the crackly voice of Garrick

Rummy. His ugly mug appeared from a shadow of the cave. "And you, Murdoch—or *Macpherson*, I should say—have ye the Grimstone?"

"I take it you haven't already found it, then?" Zale asked.

Seadread's eyes narrowed. "Don't ye be playin' games with *me*. Ye clearly weren't with yer crew when we paid our little visit. So, we'll be makin' this very simple." He held out his hand. "Hand it over, and yer crew lives t' see tomorrow."

"Rummy, you can't seriously mean to shove an entire crew from your own guild into a lake just to win a single bounty."

Seadread gave a slight tilt of his head. "'Tis nothin' personal, Murdoch. Just business."

Zale held his saber before him. "Let them go, Garrick."

"What can ye do, Zale?" Seadread said with a cackle. "Will ye fight me and a gaggle o' grimkins with naught but yer blade and an overgrown bilge rat?"

Boomer hissed.

Zale heard some shuffling along the walls. The rest of Rummy's grimkin army—around twenty—was spread throughout the cave. Zale would not take their smaller numbers for granted. Clearly even this many had managed to subdue and capture his entire crew.

"Your hired army's a lot smaller since I last saw you."

"I assure ye, this be the most ruthless o' the lot, every one armed with byrne."

"Even if I had the Grimstone to give you," said Zale, "I have no reason to trust you'd just let us go."

"Aye, ye know me well enough, Zale. I give ye this assurance. Hand it over, and I will leave back t' me ship, with half me forces. We'll even take all the byrne with us. You'll remain here, and half an hour later the remainin' grimkins will free yer crew. This way there'll be no chasin' me down before I get t' me ship. 'Tis the best I can do, ye'll understand, given the circumstances."

Zale seethed at what Rummy was doing. Carefully, he tried to consider his options. He looked around at the grimkins. One of them, dressed in dark red, wore a particularly deep glare. It kept its comrades steady with a motion of its arm. Zale realized this was their leader.

He looked all about the cavern, as though a panacea might suddenly appear to him. He ran his hand down his coat, perhaps a signal of nerves to Rummy, and felt the items still tucked within. He looked up at his crew and made eye contact with Beep and Evette and others who were watching him back.

It was time to make his move.

CHAPTER 12
VOID CONTAINMENT

8/9/3203 P.A.

Z ale gave Seadread his hardest stare. He sheathed his saber. "Fine, Garrick. We'll play at your game."

A smarmy smile crossed Rummy's lips. "I'd hoped ye'd make the right choice. Now, let's be on with it." His palm upturned, he curled his fingers expectedly.

Zale reached into his coat. His hand brushed over the lump of the Grimstone casing in his pocket. When his hand came back out, it was extended by a ghostly white glow.

Seadread stared at the light, his expression mesmerized. "Be that the—?"

"Nope!" Zale shouted.

The light of Fulgar's anelace intensified in his grasp. He pointed it directly at the grimkin commander standing by the wall behind Rummy. A blast of energy shot forth, a stream of pulsing white spheres. A few of the grimkins, along with the commander, were sent sprawling, ricocheting off the cave wall

244

along with a shower of rocks.

Zale was as shocked as anyone, but now was not the time to question his fortunes.

At first Rummy's jaw dropped in surprise, but soon his face twisted with rage, baring yellow teeth. He drew his sword. "Damn ye t' the depths, Murdoch!" He turned to the flustered group of grimkins. "Come on, ye feathered scrubs! *Attack!*"

Zale's crew sprang into action, flinging away the ropes and netting that they had managed to cut through. They descended the rocky ledge and rushed at the grimkins unarmed, their cries and shouts filling the cavern. Zale glimpsed Starlina toward the rear of the bunch, Jensen keeping close, and he felt very relieved to see her unharmed.

Yancy and Rosh and a few others claimed the dark-gray blades that had been dropped by Zale's victims. Wigglebelly slammed his girth into one of the enemies, crushing it against the wall. Hookknee decked it in the beak before it could recover.

Fulgar worked his way toward the edge of the melee, calling to Zale. "The novidian suits you, Captain!"

"Here!" Zale shouted back, tossing the dagger. "Help the crew!"

Fulgar caught it by the grip—it practically floated to his hand—and turned to engage the opposition.

Zale looked down at Boomer and the small crossbow that he held. "Boomer, you too—go help!"

"Yee, yee! *RakakaKAAA!*" he yelled, bounding off after Fulgar.

"Father!" screamed Starlina. "Look out!"

Zale turned just in time to see Seadread lash out with his sword. He stepped aside, drawing his saber, and traded a few blows with his rival.

"*Father*, she says," Seadread said. "I'm not sure which o' the two o' us wants more for honor, Zale. Me for turnin' the grimkins on ye, or you for bringin' yer own daughter to her death."

"That answer's very simple, Garrick. You're a slimy, traitorous ratbag."

"Well, we all have our qualities, don't we?" He swung out again, striking Zale's saber.

Zale was heavy on his feet, but his arms were swift and precise. He parried up high, then low, trying to sneak in a stab to Seadread's arm. There was a time in their rivalry when Zale considered Seadread merely ruthless, but never a cold-blooded murderer. That time had passed, and now Zale himself wondered how close he might be pushed to taking a fellow countryman's life.

Seadread tried all manner of dirty techniques. Jabs at the chest, swipes toward the throat, all while cackling through a throat that sounded ever parched with thirst. All his attempts were thwarted by Zale's counterstrikes.

Meanwhile, Zale's crew continued to battle for position against the grimkins. He chanced a glimpse and observed a general deadlock in the brawl.

Zale managed to rip a seam of Seadread's coat near the shoulder.

"Me best coat, Zale," said Rummy. "Ye'll be payin' for that!"

"Well, to be fair," Zale huffed between heavy breaths, "you started it."

Seadread hopped upon a rock where the ground sloped upward toward the ledge above the lake, gaining slightly higher ground. Zale determined he'd had enough of this. In the seconds Seadread spent steadying himself upon the rock, Zale grabbed a stone from the floor and launched it, hitting Rummy squarely in the head. He tumbled backward, landing hard upon the bed of loose rocks beside the lake.

Zale wiped sweat from his brow and stared at Seadread's now-motionless form slumped upon the rocks. Zale breathed a sigh of relief.

Then he looked to the battle between the grimkins—the prime of Seadread's mercenaries—and his crew. Shaking out his shoulders, he readied himself for more action.

"Starlina, stay close!" shouted Jensen from atop the ledge.

A full close-combat brawl had erupted inside the cave. Free of their bindings, most of the crew had made it their priority to charge down from the ledge and into the mob of grimkins. Jensen had made it his priority to keep Starlina unharmed.

They were relieved to see Captain Murdoch prevail against Seadread, but it was short-lived. Jensen had no weapon, and the slope leading up to the ledge was total mayhem. Behind them, perhaps fifteen feet below the ledge, was the subterranean lake. At the moment, about all he could do was watch and stay alert.

Several of the grimkins leapt forward, diving into crewmen's shoulders and pushing them to the ground. Numerous deckhands took a solid beating—Sal, Snow, Jonas, Bert—but did their best to fight back.

Evette and two of her oarsmen—Archie and Fritz—had managed to capture swords. Soon Fump, Beep, Kelvin, and Dippy had done the same, dueling and swinging as best they could manage in such a tight crowd.

Fulgar struck in blurs of light, aiming for the black amulets that the grimkins wore around their necks. When his novidian dagger hit its mark, the amulets exploded into dark-purple clouds.

At the edge of the fight, Captain Murdoch had just spun a grimkin around by the shoulders and bopped it between the eyes.

"We've got to find a way down!" said Starlina.

"Come on—we might be able to slip down the side here," Jensen said.

It was steep and rocky, and it would take them straight over the now-still lump of Seadread, but they could probably make it.

He grabbed Starlina's hand and had taken the first step over the side when a grimkin leapt out of nowhere and tackled him to the ground. It screeched angrily and punched his face and chest in rapid succession. Starlina shrieked and fell backwards.

Jensen felt stunned, his jaw throbbing in pain. The grimkin stood, lifted him by his shirt, and cuffed him again. Jensen finally gained enough clarity of mind to grapple the grimkin by its arms and push it off, taking his own swing at its face.

The grimkin swung back, and Jensen dodged. It swung again, and Jensen pushed away its arm. They traded several jabs and kicks before grappling with each other and turning a dangerous circle near the ledge.

Jensen landed a solid kick to its side and a right hook to its shoulder. The grimkin gave Jensen's forehead a sharp peck with its beak. He stumbled back and fell to his rump in dizzying pain, his hands landing upon loose rocks.

Starlina grabbed the grimkin from behind, slapping and scratching at its face. It was terribly swift and shouldered her off with little effort. She did her best to strike back, but the grimkin pushed through her hits, grabbed her by the arm, and yanked her over the ledge. Screaming, Starlina fell into the water below.

"*Starlina!*" Jensen shouted. He sprang to his feet.

The grimkin turned to him with a screech, and Jensen swung two rocks together to crack its beak, turning its face into a bloody mess. Jensen dropped the rocks and decked it three more times. It wavered, and Jensen kicked it into the rocks over the steep side of the ledge.

Wasting not another moment, he jumped from the ledge into the lake below.

Zale finally caught up with his crew as the battle in the cave raged on. Dippy ran up to greet him just beyond the edge of the battle.

"Nicely played, Captain!" said Dippy.

"And you!" Zale said. "Did someone have a knife stowed away?"

"Beep, sir! Ah, it'll be a great story to relay over a stein of ale aboard the *Queenie.*"

Zale nodded his approval. "No doubt it will. Let's get these duck-brained fools off our backs and make for the ship."

"Captain!" called Fulgar, running to join Zale and Dippy. "Praise be to Eloh that you're okay!"

"Aye, I'm fine. We need to be on our way, Fulgar. Can you and your dagger make quick work of these remaining grimkins?"

"I am trying my best, whilst not risking harm to the crew with anything too … explosive. These remaining foes are particularly strong in the Void. I aim for their byrne, but I must strike with care. Should one of them happen to turn my powers against us, it could be devastating."

Zale raised an eyebrow. "They can *do* that?"

"Powerful Creepers—those well-practiced in the Void— should never be underestimated."

"We'll not give them the chance!" Dippy said.

Zale took a moment to observe the battle.

A grimkin fell near the base of the slope with a strangled

squawk, Fump roaring in triumph.

Boomer was a pure menace to the enemies, hopping about between heads, weaving around legs, and firing the occasional bolt from his miniature crossbow. Zale heard his animalistic cackle rise above the action and couldn't help but smile.

Murdoch's Mates were holding their own so far, and Zale was pleased with their number compared to the grimkins'. He was ready to join them, but first he needed this moment to debrief with Dippy and Fulgar.

"Macpherson's hiding place was . . . interesting," Zale said, "like a sliver of the Shadow Age."

"Sir," said Dippy, "did you say the . . . *Shadow* Age?"

"That's right, Dippy. I can't tell you much from history, but *that* place felt very real and *very* disturbing."

Fulgar leaned in with interest. "Were you successful in your search?"

"That I was," Zale said.

He pulled out the Grimstone casing and showed it to Fulgar.

He glared at it, as though Zale were holding a rotten apple.

"So much evil, in so small a container," Fulgar said. "There are words on it."

"Dark opens dark." Zale pushed the casing back out of view. "Do you know what it means?"

Fulgar reared back his head and laughed. "*That*, Captain, is perhaps the easiest riddle of them all." He reached into his own pocket and pulled out an amulet containing a black, purple-veined stone. "Byrne—the Dark Ethereal."

Zale took the amulet and stared at it, hardly believing that this could be the answer.

"Where did you get this?" Zale asked.

"The grimkins use it to conjure their powers of the Void. I took this from one of them. I meant to destroy it ... but, well, you never know when a thing might come in useful ... and here we are!"

Fulgar's words were almost like a cue, for at that moment darkness exploded between the grimkins and Murdoch's crew. Screams of pain and terror filled the cavern. Several men were heaved high into the air.

"*No!*" Fulgar shouted, dashing back toward the battle, glowing anelace in hand.

There were not many grimkins remaining, but Zale realized that the gnarled-looking commander was among those still active.

Several crewmen, including Chim, writhed and howled upon the floor. "I can't feel my arm!" he bellowed. Fump hastily dragged him back.

"Regroup!" shouted Dippy. "Shield the injured!"

Murdoch's crew clustered together and positioned themselves to protect the wounded. Fulgar quickly made rounds among them, offering comfort and remedy where he could.

Zale, still slightly removed from the main action, glared at their remaining foes. He was surprised to see only five, the commander included, given how much havoc they'd still managed to cause.

"Grimkins of Akkadia!" Zale bellowed. "You've fought well and true to your charge. Enough of this! Your captain is down, and you are outnumbered. It is senseless to continue this contest! Let us reach a truce from this point, and we'll depart unhindered with our wounded and fallen, each to their own ship, so that we can leave this cursed and forsaken land behind."

The grimkins' dark eyes exchanged glances.

"What say you?" Zale asked.

"The curs-ed is *you*, filth of Tuscawny!" the commander hissed. He raised a hand sheathed within a gauntlet, in which was embedded a stone of byrne. "Standing in Gukhan, for us is honor most great!"

"Our number is handily greater than yours," Zale said.

The commanding grimkin returned a sinister smile. "For us is plenty!"

Before Zale could retort further, the commander squawked to his comrades. His hard eyes fell upon Zale. Challenging him. Mocking him.

"Is plenty for Void!" screeched the grimkin. "Watch and see!"

Using the byrne of his gauntlet, the commander created a grayish-silver, barely translucent field that completely encased Murdoch's crew. Their shouts from within were heavily muffled by the barrier.

"You yolk-headed swines!" Zale stepped toward them but soon stopped as the other four grimkins pointed their swords and byrne in his direction.

Fulgar, he thought. *Fulgar is in there with his novidian.*

He hoped against hope that their spiritual guide would be strong enough to get them through this.

Fulgar tightened his fingers around the novidian anelace and stared at the dome now surrounding him and the *Queenie*'s crew.

"What is this?" several of the men asked. They pushed and kicked and struck at the anomaly, but it would not give.

"They have surrounded us in an encasement of Void energy," Fulgar said, trying his best to remain calm even as those around him became more frenzied.

Boomer chittered and squealed like an oversized rodent freshly trapped. He kept throwing himself into the barrier, each attempt as futile as the last.

Fulgar reached down and cupped his shoulder. "That will not help, my little friend."

"You can get us out of this, right?" asked Kasper.

"I have heard of this power... although I have never encountered it."

"So... is that a maybe?" asked Yancy.

Fulgar breathed out and breathed in, gauging his aura, trying to suppress the pains and stress signals radiating throughout his body. He had nearly overdone it multiple times today. This was the risk of having honed his abilities to the extent that he had. There was an inherent risk to channeling large amounts of ethereal energy through a human's confined, mortal shell. Too much magnetism could deplete his essential metals. Too much electrical exertion might disrupt the impulses controlling his heartbeats. Much could go amiss. It was ever a balance.

He tried stabbing at the barrier. It would not puncture. He pressed his hands against it, feeling the vibrations of the energy. Whiteness surrounded his points of contact, but it was not enough to break through.

Everyone watched him.

"I've had little chance to recuperate," he said, removing his hands.

"There must be *some* way out of this thing!" said Evette.

"*Aaaahhh!*" Jaxon, being the largest of them all, charged at the wall.

"No, don't—!" Fulgar shouted.

It was too late. Jaxon ricocheted off the wall and fell like a giant lump of mashed potatoes.

Jaxon stood with the help of two crewmates, his face indignant. "That thing's tough, man. Really solid."

"Only an ethereal power can dissolve this," Fulgar said. "For a Fielder, I admit it will require much strength."

"Is there anything we can do to help you?" Daubernoun asked. "Anything that can boost your ability?"

Fulgar shook his head. "Not unless an etheretical affinity has been awakened within any of you. To my knowledge that is not . . ." He stopped himself and peered through the faintly translucent wall where Captain Murdoch stood outside the barrier, shouting words they could not hear. "Unless ... perhaps ..."

Suddenly the dome started to move. It slid slowly along the ground, moving away from the grimkins.

"They're pushing us toward the lake!" shouted Miles.

"Push against it!" screamed Evette. She threw her hands into the wall of the dome. Her oarsmen and several other crew-members joined her.

The dome was unhindered, its pace unchanged. It merely pushed the crew along, no matter how much they dug their boots into the ground. Fulgar was not surprised. Fazing this sort of contrivance would require more than any amount of physical power.

He searched his inner strength, knowing it was not enough ... but he had to try. He gripped the novidian and slammed his hands into the dome. Brilliant white energy emanated from his touch.

The dome's movement slowed a little, but it did not stop. It continued toward its target, pushing large rocks out of its path.

He looked again to the man outside the dome. He knew it was Captain Murdoch. He pounded against the wall of energy as though banging on a door, causing bursts of white light to spread from each impact.

Fulgar could only hope his signal would be grasped from the other side ... because it was the only hope he had left of gathering enough strength against their deadly prison.

Zale saw the bursts of white light from inside the dome and knew it could only be Fulgar. Feeling insanely helpless already, he was relieved to see the dome's movement slowed, if only a little, as Fulgar took his powers to it.

Still, something was amiss. The dome continued to move, closer and closer to the lake.

Fulgar's movements seemed increasingly frantic, not so much the controlled actions Zale had come to associate with the man.

Finally, it dawned on Zale: Fulgar was trying to get his attention.

I see you, Zale thought. *What under the rings do you want me to do?*

Zale looked at the grimkins. While the commander alone had initially created the anomaly, now all five of them were concentrated on keeping it intact. Keeping twenty-something men imprisoned in some hexed dome, Zale figured, must take a combined effort.

He stepped slowly closer to the barrier. Aside from the pulses of white, Zale couldn't make out anything definitive within. He could only see dark forms frantically trying to push against the dome's movement.

It was getting very close to the lake now. Soon its edge would touch the water. The horrific realization had already occurred to

Zale that the grimkins intended to drown his entire crew.

After a bit longer, the white bursts became handprints. Fulgar was pushing deliberately against the wall, so that the shape of his hands shone through. Zale got the distinct impression that Fulgar wanted him to touch the dome from the outside.

With another furtive glance at the grimkins, Zale took off and jogged toward Fulgar's position.

He was just reaching out for it when he suffered a hard hit from the side that took him down and knocked the wind from his lungs. His saber clashed to the cave floor several feet away, too far to reach.

"Zale, ye bloated gaffer, surely ye didn't think our contest would come t' an end as swift as that."

Gasping, Zale sat up, staring into Seadread's blade. He cursed the scruples that had kept him from killing Seadread when he'd had the chance.

"Now," Seadread said, "let's see if ye've finally come t' yer senses. I'll be havin' that Grimstone, if ye please."

CHAPTER 13

SELFLESS DEFENSE

8/9/3203 P.A.

Starlina emerged from the lake, dripping like a sea otter and gasping for air. Seadread loomed over her father. They were perhaps a spear's throw away, Seadread's back turned to her.

"Get away from him, you monster!" she screamed.

Seadread cackled like dry leaves. "Ah, Zale, seems we have ourselves an audience. Now, give me the Grimstone, and put an end t' this game. Show yer daughter ye know how t' lose with dignity."

"Oh, I see," her father said, still upon the cave floor. "And you're just going to let us all walk out of here peacefully, like we just lost a friendly game of tag?"

"Whatever makes ye happy, Zale," Seadread replied. "I really think we're beyond the point of exchanges and negotiations over who's doin' what. What's fer certain be this: I have ye at the point o' me sword, and yer crew be slippin' fer the water, every one o' 'em trapped like fish in a barrel."

"Not *all* of them!" Jensen shouted.

Starlina turned with a start.

Jensen—*her* Jensen—emerged from the edge of the lake like a crocodile on the hunt. He plowed into Seadread, water spraying from his clothes. As the scoundrel fell to the side, Jensen took up her father's saber.

Seadread sprang to his feet with a wild swing of his sword. Silver steel flashed as they dueled. Jensen's youthful fervor proved a challenge for Seadread, but the dastardly captain held his ground.

Starlina's father had not yet stood. His hands were busy inside of his coat, as though checking for something.

Her eyes narrowed. *Does he actually have the Grimstone here with him?*

She dared a step toward her father but then stopped, her advance halted as she noticed the strange barrier surrounding the rest of the crew.

The barrier was slowly moving into the lake. The crew's dark outlines splashed about frantically as water filled their bubble of a prison. Somehow the grimkins were able to keep them trapped inside while also allowing the water in.

She saw the whiteness of Fulgar's hands and dagger banging against the dome. *Please, Fulgar*, she silently hoped. *Please find a way to overcome it.*

Then Fulgar made the outline of a star.

Starlina's heart skipped. Was he . . . signaling for her help?

She swallowed her fear and ran toward the barrier, stepping ankle-deep into the edge of the lake. Fulgar's face was just behind the dome, looking back at her. Maintaining eye contact, he smacked his palms and dagger against the dome, the white of his energy spreading from the impact.

She had no idea what he expected. There was only one thing she could think to do.

She placed her hands over Fulgar's. It was like trying to touch through a pane of glass, typically a futile endeavor.

But it wasn't futile.

Starlina flinched as she felt an intense yet inexplicably welcoming warmth in her hands. The same white glow Fulgar possessed spread from her own hands. Fulgar closed his eyes. Her energy seemed to feed into his.

"*Ahh!*" Seadread yelled out.

Seadread and Jensen were still fighting.

Jensen had just made a bad step upon a rock, turning his ankle. As he stumbled to the side, Seadread's sword came around, slicing hard into the back of his left leg. He fell with a bloodcurdling scream, unable to stand.

"*Jensen!*" She pulled away from the barrier and leaped at Seadread.

"Starlina, no!" her father shouted. He was back on his feet.

She grappled Seadread around the neck from behind, trying to pull him backward. He wriggled free and threw his arm around her neck, tossing her against the nearby cave wall.

"*Starlina!*" Jensen shouted, wincing and holding his leg.

The entire cave rumbled. Fulgar was pushing the barrier back toward the grimkins. Zaps of white energy emanated from around the barrier, striking at the cavern, loosening stalactites and chunks of rock.

Starlina's chest heaved with exertion and terror. Seadread's sword was now pointed directly at her heart.

Seadread positioned himself to address her father. "Now ye see, Zale, we have here a final ultimatum. Give me the Grimstone if ye want t' see yer starling poppet leave this place alive."

"Garrick, you murderous dog!" shouted her father. "Leave her out of this!"

"I'll not be impugned by the likes o' *you*, Zale. Given ye chance after chance I have, and now we've come t' this!"

They had to shout ever louder as the rumbling within the cave increased. Fulgar and the grimkins were deadlocked, although the grimkins were clearly struggling to fight back. As rocks continued to rain down throughout the cavern, Starlina wondered if the cave itself might collapse.

Three of the grimkins stepped closer to the anomaly, trying to overpower Fulgar. They soon regretted it, as they were zapped by white tines of energy that destroyed their black stones and scattered their lifeless bodies like dandelion seeds.

Another grimkin was crushed by a boulder from above, leaving only the commander.

"Zale, ye damned fool!" Seadread spat. "By now it seems ye'd take me serious."

He grabbed Starlina by the collar and shoved her back into

the cave wall, giving her head a painful jolt. He reached down and ripped at her shirt, exposing her midriff. She felt the chill of his blade for only a moment as it touched her skin, immediately replaced by a vast and fierce sting as he cut a red line across her belly. She screamed in pain.

"D' ye take me serious *now*, Zale?"

Her father fumbled with his coat. "Stop, Rummy! Look, I have it...right here."

He pulled out a cylindrical casing.

"This is what I found. I just haven't been able to open it yet."

Seadread again had his sword pointed at Starlina's chest. Hands pressed against her wound, she tried to stop the bleeding. The sting was almost unbearable, but it seemed the sword had not cut deep enough to go beyond the skin.

"And why be that?" Seadread asked.

"There's a riddle," her father said. "*Dark opens dark.* It means byrne—I figured out that much. It takes the Dark Ethereal to release the shard of the Dark Entry. But all the byrne you've used against my crew has been destroyed."

"Well, Zale, not *all*." Seadread gestured toward the commander of the grimkins. "But even if he doesn't survive, 'tis but an exercise in patience. Ye remember Vidimir, I'm sure. He'll have byrne enough, just as he had when he set the dockyard aflame back in Warvonia."

"That was *him*?" Zale replied. "But why?"

"An act o' persuasion, o' course. If that weren't enough, I knew sailin' in view o' yer ship would be." He cackled. "Ah, ye took the bait as a marvel, Murdoch! We knew we needed ye—yer ancestral blood—t' get t' the Grimstone. All the rest be history now." He moved the sword tip closer to Starlina. "Now, Zale, give me the treasure... yer sacred, legendary Treasure o' Macpherson."

"Fine, Seadread. You win." He stepped closer and held out the canister. "The real Treasure of Macpherson isn't the Grimstone."

Seadread grasped the cylinder's other end.

"The *real* Treasure was his family. His daughter." His eyes met Starlina's, and she knew in that moment that he wasn't only talking about Macpherson's true treasure but *his* as well.

Starlina felt awful and touched all at once. Throughout her entire life her father had chosen time taking voyages over time with her. In truth, she'd never felt particularly valued by him over his treasures. Whether or not that was fair, he'd never really proven otherwise... until now.

Seadread gave a yellow-toothed smirk. "Very sentimental, Zale, but I'll be takin' the Grimstone."

Her father released it to Seadread and took hold of Starlina's arm before Seadread could pull any further tricks.

More rocks fell within the cavern, landing all around the grimkin commander and rolling off the barrier.

"Best o' luck t' ye, Zale," Seadread said. "Should ye make it back, I'll put in a good word for ye with the guild as a grandmaster." Laughing, he ran from the cavern.

Seconds later, the barrier lifted from the ground. Fulgar

pushed it away, quivering and baring his teeth with immense effort, and the crew took their chance to scuttle out from beneath the barrier.

Starlina laughed out, ecstatic to see Fulgar and the crew finally escaping the grimkins' deathtrap.

Zale felt a wave of relief, his crew now freed from the barrier.

His gaze fell upon Fulgar. Straining, with white energy surging between him and the dark byrne-concocted encasement, the man put his all into pushing against the power of the grimkin commander. Zale felt powerless, wishing there was some way he could help.

"There's Seadread!" shouted Dippy, pointing. "He's running away!"

"Let him go!" Zale replied. "Our priority now is getting everyone out of here alive!"

"We can still catch him, Captain!" Fump yelled. "I've got some spring in my step yet!"

Zale shook his head. "No. He still has a full, fresh crew waiting for his return. I'll not lose more of our own on account of that cursed Grimstone. Dippy, let's get everyone secured and away from that Gheol-cursed barrier!"

"Pull away our wounded and fallen!" Dippy called out.

Those who hadn't been able to escape were dragged to

safety away from the magical tug-of-war. Zale was crestfallen to see that good seamen had perished: Jonas, Ian, Sal, Clement, and Winston. Several others, including Jensen and Rosh, were seriously wounded and would need to be helped back to the ship.

Zale came as close as he dared to where Fulgar still held back the barrier. "Capital work, Healer Fulgar, no doubt worthy of Eloh's highest honor! The crew is freed, and it's time to go!"

Fulgar was covered in sweat, his raised arms shaking. He met Zale's eyes and smiled.

Then the Healer lowered his arms with a massive burst of energy, dissolving the barrier and shooting a shockwave throughout the cavern. The blast tore through the grimkin, burning away feathers and skin. Its byrne was destroyed with a puff of violet smoke.

A mighty rumble followed the blast, and an avalanche of rock fell directly upon Fulgar's position. Everyone in the cavern fell silent as a huge cloud of dust kicked into the air.

Shouts of anguish erupted from the crew.

"Quickly, uncover him!" shouted Zale. "Now!"

They swarmed the rubble, pushing away cave rocks and shards.

"Sir!" Fump shouted. "He's still alive ... but just barely."

Zale came at once to their location. Fulgar had been badly pounded. His breathing was labored and rattled. A very large chunk of rock had fallen right over his torso—lungs, ribs, and everything around them.

"Fulgar!" Zale chewed his lip as he took in the grim state of their healer and spiritual guide. "Hang on. We'll get you back to the ship."

"Nonsense, Captain," Fulgar muttered. "Waste no resources on my account. There is . . . no point."

"Your head is jiggered," Zale said. "We leave no man behind. We'll get you back to the ship, get you rested, get you fed . . . and you'll be shipshape in two shakes of a stick."

Fulgar smiled weakly. "Such optimism, Captain." He coughed, wincing. "The Grimstone . . . . I know . . . you will do right . . . . Your heart . . . is good."

Zale sniffed. He fought his emotions. No captain worth his salt would be caught tearing up over a newly initiated physicker.

"You know me," Zale said shakily. "Always helping others."

Fulgar opened his hand, the novidian anelace resting within. "Please . . . take it, Cap . . . ." He sucked in a breath with great effort. "Take it."

Zale did.

"Seek the Order of Aether . . . Diamond . . . . Tell them . . . of . . . Grimstone . . . ." Fulgar swallowed. "Captain Zale . . . may Eloh's brightness . . . shine . . . on . . . you . . . ." His eyes fluttered. "Such light . . . ."

His last words were merely a whisper within his final breath. Fulgar's head fell aside in death. His lips remained smiling, as though he were merely in peaceful slumber.

Anyone wearing a hat had removed it. Sniffles echoed throughout the cavern. Zale brushed away his tears. This man had been so much more than a physicker.

"I imagine he saw the light of the Ethereal Realm just then," Fump said.

"Of that, good sir," said Zale, "there is no doubt."

Seadread's ship was long gone by the time Murdoch's crew was fully aboard the *Queenie*. By the soft light of the moon and rings, they loaded the last of their dead and wounded. Many situations might have called for land burials prior to departure. Zale, however, with his crew in full agreement, was not in the least bit inclined to leave his fallen in this cursed land of Gukhan. They would sail well beyond its borders and give them an honorable burial at sea.

Their fallen crewmen were wrapped in their own hammocks and kept upon the forecastle. Six souls lost in the cave, added to the three taken when the grimkins had boarded their ship. Nine lost in total. It was the worst single-voyage death toll Zale had experienced during his entire career in the seafaring guild.

It seemed no small stroke of luck that they had avoided any further encounters with Gukhanian soldiers. Word of the overtaken fort might not yet have reached other strongholds or authorities, but Zale knew this would not be the case for much longer. If retaliation came, it would be swift and ruthless. With everyone aboard, there would be no loitering or rest, no good night's sleep to prepare for an early-morning sail. Rather, the ship would be turned about and sailed at once, for as long as needed until they were clear of Gukhan's shores.

Fortunately the river's current naturally flowed toward the ocean, making their exit faster. Once back at sea they took full advantage of a southeasterly wind and cut the waters as quickly as the elements allowed. It was not a direct course back to Tuscawny, but it was the fastest course away from Gukhan. They could correct for direction later.

The crew stuck to their tasks, with few words spoken between them. They were tired and hungry and sorely aggrieved, and every one of them was driven by the innate instinct to get away from this place as fast as they could. It would be a long haul from here.

With nine fewer, there would be more work and longer hours for everyone.

"All for naught," grumbled Beep from the helm. "We don't even have the Grimstone to show for it."

Zale stood by the larboard railing of the quarterdeck, gazing out to sea and watching the dark mass of Gukhan shrink in the distance. "Are you familiar with the concept of a 'blessing in disguise'?" he asked. "You didn't see what I did. That Grimstone is nefarious business. Fulgar was right to warn us of its danger."

"If it's such a powerful, dangerous thing, I can't imagine it being better with Seadread."

"Maybe it'll prove too much for that black-souled tyrant." Jensen leaned upon a crutch, his leg splinted and bandaged. "Perhaps he'll get just a little too careless and turn into stone."

"Or perhaps he'll melt into a puddle of ooze," said Evette. The loss of oarsman Winston had fueled in her a special hatred for Seadread.

"He'll burst into flame and burn to ashes," Miles said.

"Boils will cover his skin and all manner of bugs will bite at his wounds," said Hookknee.

"Bah," said Beep, "we still have no prize to show for this voyage, with not enough time to take new jobs before the bar goal expires . . . or before Seadread beats us to it."

"There will be more prizes," Zale replied, clapping Beep on the shoulder. "What we've lost here in spoils, perhaps we'll have gained in scruples. That's much more than can be said of Seadread. I have a feeling he'll get what's coming to him."

He descended the stairs to his cabin. He heard one final grouse from Beep as he walked away.

"Perhaps, but they don't pay well for scruples back at port."

"Today, friends, the sun smiles upon us!" Captain Murdoch shouted from the forecastle. Jensen joined in a chorus of *ayes* with the crew.

Everyone was gathered upon the deck under the light of late morning, the salty air mild and comfortable. They had sailed hard all night, working to put as much distance as possible between them and Gukhan.

Some of the crew had managed to sleep. Some were wobbly on their legs with fatigue. Tired or not, none of them would miss this moment for anything. Every one of Murdoch's Mates held a mug of ale, even Chim out of solidarity.

Jensen appreciated their captain's cordial demeanor. The long voyage back to Warvonia had only just begun, and spirits had never been lower aboard the *Queenie*. Starlina stood nearby, her hand holding tightly to his.

"If there is ever a good day for bidding farewell to lost comrades, it is a day like this one," Murdoch said. "Men, we have suffered much. Murdoch's Mates are known for success, for being the best, for beating the competition. You may feel bested, like we have lost to Garrick Rummy . . . but there is no honor in being a turncoat and a murderous fiend. That is how the weak-minded *think* they win. That is how they dig such a hole that, eventually, they fall in and bury themselves.

"You feel beaten, but let me give you this assurance: we are *still* the best!"

"*Aye!*" roared the crew.

Captain Murdoch pulled a folded page from his pocket.

"If I'm being totally honest," Murdoch said, "last night I had to make the most emotionally trying and painful updates of my life to a crew roster. All of you performed beyond your charge on this cruise. You fought like champions. You sailed like masters. You stared into hellfire itself and emerged stronger for it. Nine souls among us gave it their all, and today we put their bodies to rest. It is said that the ocean's floor is of the purest sediment in the world, the first soils of creation. These bodies are but the corporal shells of our comrades. Today we commit these shells back to the sea ... back to creation."

He positioned his monocle, lifted the page, and began to read.

"Three souls lost to grimkin invaders aboard the deck of the *Queenie*. Redvers Hardy, age twenty-six, deckhand and one of the best sailors to ever man the braces. Tate Woodard, age twenty-eight, a boatswain's mate who could've sailed us through stacks in the fog of a blizzard with both hands behind his back. Elihu Jones, age twenty-nine, deckhand and the reason half of Wigglebelly's soups passed edible."

Wigglebelly sniffled and wiped a tear. "It's true, man."

"Five souls lost to grimkin mercenaries in the cave of Gukhan," Captain Murdoch said. "Ian Hopper, age thirty-two, ropemaster and none skilled the better at rigging. Winston Clergy, age forty-one, oarsman and coxswain's mate, a true honor to have had in our crew. Sal Wiggins, age thirty, deckhand and the most eager lookout I ever did encounter. Jonas Singleton, age thirty-nine, one of the best deckhands I ever saw with a sword. Clement Gardina, age forty-four, deckhand and most honorable swab-master ...."

Captain Murdoch paused a moment, preparing himself to read the last name.

"And Fulgar Geth, age fifty, lost in selfless defense of the crew against grimkins in the cave, physicker ... healer ... spiritual guide ... and the reason we stand here alive today."

Every head lowered, every hat was removed, and solemn moments of silence followed. The captain raised high his stein. "Raise your ales and drink a toast! May their journey to beyond be one of fair winds and following seas."

"Hear hear!" shouted the crew with a coinciding draft of ale.

Then, one by one, large stones were tied to the hammocks, and the fallen men were committed to the sea.

It might've been the way the sunlight glinted in descent, but Jensen could've sworn he saw a nimbus of faint, white light surround Fulgar's hammock as it splashed into the water.

CHAPTER 14

MURDOCH'S CHOICE

8/22/3203 P.A.

J ensen was counting the days. By Beep's calculations, they were about one week away from reaching Warvonia. The past twelve days had been hard ones at sea, with constant reminders of the crew they'd lost and the extra work everyone had to do.

Fatigue ran rampant, but camaraderie between the *Queenie's* core group of officers and shipmates seemed as high as Jensen could remember. They'd had their share of victories in this quest, all of them hard fought. In the end, their efforts were marred by the losses of both crew and bounty, and somehow it seemed to be that collective defeat that brought them closer together.

It had been a loss at the hands of a traitor. Yet, it was by pure selflessness that they had survived—the sacrifice of Fulgar. As a crew, this brought solidarity to an all-time high.

Still, there were the grumblers, the handful of surly crewmen who stomped about disenchanted by the voyage's lack of success.

No one could entirely fault them such feelings.

Loss of their bounty stung them all like a barbed dagger to the gut. It might be the first ever such loss for a Murdoch voyage, and not one they'd forget. Most of them knew it was best to put the pain of defeat astern and set their sights to the horizon, ready to face their next job, and Eloh help Seadread should they again cross paths with the reviled captain.

If many of the crew were being honest, it was a relief to be free of the pressures of trying to attain the mastery bar. For Jensen, the hardest thing was coming to grips with the reality that Seadread and his crew would be the ones to reach it.

"Surely, once the guild hears of what they did," he said one day to Beep, "they'll strip him of that privilege."

Beep merely shrugged. "Crews never speak of how they win or lose their charges, *especially* if they lose to each other. Sort of an unwritten creed."

"Even if they did," said Fump, "the guild wouldn't listen. They don't bother their precious selves with anything that happens offshore, least of all squabbles between crews. It would be the word of Seadread's crew against ours. They'll just deny ever having hired grimkin mercenaries—they're all dead, anyway—and they'll say the deaths of our crew are our problem. No help to be gained from those goons."

"Aye," said Chim. "Lick your wounds and get ready for the next job. That's all they're about."

"Bottle in your afflictions, and they bottle in their questions," Jensen said, knowing the ways of Warvonia's guild. "It seems ghastly."

Harsh as it was, however, he knew it was reality, particularly within the league of specialized, high-value seafarers that counted Murdoch among them.

"It goes both ways," said Dippy. "It's just as well for us if the guild never knows that we had to rescue the captain from a Gukhanian prison, taking down dozens of their soldiers in the process."

Simply losing to Seadread was one thing. Jensen felt especially concerned that Garrick Rummy was about to be deemed a grandmaster in the guild. This had not happened since well before any of their lifetimes, so it was hard to know with certainty how this would affect their crew. It was a designation supported by ancient kingdom decree—not officially above the provincial guilders, but Chief Pratt might have limited influence should the grandmaster appeal to higher authorities.

Thus, Jensen wondered with grave concern how Seadread's new status could influence the jobs they took, the oversight received, changes to the crew, provisions allowed, and any other matter of guild business. Life in Warvonia's seafaring guild might be much tougher from here.

As much as that bothered Jensen, life otherwise aboard the *Queenie* had turned some interesting corners. Relationships managed to develop, if even in a furtive, hole-and-corner sort of way. Evette had been seen passively stroking Beep's beard, endearing him with the occasional coquettish smile.

"Fishin' for more daggers, Shrew?" Fump called out one

afternoon as Evette hung about the helm for no conceivably productive reason.

"Only to shove it down your grog-hole," she answered with mock geniality.

Boomer seemed to be having the time of his life. He'd fashioned himself a headscarf out of scrap cloth and strutted about the ship holding his miniature cutlass, echoing orders issued throughout the ship.

"Steady the braces there!" Dippy called out.

"Stee-ka bracees, *keekeekee!*" Boomer repeated, adding his animalistic cackle.

"Heave ho the starboard lines!"

"Hee-ho star-sta leens, *keekeekee!*" And so it went.

Boomer also had an enduring infatuation with the chickens. At first, Wigglebelly shooed him away. "Get down, furball!" he shouted, waving a ladle. "Those chickens aren't snacks, man!"

Boomer shook his head fervently and chittered back at them as though trying to make a serious point.

Then one morning a chicken managed to escape as Wigglebelly gathered eggs. He squealed in panic as Boomer ran up to it. When Boomer delicately stroked its feathers and carried it back to its cage, cooing all the way, everyone realized that he meant the poultry no harm. It turned out their fitful little mascot didn't want to eat the chickens. He was simply being affectionate.

Captain Murdoch, for his part, spent more time than usual in his cabin. This job, most assumed, had been especially hard on him. His biggest rival had prevailed, and they had suffered heavy losses, with no prize but a pile of battle-used Gukhanian swords and armor to show for it. Most days he emerged from his cabin, made his rounds with curt greetings and status inquiries, and then no one would see him again for hours.

On one occasion the captain approached Jensen. "How fares the leg, young sir?"

"Slower recovery than I'd like, but coming along," Jensen said.

The captain lifted his left pant leg, patting the dark-gray graphenite beneath. "Keep it up, and you'll soon earn one of these beauties."

"I'll consider it an honor, should it come to that."

"Everything copacetic with our course?"

"Certainly, sir," Jensen said, a bit tentatively.

Zale grunted, lingering a moment. "There's a matter I wanted to speak with you about, related to this resilite of yours."

Jensen swallowed. "Captain, I don't mean to cause a stir by having it, but—"

"Say no more," Murdoch said. "Fulgar informed me of your talk before the whole cave debacle. I just wanted to apologize for giving you grief about it."

Relief swept over Jensen. He had worried that punishment was coming for his having the resilite. Now the captain was actually apologizing to him. "Oh, please, sir . . . think nothing of it!"

"Also . . . I want to thank you for helping to protect my daughter through all of this. I know she can be headstrong and contrary, but you always stuck by her."

"I'd give my life for her, sir. Please know that."

Murdoch nodded. "I know you would, and I take comfort in that."

Jensen felt he should tread carefully here. Through experience he knew that this was a delicate subject to speak of with Murdoch.

"She is much conflicted about being with a sailor," Jensen said. "I had hoped, perhaps over time..."

"... that she might change?" Murdoch said with a light chuckle. "We Murdochs are a stubborn lot, thick-skinned as hippos."

"Yes, I have noticed." He said this to be lighthearted, but truly his heart felt heavy, worried about how he could ever truly be the man Starlina deserved.

Murdoch looked out over the railing. "Starlina wants someone she can feel close to, someone accessible. If I'm being truly honest, she wants what I haven't been. It's not unreasonable for her to want that."

Jensen looked down. "I suppose you're right."

"An old wise sailor once told me," Murdoch said, "that enough time spent on the sea will give anyone a new perspective on life. Add that to the already profound effects of love and, well, I guess you just never know."

"Indeed, sir. You never know."

Murdoch clapped Jensen's arm. "Things have a way of working out, Jensen. And, just perhaps, it could be possible for a sailor to sit out a voyage every now and then. A captain's daughter must be well looked after, you know." He winked. "And we have the needs of Starlina to consider, don't we?"

Jensen felt a spark of hope at the possibility that Starlina's father might actually be rooting for him. "We absolutely do. A huge responsibility, to be sure."

"One more thing," Murdoch said. "You once asked for my blessing to propose to her. I want you to know . . . you have it."

Jensen felt like leaping as high as the crow's nest. "Thank you, Captain! That . . . means the world to me, sir."

Murdoch clasped Jensen's hand in a firm shake. "*Ah hahaha! You're a good man, Jensen!*"

"Not so good as you, sir!"

"You just might get there," said Murdoch with a chuckle. "Right. Good luck, sailor."

With that, Murdoch walked back toward his cabin.

Amazing as that was, Starlina had perhaps surprised Jensen most of all. She had, during most of the voyage to Gukhan, kept to her quarters and to herself. On this voyage home, she actually pitched in as one of the crew. She helped to pull at the sailyards. She helped Wigglebelly in the galley. She helped swab the deck and coil the lines.

The cut she'd received across her abdomen from Seadread stung severely and often for a while. Fump, who had learned some basic medicinal remedies in his time as quartermaster, helped her to bandage it with a poultice of herbs and honey.

"And when you're done with it, you could eat it," Fump said.

"I wouldn't, personally, but you could."

The cut itself was no joking matter to Starlina, though. It was likely to leave a lifelong scar.

Late one evening, she stayed upon the quarterdeck with Jensen as he took his shift at the helm. The breeze was warm and pleasant, the sky a beautiful twilight banded by the rings high above, and the closest crewmembers were busy down around the mast.

Jensen had much on his mind, not the least of which was his earlier conversation with the captain. He felt inexplicably nervous. Although he had the blessing of Starlina's father, Jensen still worried that it wouldn't be enough. Jensen was still a sailor. He would still be gone for long voyages. She might never be able to accept that, and he realized it might not be fair to expect her to.

"It really doesn't look all that difficult," she said.

"Is that so?" Jensen laughed, holding the wheel steady.

"You're just standing there."

Jensen made a show of indignation. "It's not *just* about standing here."

She stepped up closer. "How do you know where you're going?"

"Are you asking me how to be a sailor?"

"I merely wonder how you know we're going in the right direction, that we won't end up ashore on the tip of Akkadia."

"Ah," said Jensen, "then you've taken an interest in how to navigate at sea."

She raised an eyebrow. "We *are* at sea, aren't we?"

"That we are, milady. Very well, then—a crash course."

Starlina chortled. "So long as we're not *crashing*, of course."

"The rings, you see, are our primary navigational tool. We can measure their position from the horizon to determine where we are against Kasper's maps and charts." He knew she preferred to address the crew by their real names, thus avoiding their boatswain's usual moniker of "Beep." He looked into her bright, gorgeous eyes. She was watching him intently, so he continued. "We've oriented our map and compass, and using that Kasper currently has our bearing at two hundred twenty-five degrees, which happens to be southwest. Visually, a bit to the right of the rings' apex, which of course mark the south."

"How fascinating," she said, smiling.

"And so, this is me—standing here, yes—but also ensuring we stay on our determined course. Sometimes it takes quite an effort to keep it steady, you know."

"May I give it a try?"

It was a question he never thought he'd hear from her. His heart pounded with joy.

"Starlina the Anti-Sailor, asking to steer the ship. Now I believe I've seen it all." He stepped to the side, taking care not to allow the wheel to careen.

She took hold of the wheel, momentarily struggling against its pull. "It really doesn't like to stay in position, does it?"

Jensen laughed. "Staying on course is ever a balance between the wind, the sail, and the currents. Veering even a small amount could take you miles in the wrong direction. Here, allow me ...."

Reaching from behind her, he placed his hands over hers. Her hair streamed about his face, and he breathed her in, a scent remarkably exhilarating despite the limited hygiene of sea life.

"I can feel that you are very much in control, Jensen Karrack," she said.

"Of our ship's navigation, I suppose you're right."

"But of nothing else?"

"Of the rest of life, who am I to say?"

He inhaled deeply of the warm breeze. He watched his hands upon hers, together, and in this moment, solely responsible for the direction of their course.

"I suppose only time will tell," he said.

Starlina entered the captain's cabin to find her father sitting pensively at his desk, looking over papers.

"I thought I'd find you here," she said.

"Ah," he said after a moment, "pleasant afternoon, Starlina. Is everything okay?"

She took a seat in one of the cushy armchairs. "You tell me."

"What do you mean?"

"Clearly you're not yourself. We barely see you out on the deck anymore."

He rubbed at his chin. "Just had a lot on my mind."

Starlina looked upon the desk, where Fulgar's anelace rested. "What do you intend to do with the novidian?"

He turned in his chair and picked up the weapon, looking it over. "In all honesty, I have no idea. Fulgar told me to seek out his Order."

"Will you?"

He shrugged. "Maybe I will."

"Once he had me hold that dagger." She stared at it in remembrance. "It wasn't anything like when Fulgar held it, but it glowed for me. He seemed to think that meant something."

Her father was watching her, expressionless.

"Then, in the cave, he had me touch that"—she shook her head—"cursed dome thing, and somehow he drew energy from me."

He nodded. "You and I . . . we have something unique in our lineage, going back to when our ancestor Augustus Macpherson banished the Grimstone from Tuscawny and sealed it away in Gukhan to save the land. It's that something in our lineage that gives us a connection with novidian."

She leaned back, thoughtful. "Does it concern you at all? I mean, Macpherson removed the Grimstone from Tuscawny, and now Seadread is taking it back there. *We* would've taken it back there. Couldn't that be dangerous?"

Her father blinked, seeming to consider that. "Fulgar wanted it to be back under the watchful eye of the Order. He seemed to think that Gukhan had become such a dark place that it was no longer safe there. I saw visions associated with that

Grimstone there ... and it is not to be trifled with."

"*Dark* is right," Starlina said. "I have to wonder, though, if the order Fulgar belonged to is really safer than where Macpherson hid it."

He smirked. "That kind of doubting is usually *my* job. I came to trust Fulgar."

"And so you trust the Order?"

His mouth flat-lined. "I don't trust anyone until they've earned it."

"Not that it matters now," she replied. "Seadread is taking it right to the person who wanted it. Maybe the man thinks it'll help the kingdom ... but it just doesn't quite *feel* right. I mean, Dark to help Light? It seems awfully backwards."

"Yes, well, personally I think Seadread will find he's bitten off more than he can chew." He gave her a hard stare, as he might when assessing a new crewmember. "You've a keen instinct about you, Starlina."

She brushed aside a braid of hair. "Well, I am a Murdoch after all."

Her father's eyes softened, and the look she got from them was one of great pride. "Ah, that you are, my dear ... but not just a Murdoch. A *Macpherson*."

Jensen looked out from the taffrail of the stern deck, watching the sun as it crept below the horizon. His ears took in the tranquil sound of the ship cutting through the water, chasing white waves from the hull and leaving a trail in its wake.

They were less than three days away from Warvonia. Nobody knew how long they would stay ashore before their next voyage. There were already whisperings among the crew that some would seek a transfer, following the epic failure of this trip. This, of course, came from those of lesser experience and, generally, lesser ability.

Jensen was not among them. As with the officers—Dippy, Beep, Fump, Chim, Evette—he was a Murdoch's Mate through and through. They all knew the outcome of this voyage wasn't a failure of their captain's. Rather, it was a sabotage of Seadread.

Jensen very much wondered what would transpire if and when their path crossed again with Garrick Rummy. Whether or not Captain Murdoch would ever condone any open acts of revenge, the crew of Murdoch had no small score to settle with that fiendish rogue.

Jensen felt absently for an object in his pocket. It was a thing that he had quite meant to be without before this voyage even began, if only he'd been able to get Starlina to accept it.

"I find it special, you know," Starlina said from behind, "to be aboard my father's ship as it returns from a daring voyage such as this."

Beaming, Jensen turned around. Once again the pendant of lilac kuntupite hung below her neck. "You never know where we'll sail to next. It'll be somewhere away from Warvonia..."

"...and it'll be somewhere grand, I'm sure," she said.

She joined him beside the taffrail, standing right by him, so that their arms touched. Her makeshift shirt had no sleeves, and her skin was warm and soft against his. "Being surrounded by this view on all sides—the absolute perfect backdrop, isn't it?"

"It *is* beautiful," he said.

"It's what every sailor dreams of," she said. "These open waters, the horizon laid out before you. It's like freedom." She looked at him with an impish smile. "That's what someone told me once."

He chuckled. "The words of a wise man. A real keeper."

His fingers were restless inside his pocket.

"I love the ocean," he said. "I love this ship...and the adventure...and sailing under your father."

He looked into her eyes, bright and wide and staring back into his.

"But I would give it all up for the greatest love of them all. *You*, Starlina."

"But then you wouldn't be *you*, would you? And we can't have that."

"I'm not me without *you*," he said.

He took her hand, his heart pounding.

He took a deep breath. "I...I have a question for you...."

She placed a finger over his lips. "Sailors don't ask questions," she said, leaning in very close. "They take action."

And with the water all around them, they kissed, longingly. He swam in her goodness, drinking her in, forgetting everything he'd ever been worried about. His hand cradled her cheek, and his nostrils filled with her scent. Long gone was the smell of rosewater. It had been washed away, replaced by something even more invigorating.

The sea.

It was about the fourth hour of the morning when Zale stood atop the stern of his ship, leaning against the aft ballista in thought. He was alone. Beep had just relieved Jensen of helm's duty on the quarterdeck below. When they reached Warvonia in about two days' time, their rest would be well-deserved.

He and his officers would have their work cut out for them once back ashore. He already assumed several of the deckhands would attempt to transfer, hoping for captains who take jobs with less risk and danger. They would need to be replaced, but this was not entirely unfamiliar to Zale.

Then there was the far more unpleasant business of having to inform the guild of those crewmembers lost in action. That was a relatively sterile process—mostly paperwork, and no questions asked about the details. Any family and loved ones of those men, however, would demand ... and deserve ... more answers.

He couldn't bring himself to even think about the mastery bar anymore. He figured the guilders would want to work him to the death. He had already decided that, if he wanted a month off with his wife and family, he would take it, and to Gheol with the guilders.

By now the choice of family over career was an easy one for him.

The harder choice—the one he'd wrestled with over their three-week voyage home—had to do with the object in his pocket.

He pulled it out, an object like a small, flat slab of shale in his hand—clearly the broken shard of something larger.

It was the Grimstone.

Either now or very soon, down in Miskunn, Seadread was about to present an empty canister to what would certainly be a most displeased Vidimir. It seemed that ol' Puffypants would not reach the mastery bar this year after all. That afforded Zale a most satisfying chuckle.

He stared at the Grimstone. "So much evil in something so small," he whispered, thinking of Fulgar.

"*I know ... you will do right,*" he had said. "*Your heart ... is good.*"

What, exactly, was *right* was what Zale had deliberated with himself over and over again all the way home. His crew had every right to the payoff this object could bring. It was for this object that Zale had turned away two easier charges. It was for this job that nine men had died.

But the lives of nine could pale in comparison to what Zale had seen in the visions. If true, the destruction this object was capable of might affect the entire kingdom, maybe even beyond.

This concept of saving the land by replacing the Light with *this*....

If the land needed saving at all, there had to be a better way.

His daughter and his granddaughters would not grow up in a haunted, lightless world like the one in those visions, not if he had anything to say about it.

To bring the object back to Tuscawny seemed to be what Fulgar had intended. It would be under the Order's watch, supposedly safe.

But his own ancestor, Macpherson, had gone through great lengths to take it far from there... far from the Light.

And so he had a choice, perhaps the greatest choice of his life.

"What to do with you?" he spoke softly. Even in his hand, he somehow felt a sort of contempt from the object, as though it hated being within his grasp.

He closed his eyes in thought. He saw the gentle smile of his wife, Lola. He heard the joyous laughter of his young granddaughters. He saw Starlina and Jensen, his crew, the city of Warvonia that he loved.

Not even opening his eyes to see it again, he threw back his arm and launched it to the sea.

"You, Fulgar, are of the Order," he said. "Now you keep it safe."

Zale Murdoch had made his choice.

HEROES OF TIME LEGENDS

A NOVEL OF THE HEROES OF TIME SERIES

MURDOCH'S SHADOW

BONUS PREVIEW

BY WAYNE KRAMER

ONLY THE WORTHY

2/9/3203 P.A.

Jagged lightning speared through the sky like tridents of doom.

High Count Carnelian Shaw craned his neck outside their carriage as it bumped along the rugged, precipitous route to Astralsin Citadel, built within the ledges of dueling mountain ranges. To call this a road would be generous. It was more like a trail, with unkempt ground beaten down by the years and elements, better suited to ibexes and mountain goats than humans. Few dared this climb, a trek reserved only for the most worthy.

Some considered the ancient site to be the anchor which pulled the Ba'ar and the Cairn Mountains together, bridging them, forcing accessibility from one range to the next where there was otherwise a deadly chasm.

This site was a prize of the Brumm province within the kingdom of Tuscawny. Brumm was unlike the other provinces in that it was further divided into five enclaves, each ruled by a kith, among the kingdom's highest houses of nobility. Carnelian presided over Kith Shaw of the Gaul enclave, a beautiful domain with plentiful forests and an expansive coastline.

Today, Astralsin Citadel was the location of a lavish gala, the perfect place to meet with his long-time rival, Vidimir Tefu, high count of the Volga enclave.

For over two years, both Carnelian and Vidimir had sought the same treasure: the Grimstone, a powerful relic of the long-past Shadow Age, when the power of Void first entered the world of Eliorin.

Most considered it fable. Others believed the Grimstone was long gone. Plenty of fools dismissed the Shadow Age entirely. Vidimir, just like Carnelian, not only believed the Grimstone existed but that ancient forces of darkness churned within the world even now, seeking their chance to rise again.

The ascension of Shadow was but a matter of time. Most were deaf to it. Vidimir, however, had kept a sharp ear. As with Carnelian, he had heard the subtle siren of bygone voices in the air. Ancient things long thought dead were stirring, rallying allies.

How great the promise of power and dominance to those who answered the call!

No greater opportunity for influence existed than the Grimstone. Carnelian was not about to let Vidimir beat him to it.

Not only that, but by the end of the night, he intended to convert Kith Tefu's rivalry into loyalty.

Rain pattered about Carnelian's face and splashed against the white teeth of his grinning mouth. He smoothed the water through his cropped, silver-brown hair and relished in the danger of their flight. It was a story in the making, a rush of adrenaline propelling them to the realm of the upper echelons.

Wet dapples formed rapidly upon his tunic of orange velvet. Patterned upon its breast, in tiny-faceted gemstones, was the familial crest of Kith Shaw: a gryphon in flight, with a fish in its talons.

At Carnelian's orders, the carriage sped along the route, even as it became ever more treacherous. They were not far now. It was time to be ready.

Beside him, rigid as a board, sat his latest mistress, Zuzanna. The elegant plaits of her dark-brown and golden hair rested stiffly about her shoulders. Adorned with hundreds of hand-polished sapphire shards, her gown sparkled with each lurch and jostle of the carriage. Her magnificent dress left bare one shoulder, the sides of her waist, and a circle around her navel, tailor-made to fit her form perfectly.

Across from Carnelian sat Tack, his tweedy butler, legs crossed and a book in his hands. Tack had been on at least a dozen such trips with Carnelian before. He was well-tempered, fully acclimated to the charge, accepting of the risk. You would make it to the gala or die a glorious death in the process. Might as well enjoy a good book along the way.

This was Zuzanna's first gala. To her credit, she had the good sense to keep quiet as the carriage bounced ominously forward.

No yelps or squeals like so many before her. It was much more than could be said of the last woman he was with. She had never made it back from the noble soiree preceding this one. After she'd stumbled into the chasm like the klutzy trollop she was, he hastened to distance himself from the screams, and he never looked back. He immediately shoved her name to the back of his mind—a thing not worth remembering.

The carriage jumped with such force that his head bumped the ceiling, Tack's book launched from his hands, and one of Zuzanna's shoes flew across the carriage, nearly spearing Tack with its heel.

Carnelian reared back with laughter, even as two of the carriage's wheels nearly slipped over the ledge, where naught could be seen but an abyss of fog. Up ahead and to their right, he glimpsed the peaks of turrets hewn from the mountain's rock.

"You see that, my darling?" he said as Zuzanna fumbled with her shoe. "A fortress rooted in the rocks of *two* mountain ranges! What could possibly be more majestic?"

"I'm sure I don't know," she said with a taut voice. "Living, perhaps?"

"Keep us at full speed, Reyson!" he called to the front, his window open again. He squeezed Zuzanna's thigh with a glower of mischief. "Not a hair slower until we're right upon the entrance!"

"Sir, there's mud t' be considered!" Reyson replied in the common dialect of Brumm serfdom. Most nobility throughout the province avoided this speech pattern to distinguish themselves, instead leaning into the more refined influence of Sharm, the province which housed the Throne of Light within Metsada Palace.

"Right!" Carnelian called back. "Do try to keep the splattering to a minimum." He turned to his fellow riders. "We are attending a gala, after all, not a gulobeast rodeo. *Ha HA!*"

They rounded the apex of their climb, and the carriage ground to a halt. They had arrived. At least, it was as far as they could go by carriage. From here, they could not see the façade of the citadel. Instead, a narrow walking path of bare dirt stretched before them. That path converged with a long series of switchback stairs that scaled a rocky wall all the way to the top, continuing beyond their current view. Other attendees of the gala already traversed the stairs, many of them looking toward the newly arrived carriage.

Carnelian's hand rested upon the door handle. "I shouldn't need tell you that some of the most influential eyes in the province are now upon us. We shall exit, composed … calm … unaffected. Do you understand?"

"Of course, sir," Tack said at once.

Zuzanna merely nodded.

Carnelian surveyed her face. She was far too stiff, too pursed, like a lemon had been shoved in her mouth. He brushed her face with the backs of his fingers, gently running them up and down her jawline, then her cheeks, back down aside her nose, and to the corner of her mouth. "Relax, my dear. You came a mistress. You shall leave nigh a princess."

He shoved open the door and let it slam conspicuously against the side of the carriage. The rain had reduced to a mist, but the ground here was a muddy disgrace.

He inhaled a quick breath of revulsion. "Tack, the vaporite."

"Right away, Your Excellency." The butler produced from his pocket a translucent-white, rectangular rod, which appeared to have tiny bubbles entombed within. He placed thin, gray gloves on his hands and stepped out onto the iron footplate.

Tack snapped the rod like a twig. He placed the two pieces between his hands and rubbed, faster and faster, until the vaporite glowed—softly at first, then brighter and brighter. Once at their peak brilliance, Tack dropped the pieces of vaporite onto the path.

A blast of energy rippled through the ground, spraying water droplets into the air from the carriage to the base of the stairs some fifty yards away. The result was a walkway of perfectly dry dirt cutting through the surrounding mud.

Carnelian cackled. "Very good, Tack! Very good, indeed!" He proffered an arm to Zuzanna. "Come. Let us dazzle the peerage."

They emerged from the carriage, tall and dignified. Stray rays of sunlight jabbed through the clouds and made their outfits glisten. "Even Zun smiles upon us," he said quietly.

By virtue of their now dry and easy path, they soon reached the stairs. A short, balding man with a thick, yellow and gray mustache, a pipe in hand, and a black, red-trimmed coat nodded in greeting. "Peace be the day." Carnelian recognized him as Lord

Mayor Bannister of some midgrade town in the Wolof enclave.

This was no mere salutation. It was code for "the baron of Brumm, Arlo Day, is on his way out." Of course, among this crowd, the even deeper meaning was implied: "and I shall be the one to succeed him."

Baron Day, a feeble-minded old man, had entered a rapid state of physical decline over the past year. He rarely appeared in public. When he did, he might wave to the masses and stand for a few minutes before retreating back out of sight. His end was but a short amount of time, and the kiths of Brumm smelled blood in the water.

Carnelian gave the mayor a curt nod, and they continued up the steps, passing by the man as he puffed his pipe.

Once atop the first round of stairs, Carnelian set his eyes upon the massive, gaping façade of Astralsin Citadel now visible in the distance. Exactly one thousand seven hundred and seventy-seven steps comprised the ascent. They were relatively small steps, most of the stretches not terribly steep, but still the climb was not for the faint of heart. Their path would take them to the chasm's edge via a series of narrow arch-bridges and landings of precipitous rock spires.

The structure itself was suspended over the chasm atop a massive, protruding formation of rock that was said to have been reinforced in ancient days by some of the world's hardest substances.

It was, in effect, a portion of manmade mountain.

Carnelian felt Zuzanna's arm tense as their route came

clearly into view.

"You ... come here often?" she asked.

"Enough to be familiar," he answered. "Not so often that the sight is any less majestic."

Halfway up their first arch-bridge, Zuzanna slipped on one of the steps. Her startled yelp carried into the chasm, an echo of Carnelian's boiling vexation. Their arms were still locked, but he held his footing, quickly yanking her upward.

He pulled her closer, until his mouth was just beside her ear. "Remember, my sweet, *we* are the dominance here. Others think the same of themselves, yes, but we prove it in our steps, in our fearlessness, in our every move and interaction. There is a saying: 'The daring may reach the citadel, but only the worthy return from it.'" He gave her ear a kiss, and they continued.

Minutes later, the rain returned.

The route's final stretch was a straight, narrow bridge from the mountain's natural end to the citadel's platform. They stood ten steps above it, where they could see its entire length. No more than two people could walk it abreast. There were no rails. It appeared as a mud-covered plank, longer than a fallen roast-wood tree, made increasingly treacherous by the falling rain.

Carnelian and Zuzanna watched for a moment as others made their way across. They all attempted to appear indifferent to the danger, most of them failing by their uncertain, teetering steps.

Just beyond the halfway point, a tall man in a silver jacket slipped on a muddy patch. As he staggered, he attempted to grab his escort, who stepped nimbly aside and allowed the man to tumble over the edge.

"That was the lord mayor of Helkath," said Carnelian. He chuckled. "An old fool, and clearly his accompaniment knew as much." The man's scream vanished into the fog below. "He will be succeeded. It was time." He urged Zuzanna down the steps.

"Sir," said Tack, "shall I use the vaporite?"

Carnelian glared at the muddy path. "No, Tack." Zuzanna gasped, her wet head whipping to face him. "Falter not, the both of you."

"Very good, sir."

Carnelian felt dozens of noble eyes aimed at them from the stairs and balconies of the citadel. He knew that Vidimir could well be among them.

Zuzanna played her part well. How powerful the forced, multipronged sense of self-preservation—that primal, inevitable urge to simply avoid death.

They made their way across, maintaining an air of confidence. Carnelian paid special attention to Zuzanna as she stepped over a small pit in the surface. With a half-smirk, he remembered exactly where his escort of the past had tumbled to her disgraceful end.

Then they were on the other side, with only a single broad stairway between them and the citadel's gallant entrance.

"Now use the vaporite, Tack," Carnelian ordered.

"You are truly maniacal," Zuzanna said.

It was as grand an entrance as he'd hoped for. Sprays of water erupted from the stairs, forcing loiterers to shield their faces and their dignities. A fierce gust blew the moisture from their clothes and bodies.

They returned scowls of loathing. Carnelian didn't care. These were not people that currently mattered to him.

Like figures of imperial power, Carnelian strode up the stairs with Zuzanna in tow, dry as fallen leaves in the sun.

Like a figure of legend. By the end of the night, he would be just that.

Crossing the threshold was like entering another world. Dark-green and white-veined marble slabs made up the floor before them. The interior was a massive, open expanse tiered with balconies and stairways running throughout the walls. Huge columns of red and silver travertine appeared throughout.

Straight ahead was the peak of the main staircase, with thick banisters of white and gray quartzite and stairs of green marble. It led to the citadel's lowest level, where gleamed the ballroom floor of brilliant white basalt. Around all sides of the white floor were round tables set with the finest of crystal glassware and utensils of handcrafted, translucent-green peridot.

"Down there," Carnelian said softly, pulling Zuzanna gently toward the stairs. "That is where my quarry will be, down where squirm the slugs and worms, where the gryphon may feed of the lesser creatures." He surveyed the area below, maintaining his paced descent. "The crest of the Dark Diamond is in our midst. The slithering tongue of Tefu is nigh."

He kept in his expression a cool indifference as they

descended the last step. A nod to a guild chief on his left. A one-word greeting uttered to a mayor on his right. They made their way around the dance floor, currently empty despite the veiled whispering of stringed instruments in the air. Sycophantic chatter and ringing crystal reached their ears as they strode between the tables.

Carnelian stopped. His eyes locked on a table just ahead. There sat Vidimir Tefu, a tall-faced, pallid man with slick black and white hair, his mouth ever fixed in a smarmy grin. His suit jacket was dark purple with twists of black, while the lapels were black and lined with tiny black and violet-veined gems. A pendant containing a larger cut of the same gem rested snugly between the flaps of his collar.

Does he even keep byrne *within his attire?* wondered Carnelian.

Carnelian briefly watched from afar. Vidimir swirled his wine and took a sip, looking around with confidence in his eyes that seemed to suggest he owned the place. Little doubt he believed he did.

Carnelian allowed not another idle moment to pass and broke into long, deliberate steps toward the table.

"High Count Tefu," said Carnelian, pulling a chair back from the table. "Just the man I'd hoped to see here today."

"No need for such formalities among friends, Carnelian," replied Vidimir. "We are on a first-name basis, are we not? Please, have a seat."

"Very much obliged ... Vidimir."

Vidimir scanned Zuzanna up and down, and up and down again, showing no restraint. "What a lovely associate you've brought along. I daresay my favorite yet of yours. I do hope this one lasts."

Zuzanna took her seat. "A pleasure to finally meet you, High Count Tefu," she replied in her rich, sumptuous voice.

"This is Zuzanna. I had the fortune of finding her after a march through Lozellien. She stood out from the townsfolk like a diamond in the rough."

Servants, having noticed Carnelian's arrival, rushed to bring a selection of wine bottles for his choosing. "I'll have the Oden Valley White."

"The same," said Zuzanna.

Vidimir showed white teeth, a playful glint in his eyes. "And why tarnish yourself with one so blemished as him?" he asked Zuzanna.

"I take a keen interest in political hierarchy," she replied. "It has always fascinated me. Before him, I was promised to a high reeve. Far too boring. Far too limited." She leaned enticingly toward Carnelian. "High Count Shaw enchanted me with his charm, and I traded up."

"Ah yes... *charm*," replied Vidimir, raising his glass. "Another word for riches and influence." He gave a slight tilt of his head, prodding Carnelian with a sharp eye. "And I'm sure other redeeming qualities. Ambition, for a start."

Carnelian relaxed against his seat. "My dear Vidimir, is there a single enclave leader among us who lacks ambition?"

Vidimir swallowed a draft of wine. "Well stated. It is not so much the ambition as being worthy to flaunt the ambition. *That* is what separates us from the other enclaves, even from the other provinces. Would you not agree, Carnelian?"

"Of course I would," he replied.

"And so we are in good company, you and I," said Vidimir. "The dominant among kiths. The alphas of the pack."

Carnelian took a swig of his wine and sat it gently back on the table. "And yet, every pack has only *one* alpha." His eyes met Vidimir's, daring his next response. It came even sooner than he'd expected, but his position among the enclaves was soon to be cemented. Carnelian's moment of triumph was nigh.

"Are we wolves, that we must adhere to such primal ways?" Vidimir lifted his glass, swirling his wine absently but not taking a drink. "I suppose some laws of nature cannot be broken. Even so, there is one thing I am very sure of. This night will not go as you expect . . . and I am so sorry if that disappoints you." In these last words, he broke into a laugh, an open-mouthed chuckle.

It was a laugh of mockery.

Carnelian frowned, his mouth a flat line, a sudden lump in his throat. He swallowed, recovering himself. This was no time to falter. "I rather think tonight will be splendid. You see, we of Kith Shaw have made a significant stride toward finding the Grimstone."

"Oh?" Vidimir steepled his fingers over the table, looking calmly back at Carnelian. "You have my rapt attention."

"I have the Eye of Shi'kha. By now, my men have already

secured it within one of our vaults. I almost didn't believe it to be real, you know. But I have seen it ... held it ... felt of its power. It is like having a piece of the Shadow Age in my grasp. Remarkable to behold."

Vidimir slowly tapped the table with his fingers as he listened to Carnelian's every word, his face a blank slate. Finally, he straightened himself. "That *is* remarkable. I am ... intrigued."

"I thought you might be." In truth, he'd hoped to see Vidimir more rattled by this revelation, but he was not surprised. The high count of Kith Tefu was a master of the game. "Of course, you know what this means."

Vidimir placed his elbows on the table, folding his hands. "When it comes to matters of the Void, I know a great deal."

Carnelian took a sip of wine. "Then you know that I have the one thing that can locate the Grimstone."

Vidimir raised a finger. "Careful that your ambitions don't get the better of you. No eye, even a mystical one, can see *everything*, if what you seek is too well obscured."

"*Ha!* No, Vidimir. My ambitions are the *best* of me, but I do try not to be shortsighted. I must admit that your grasp and knowledge of the Void are far greater than mine ... and I have heard of this powerful mage you keep by your side."

"Mazek?" asked Vidimir. "It is true—his devotion runs deep. What is it you want?"

"The Eye of Shi'kha ... the Grimstone. ... These are no mere stones of byrne we are talking about. They are Void relics of the absolute highest order. They require great care. What I would like is your cooperation—that, together, we can ensure the Shadow Age rises again, with me at the forefront of it . . . and, for you, Vidimir, a lofty and safe position within the realm reborn."

Carnelian paused for another sip of wine. "Of course, this also means Kith Tefu must renounce any claim to the barony and leadership over Brumm, and you will swear fealty to me."

Vidimir arched an eyebrow. "It would seem you have the upper hand, Carnelian."

Carnelian allowed himself a small chuckle. "It was inevitable, really."

Vidimir stared calmly back at Carnelian. There was a sudden swell in the background music from various stringed and woodwind instruments. All around them, attendees stood from their chairs and made for the central dance floor.

"Well," said Vidimir, "we must not breach decorum, after all." He stood, came around the table, and offered his hand to Zuzanna.

Carnelian frowned. "You do not strike me as the dancing type, Vidimir."

"Sometimes one must learn to play the part."

Carnelian nodded to Zuzanna, who then accepted Vidimir's hand and followed him to the dance floor. Carnelian, wine in hand, stood in silent watching from just behind the edge. Zuzanna was like a beacon of beauty, drawing looks from everyone around. Her movements were graceful and immaculate. Vidimir, in contrast, was precise yet stiff, with all the alacrity of a statue. She made him look better in every way.

As Carnelian watched, sipping his wine, he contemplated Vidimir's reactions. He wasn't quite sure what he'd hoped for. Upon learning that the Eye of Shi'kha was under the control of Kith Shaw, he had looked for some falter, some misstep, some hint of surprise. He got none of that. Vidimir remained calm as ever, and now he had Carnelian's own mistress out on the dancefloor. Something seemed off, some detail that Vidimir had not yet revealed.

Tack appeared by his side. "Is everything okay, sir?"

"Ah, Tack! Keep a close watch on the company and carriage of Kith Tefu. I need to know if they make any sudden or unusual moves." One could never be too cautious, not among this crowd. A sudden retreat or a stir within Tefu's servanthood might indicate a rash move.

"Right away, sir." The butler scurried off.

Three songs in, Carnelian's patience had finally worn thin.

"Count Tefu," he called as Vidimir and Zuzanna swayed near, "I should very much like to recover my date."

Vidimir walked right up to Carnelian and gave his shoulder a firm pat. "Of course, Carnelian. We should discuss this matter of the Eye." He walked in the direction of the main staircase, Zuzanna trailing just behind. "Let's find a quieter place to settle this."

Overcast sunlight and the tall, majestic entryway scrolled into view as they ascended the stairs. Once at the top, Vidimir led them to the threshold, where few of the attendees congregated. It was not a typical location for conducting noble business.

"I am impressed that your doddering brood would manage to procure the Eye of Shi'kha," Vidimir said.

Carnelian cackled. "Call us what you will, Vidimir. It was our spy network that found it...in a remote anthropod village, of all places. For a good while there, I honestly believed you would beat us to it."

Vidimir leaned in very close. He spoke just over a whisper. "Oh, but I have."

Carnelian's smile faded. "We have the Eye. Of this there is no doubt."

"I am sure you're correct," Vidimir replied. "But the thing is, Carnelian...I have no need of it. How can I put this? You have followed a red herring...a misdirection...a set of clues which are no longer of consequence. You kept your focus on but one means to the end. I kept my sights on the end itself."

Carnelian exhaled nervously, fighting to maintain his composure and the upper hand that he was so certain he'd held just moments before. "That is absurd. Only by using the Eye of Shi'kha can the Grimstone be located."

"The Eye is... *one* way to locate it," Vidimir answered, stepping slowly toward Zuzanna. "I have already located it. It turns out legend paved the way all along."

Vidimir clasped his hands around the sides of Zuzanna's waist, pulling her in for a firm kiss on the lips. She showed no distaste, no unwillingness. She made no move to pull away.

"Zuzanna, away from him!" Carnelian ordered.

"Come now, Carnelian," said Vidmir, the words slithering

from his mouth. "You would not steal away my promised, would you?" With a lick of his lips, he slid his hands down the stones lining the lapels of his jacket, Carnelian gaping at him.

"Your *promised*? What is this?" Carnelian said. "I demand to know what is going on here!"

"Byrne," said Vidimir, fingering the larger stone of his pendant, "another gift of the Shadow Age. Its capabilities are multifaceted, really. So . . . untapped."

"*Tack!*" Carnelian shouted into the vastness of the citadel. His butler was nowhere in sight. "You fork-tongued infidel. You will answer for this treachery! The fury of a thousand torches will be upon your doorstep. We shall rip you from the noble ranks like a helpless fish in the talons of a great eagle!"

"A pity you are not more graceful in defeat. Have you never followed the roadmap of legends? If you know where to look, it can be as reliable as history itself."

Carnelian clenched his fists, his face flush with rage. Yet, he slowed his breathing, hoping that Vidimir might let slip some critical secret behind his claims. "And what legend is this?"

"The legend of the Heroes of Time, of course."

Calmly, casually, Vidimir began to draw in the air. Carnelian squinted as thin purple lines formed a box between the man's fingers.

"And that roadmap led me clearly to one name," said Vidimir. "Think on it, as you leave this place."

"What name?"

"Macpherson."

Carnelian had time only to arch an eyebrow before the surge of biting cold overtook him. In that instant he was surrounded by dancing hues of purple. With each flail of his arms, the flames bit ever harder, driving through his skin like a thousand needles, bringing a frostbitten numbness.

He stumbled his way down the stairs from the citadel. The laughter of Vidimir and Zuzanna and other bystanders landed heavy in his ears.

He reached the narrow, mud-covered bridge and dashed forward to cross it. If he could move fast enough, perhaps the mountain breeze would relieve him of this misery.

He tripped over a pit in the pathway, and suddenly there was nothing solid beneath him at all. The breeze came from underneath. He saw all of his skin turn to frosty white before he saw nothing at all.

Suddenly he remembered the woman he'd watched fall from the cliff at his last gala.

Scarlet, he thought with grim recollection. *Her name was Scarlet.*

He could only hope the end would be swift and absolute. It was far too humiliating a defeat to live with.

CREW LOG OF
"Queenie"

Name	Station	Remarks
Zale Murdoch	Captain	Nicknamed "The Gale"
Daubennon Doyle	First Mate/Deck Boss	Nicknamed "Dippy"
Kasper Gibbers	Boatswain/Navigator	Nicknamed "Beep"
Yancy Willigan	Quartermaster	Nicknamed "Fump"
Kosh Pureblood	Master of Arms	Nicknamed "Chim Chum"
Evette Cashmore	Coxswain/Rowing Chief	Nicknamed "Shrew"
Jaxon Harper	Senior Deckhand/Victual Chief	Nicknamed "Wigglebelly"
Fulgar Geth	Physician/Healer/Chaplain	
Jensen Karrack	Boatswain's mate/Carpenter	On-hand oarsman (OHO)
Tate Woodard	Boatswain's Mate	On-hand oarsman (OHO)
Kelvin Turner	Quartermaster's Mate	Also a skilled cooper (OHO)
Ian Hopper	Quartermaster's mate/Ropemaster	Also skilled in rigging
Rowan Brun	Quartermaster's mate/Sailmaker	Also skilled in tailoring/textiles
Levi Buckett	Quartermaster's mate/Carpenter	On-hand oarsman
Archie Hunt	Coxswain's mate/Oarsman	On-hand Deckhand
Cal Norton	Coxswain's Mate/Oarsman	On-hand Deckhand
Winston Clergy	Coxswain's Mate/Oarsman	On-hand Deckhand
Fritz Flitter	Coxswain's Mate/Oarsman	On-hand Deckhand
Miles Ashmore	Deckhand	On-hand oarsman
Rolt Cone	Deckhand/lookout	Nicknamed "Hookknee"
Snow Gunnison	Deckhand/lookout	On-hand oarsman
Sal Higgins	Deckhand/lookout	
Chester Coffer	Deckhand/Purser	
Abel Weekman	Deckhand	On-hand oarsman
Edgar Oakes	Deckhand	On-hand oarsman
Jonas Singleton	Deckhand	On-hand oarsman
Elihu Jones	Deckhand	
Radvers Hardy	Deckhand	
Clement Gardina	Deckhand	On-hand oarsman
Bert Mooring	Deckhand	On-hand oarsman
Owen Huckstep	Deckhand	On-hand oarsman

TIME AND SEASONS OF ELIORIN

Dates and times are referenced many times throughout this book. Eliorin has both longer days and longer years compared to Earth, taking 28 hours per day, and 425 of these 28-hour days to make a year. (Seconds, minutes, and hours are the same length as on Earth.) A leap-year occurs every five years, adding one day to the month of Sivarch.

A typical clock on Eliorin might look like this, with a single hand pointing to the hour:

The calendar used throughout Grandtrilia, and almost universally throughout the Great Crescent, is divided into twelve months with three seasons, four months each in length, as well as six two-month sub-seasons:

Month	Number of Days	Season	Sub-Season
Janiose	34		Spring
Febtose	34	Sprout	
Sivarch	35 (Leap-Year: 36)		Sprung
Avreal	36		
Mav	37		Summer
Jervens	37	Harvest	
Jovidor	38		Fall
Agust	38		
Sleptindor	35		Fallen
Octcolore	35	Lull	
Novashtay	33		Winter
Freezindor	33		

AGE IN ELIORIN COMPARED TO EARTH

Those longer days and years in Eliorin amount to more hours of life!

Inhabitants of Eliorin are older than you might think. Nova turned four years old in Chapter One of Murdoch's Choice, but she had actually lived about five and a half Earth years.

Zale turns 55 during Murdoch's Shadow but would be 74 on Earth. However, this does not mean he actually looks like a 74-year-old as we would imagine. Eliorin's purer atmosphere keeps its inhabitants looking younger for longer. So, Zale still looks about like we would expect a 55-year-old to look. Starlina begins the Murdoch's Choice's prologue at 14 years old, but she is actually 19 in Earth's years. Following that prologue and throughout Murdoch's Shadow, she is 16, or just shy of 22 Earth years. Similarly, Jensen is 19, but he would be 25 on Earth.

A person on Eliorin is considered a child up through age nine—nine Eliorinian years, that is—an adolescent at age 10, a young adult at 15, a prime adult at 20, and an elder adult from 60 and up. The official legal drinking age in the kingdom of Tuscawny is 15, at the start of adulthood, and slightly over the age of 20 in Earth years.

If you'd like to know your Eliorinian age, check out the age calculator on HeroesOfTime.com in the "Fun Stuff" page under Features!

The chart on the next page provides age groups and conversion examples (Earth ages are rounded).

	Eliorin Age	Earth Age
Childhood 0-9	4	5
	7	10
	9	12
Adolescent 10-14	11	15
	14	19
Young Adult 15-19	16 Starlina	22
	19 Jensen	26
Prime Adult 20-59	25	34
	35	48
	45	61
	55 Zale	75
Elder Adult 60+	65	88
	75	102

Jovidor

Soulsday	Lunsday	Tunesday	Whitesday	Thorsday	Flamsday	Sitsday
1	2	3	4	5	6	7
8	9	10	11	12	13	14
15	16	17	18	19	20	21
22	23	24	25	26	27	28
29	30	31	32	33	34	35
36	37	38				

Agust

Soulsday	Lunsday	Tunesday	Whitesday	Thorsday	Flamsday	Sitsday
			1	2	3	4
5	6	7	8	9	10	11
12	13	14	15	16	17	18
19	20	21	22	23	24	25
26	27	28	29	30	31	32
33	34	35	36	37	38	

ABOUT THE AUTHOR

Wayne Kramer lives in the Southern Indiana countryside. He loves the open spaces and fresh air. His family keeps a small greenhouse, usually a little garden, chickens, and an overweight cat. He has been married to his wife and best friend, Kaly, since 2004. They have five daughters with the nature-themed names of Dawn, Brooke, Holly, Ivy, and Jade.

Wayne wanted to be a published author for nearly 25 years before finally publishing *Heroes of Time Legends: Murdoch's Choice*. Life finally afforded enough flexibility that he is able to focus a lot more time developing the "Heroes of Time" series that he is very passionate about. Another major novel in the series has already been written.

From early on writing was one of Wayne's favorite pastimes. He wrote short stories throughout middle school and high school for Young Authors contests and group projects. Before "Heroes of Time" dominated his mind, he worked extensively on creating an epic-fantasy novelization of a popular role-playing video game. Over the years Wayne received frequent feedback on many revisions of this novelization, making it one of the primary vessels through which he fine-tuned his writing.

He graduated from the University of Louisville in 2005 with a Bachelor of Business Science degree. He worked for his parents' company in the field of medical imaging equipment and parts for a total of fifteen years. Wayne also pursued business opportunities in licensed products, which included helping to run a traveling retail presence, ecommerce, and product design.

Wayne currently owns and runs his own business, W7 Global, which sells parts for medical imaging equipment all around the world. Throughout his professional and personal endeavors, Wayne has visited nearly 40 countries and about 25 states in the US. He especially loved visiting Hobbiton in New Zealand.

Wayne feels truly blessed by God to pursue his dream of writing and publishing stories. The world of Eliorin was inspired by Wayne's love of stories of classic fantasy and time travel, and he is incredibly excited to share this rich world with you.

FOLLOW THE LEGEND
OF THE HEROES OF TIME

Thank you for reading
Heroes of Time Legends: Murdoch's Choice!

Watch for more to come in the
Heroes of Time series!

www.heroesoftime.com

Please leave this novel a review at Amazon, Goodreads, or
wherever you bought this book.

Follow Wayne Kramer and Heroes of Time at…

Facebook:	http://facebook.com/heroesoftimeseries
Facebook	https://facebook.com/groups/ heroesoftimeseries
Instagram:	http://instagram.com/heroesoftimeseries
Discord:	http://murdochschoice.com/discord
YouTube:	https://youtube.com/@HeroesOfTime
Goodreads:	http://goodreads.com/waynekramer
Amazon:	http://heroesoftime.com/amazon

Follow http://murdochschoice.com/amazon to go
directly to the Amazon review page.

May the winds fare you well!

Made in the USA
Las Vegas, NV
20 August 2023

76340439R00196